Marisa's World

Also by Lorna Hopkins Keith

Lyn's Talent

Perri's Gates

ISBN: 0996613129
ISBN 13: 978-0996616125

For Daddy

CAST OF CHARACTERS

Born on Earth:

Lyn, matriarch of the clan (Granlyn)
Larry, her cousin and mate (Grampa)
Bay, her second cousin (Grampa Bay)
Pauli, her niece and Bay's wife (Granli)
Maria, Bay's sister
Chad, Bay's cousin and Maria's mate
Art, Bay's cousin
Betty, Art's wife (taken by alien)
Bill, Pauli, Allen, children of Beth, Lyn's sister

Born on Ruthor:

Adam, Lyn's half-brother (deceased)

Born on Brama:

Gabe (Gabriel), son of Adam and Kareth, a Bramite
Amy, Gabe's half-Bramite sister

Born on Harmony, second generation:

Perri and Peter, twins (to Lyn and Adam)
Charley (Perri's mate), to Bay and Pauli. Siblings: Beth
(Gabe's mate), Christi, Megan and Mandy (twins), Bobby
Art Junior (to Art and Betty). Siblings; Joan, Anne,
Cory, Mary
Chad III (to Chad Junior and Maria). Siblings; Fred,
John, Barbi, Dick

Born on Harmony, third generation:

Marisa (to Perri and Charley). Siblings; Laurie, Ricky
Will (to Beth and Gabe). Siblings; Dottie, Gary, Pam
Mike (to Peter and Anne). Siblings: Carla, Marti, Doug
Susan (to Christi and Art Junior). Siblings; Betty, Sam, Seth
Ruthie (to Joan and Chad III). Siblings; Joey, Sally, Jimmy
Freddie (to Megan and Fred). Siblings; Andi, Forrest, Tommy and Tessa (twins)
Barry (to Mary and John). Siblings; Jeanie, Nancy, Gwen
Jeff (to Barbi and Cory). Siblings; Cindy, Donnie, Kayla, Bonnie
Sara (to Mindy and Dick). Siblings; Tina, Greg, Kenny, Alice, June

Born on Harmony, fourth generation:

Willie (to Ruthie and Will)

Born on Peace, fourth generation:

 Brian (to Ruthie and Will)
Janice (Janny) (to Marisa and Will)
Glori (to Susan and Mike)
Lucy (to Dottie and Freddie)
Curtis and Leona, twins (to Lyn and Larry)

The quines:

Qione, matriarch – Marisa's partner
Kiong, her mate – Will
Quest, their son – Laurie
Qiola, Qione's aunt – Lyn
Qilla, Qione's daughter, born on Peace
Many others

From Brilt:

Roroy and Beast
Roroy's father
Villagers
Gate people

Bramites:

Kareth, Gabe's mother
Noa, friend of Lyn, master healer
Karil, Noa's mate
Treesa, accompanied Lyn and Noa on first trip
through tunnels
Old Emek, former leader
Gan, his son, current leader
Young Emek, Gan's son

Wati:

Judee, matriarch of tree people, rescued Lyn,
(deceased)
Dela, her daughter
Suli, Dela's daughter

Gatekeepers

Other aliens:

Minis
Asiram of parallel Peace

Marisa's World

CHAPTER 1 – LYN

As I watched my little granddaughter play with a lopsided cloth ball, I had no inkling of the havoc the child would cause for our colony here on Harmony. Marisa was only three, and none of us knew that her growing pains would cause a fatal disruption of our world, least of all, her. For now, however, her mindTalent was no more than the mental link she had with her mother and the rest of our clan from shortly after her birth.

In a doze in my rocker on the back porch of the child care center, I listened to her giggles rather than actually watched her. Faces of little third-graders I'd taught back on Home Earth drifted through my mind. Although I'd lost most of my childhood memories, I did enjoy being with children.

Marisa let out a yell. I opened my eyes in time to see the ball sail over the log fence at the bottom of the yard.

What is that child up to, I thought, pushing myself to my feet. A premonition of danger and major changes flowed over me. I shivered. No, she couldn't be doing that, she's much too young. Marisa was spunky and bright, but no, not this. Not yet. The thoughts scrambled through my mind.

Presently Marisa leaned over and picked something up. She turned and held her hand out with the ball in it. "See, Granlyn, I got it."

I never cared for this Talent foisted on my family, even though I didn't discover mine until I was twenty-five. My daughter's Talent of teleportation was scary enough, but I couldn't accept this. I felt like my children and their children were leaving me behind.

"I thought it to me." Marisa trotting over as I stood on the porch, shaking inside. "I made it come to me."

"How?" I had to know.

I *reached* into her delicate little mind and *sensed* a nub of something that should not have been there. Something not of us Terrans. My grandchild, my daughter's child, was no longer wholly human.

I sighed. I always thought of our mind link as a convenience and glad it came in handy when I had to use my Talent to escape from the Centar before we came here to Harmony. But that has still been part of our humanity. This new thing in Marisa was alien, other. We, my clan, were beginning to change.

"No," I cried, and told myself to calm down, I was imagining things. The change wasn't supposed to begin happening for several generations yet. I had to talk to Bay, the leader of the other half of the clan.

"Granlyn?" the little girl asked. "You hurt?"

"No, dear. I'm all right Let's go in now." I took the ball and grabbed the little girl's hand.

Trotting through a yellow playroom with its shelves of toy animals and rag dolls, I led Marisa to the room we call the office. The brown walls wore a mosaic of children's drawings. I sat her down at the little blue talk table. This was where we child when he needs a talking-to.

"I'm hungry," Marisa announced climbing up onto the chair.

I tamped down my emotions. I had to deal with her first.

"It'll be suppertime soon," I said, smiling at her. "You know you were a naughty girl."

"Why?"

I hunted for words. "You used a Talent that you were not supposed to use. You are only supposed to use the mind link until you get older."

"Why?"

"Because that's the rule. We have to be careful not to hurt anyone. The Bramites, like Miss Kareth, don't have our Talents, and we need to be careful around them."

"I got my ball. Didn't hurt anyone." Marisa stuck out her lower lip.

I sighed I wasn't sure how much she understood of the gulf between us and the Bramites. We had to be careful not to flaunt our Talents.

"Well, try not to do it, but if you must use your Talents, do it where none of the Bramites can see you."

How much did she really understand? How much did her mother understand about the situation? I remembered how confused Perri was when she was a child.

Thinking of her, I wondered how she was doing. My daughter had just given birth to Marisa's little brother. I knew they were all right, because I'd been *linked* with her, but I wanted to go and see her in person. Should I tell Perri what her daughter did, or wait for a few days? I was scared deep inside, Marisa was such an innocent little child.

"Tell me a story," Marisa demanded, bouncing up and down. "Where did you live when you were little like me?"

"I lived on another world called Earth" I sat beside her. "In a house much bigger than this." I waved my hand around. "The kitchen was almost as big as this whole room."

"How did you get here?"

"The aliens, who are changing us to look like them took me to my half-brother's world without my memories. From there, we went to a big city called Centralia, where I met Judee, the Wati. Then we went to live with the Bramites for a while, then Judee took us back to Earth on her spaceship. We picked up our cousins, and Judee brought us here."

I'd told her this before, but the child love to hear about Home Earth. "Our kitchen in our house on Home Earth had two big windows. One looked out on the patio, full of flowers, and the other, through the screen porch and the wisteria covering it, to the street."

"Whats wist whatever?"

"A bunch of little purple flowers that hung down like this." I held my hands about a foot apart. The only reason I remember them was because went back to collect cousins. I still couldn't remember much of my childhood.

Kareth, the Bramite, who ran the childcare center, and several parents arrived. "How's our little one?" she asked, picking up Marisa. The others headed out back to collect their children.

"I'll start supper," Kareth said as she put the child down and poked her head out the back door. "Everybody in, now," she called. Marisa climbed up on the couch and cradled her rag dolly. I stood where I could watch her and talk to Kareth in the kitchen.

"How's things down there?"

I missed being with the others, but knew we had to keep the little girl away from the Bramites is much as possible. They did not have, and mostly did not understand, the mind link Talent that I and my fellow Terrans had. Perri and her twin Peter, had learned to keep their abilities under control, each new generation's talent was stronger, and we had to keep a sharp eye on Marisa.

And now we have this new worry. How could we keep it under control? I shivered again and went to the kitchen to help Kareth.

As I was putting food on the table, Charley, Marisa's father, stopped by.

"Papa!" Marisa ran to him. "Where's Mama?"

"Down in the clinic with your new little brother." He swung her around.

"I want Mama!"

"She's asleep now. Maybe tomorrow."

"How is she?" I asked, although I knew, I'd been mentally *linked* with Perri most of the day.

"Good," Charley said, kissing his daughter and putting her down. "I have a son." He stretched his arms upward.

After he left, and I took Marisa to her other grandmother for the night, I went home to Larry. Although he had no Talent, he knew very well what I was feeling. Yellow walls decorated with pictures from Home Earth were as comforting as his arms.

"What's up babe?" he asked as he hugged me. He'd always been there for me, even as children.

"Marisa," I said. 'She's…" I couldn't go on.

"Now, there can't be anything wrong with that little angel."

"She used a Talent she shouldn't have been able to for a long time yet."

"Hmm." He kissed my hair. "Well if it doesn't hurt anything …"

"It didn't this time," I looked up at him, "but what about next time?"

"Don't worry about it. Kids are resilient. If you told her not to again, I'm sure she will."

"I hope so." I couldn't blame him for saying that, I'd always known he hadn't quite gotten all the nuances of having talent.

I slept uneasy in his arms that night.

***

The next morning, when I arrived at the childcare center, Marisa was already there, and Kareth was fixing breakfast for the children being dropped off.

After we ate, I gave Marisa a bath and took her down to see her mother. Marisa danced along, singing, "Mama, Mama, Mama." A cool early spring day, pale green leaves sprouted on Harmony's version of oak trees, and we heard the first voices of the little brown chitterers.

Noa greeted us at the clinic. One of the few Bramites who understood the mind link, her round face, with eyes at the edges, split in a smile. "He's a healthy little guy, sounds just like Gabe when he was born. Remember?"

"Oh yes." Gabe was Kareth and Adam's son, a grown man now. I returned her smile as Noa led us back to the big corner room. Sunlight streamed in the east window, lighting up Perri's face.

"Mama," Marisa yelled, ran to the bed and climbed up on it.

"Careful," I said, as Perri gathered her in with the arm not holding the baby.

"Marisa, meet your little brother, Laurie," Perri said, pulling the blanket down so the little girl could see his face.

"He's ugly. Give him back."

"I can't. I'm afraid we're stuck with him. Don't worry, he'll look better in a few days."

Before Perri and I could stop her, Marisa mentally *reached* into the baby's mind. He screamed, and we *clamped down* on the little girl, *shutting down* her mindlink.

"No," I cried out.

"Don't you ever do that again," Perri growled. "You are not to ever go into his mind again until I tell you okay. Understand?"

"He's too little now to deal with it," I added, still shaken from the day before, and appalled my granddaughter's action.

Marisa shrank into her mother's shoulder.

I touched the little girl briefly, and sensed pain, confusion, and the feeling of being shut out. Soothing her, I looked at Perri. She needed to know about her daughter. I decided to come back when the child was down for her nap.

"I see a sibling problem," I said. "You'll need to keep a close eye on her. It was different with you and Peter, being twins and the same age. We'll have to start training her soon. She won't wait till puberty like us."

Once again, I shivered.

CHAPTER 2 – PERRI

Beth and I sat on a bench in the plaza doing mending while a bunch of screaming kids played hide and seek among the buildings and trees. Our youngest, my Ricky and Beth's Pam, played at our feet. A spring breeze tousled our curls. I heard the sounds of my world through my mindlink with Beth, or whoever was closest. My ears didn't work, something had been missing when I was born.

I remembered playing the game here with my twin, Peter, Beth, and others, when I was about Marisa's age. Peter always hid the best. I always knew where he was, but pretended I didn't.

Our plaza, surrounded on three sides by the meeting hall, warehouse, healers' clinic, crafthouse, schoolhouse, and communal kitchen, was the clan's general living area. The fourth side opened to the river and the crop fields beyond.

A new game started, with seven-year-old Marisa as 'it'. The rest of the kids scrambled to find hiding places. Will, Beth's oldest, had been 'it' previously and found everyone.

Marisa wandered around, found a few of her friends, and stopped on the side away from us.

I stared at my daughter, turning around slowly. 'No. Marisa,' I *called* mentally. The girl ignored me. She was getting good at that.

Presently Marisa said, "Meggy, I see you in the wood box." Meg, a Bramite child, climbed out, eyes wide and mouth open.

"What is she doing, Perri?" Beth asked.

I knew. Marisa was using her Talent. I stood up, my needlework falling to the ground, and pushed back the fear that I was unable to control her.

Before I could speak, Marisa called, "Joey, you're up in that tree."

A small boy shimmied down the trunk of a large oak-like tree. "How did you know?" he asked.

"Marisa, stop that. That's cheating," I yelled, trotting over to her.

Marisa ignored me and called out three more children.

A couple of Bramite women emerged from the crafts building. Their eyes widened as the girl called out the rest of the kids.

"No," one of women cried. "That's not right."

The other one said, "Miss Perri, keep your daughter away from our children." They collected their offspring and stalked off.

"Well," I said, as I stormed over to Marisa and took her arm.

"Now see what you've done."

"I was tired of walking around when I knew where they were."

"No more hide and seek for you, young lady. Where's Laurie?"

"Here, Mama," said a four-year-old copy of his father.

I took his hand and led the two children back to the bench, furious and scared. Marisa had always been an obedient child. Every now and them, though, she'd strike out on her own with some new twist of her Talents, and we'd have to corral her. This time, it was in front of the Bramites. I had a bad feeling about this.

Will crawled out from under the bench. "You missed me," he taunted.

"No, I didn't. I just didn't choose to find you yet." Marisa stood on her tiptoes and stretched out her arms.

She and Will were destined to be the leaders of their generation. That scared me even more than her misuse of Talent.

"That's enough, Marisa," I snapped. "We're going home now. Beth, tell your kids to let you or me know if Marisa pulls anymore tricks." I picked up Ricky's wooden toy boat and dropped it in my bag. He scrambled to his feet.

As we left, I saw Will stick out his tongue at Marisa's back.

Although they were still children, they both claimed they were the best at whatever they were doing.

"I thought you understood you were not to use your Talents in play," I told Marisa as we trudged up the hill to our cabin.

"I don't like playing with the Bs. They're too dumb." Marisa skipped a few steps. "Mama, why can't we have a place of our own?"

"Because there's not enough of us to make two colonies." I thought of the Bramites, whom Marisa called Bs. They'd gotten along well with Mama's generation, but my generation was far enough ahead of them to make things uncomfortable at times. And now, Marisa and her friends…

Maybe she was right, we did need a place of our own, where we could grow without impinging on anyone else.

***

That evening I left the kids with Charley and went over to Mama's house. The pale walls with their mosaic of pictures from Home Earth, wooden furniture, and yellow curtains were all welcoming.

"Mama, we've got a problem." I told her what had happened at the plaza. "What am I going to do with her? She's only seven. What's going to happen when she gets older?"

"Good question. Come sit down and we'll talk."

I joined her on the faded green couch. "It's like Marisa has two sides. The normal little girl who does little girl things, and someone else who wants to do these crazy things."

"I know." Mama shivered. "It was hard enough raising you two." She looked around. "Frankly, she's beyond me. All I can suggest is treat her like a normal little girl. You can always ask the Fours for help."

"Mama!" I couldn't believe she was saying these things. "But she's not a normal little girl. Please tell me what to do."

Mama sighed. "I can't, I don't know myself." Mama sighed again. Have you reached inside her mind recently? It's not something we should be doing, but sometimes it's necessary."

"A few weeks ago, when she skinned her knee. Mama, there was a place I couldn't *reach*. It was like something not even of us."

"Not human," Mama twirled a curl. "Yes, I saw that when she was little. I think it is the beginning of the change from human to watcher."

"But that's not supposed to happen for a long time yet." I pounded the arm of the couch.

"I know. My Four knows. You need to tell yours. I think we need to keep treating her as a normal child, keep an eye out for these other things. We need to set up some kind of Guardian ring around, loose enough so that she won't sense it, but to be there when it is needed."

"How do we do that?"

I didn't like having my child watched but she wasn't totally my child anymore. There'd always been something about her I couldn't control, but now it was more than I could handle.

"After she's asleep tonight, we'll call our Fours and see what we can do." The Fours were entities composed of four people whose combined talent was stronger than each individually. Each generation had its own.

"Okay. But you know what she asked today? Why can't we have a place of our own."

Mama looked at me. "That child is smarter than we think. I've seen that displeasure among the Bramites. Don't worry about it now. Just keep an eye on Marisa, and we'll talk about these things when you need to."

"Okay, Mama." I felt I had been stranded in a strange place on another world, with a young one I couldn't control.

"How are the boys behaving?"

"Other than linking with Charley and me and you, I haven't seen any other evidence of talent."

"Good. Let's hope they stay that way." She stood. "I need to start supper for Larry, and you need to do the same for your family. Call me when she's asleep."

"Okay, Mama." I hiked home in a state of disbelief.

***

That night, after the children were asleep, I told Charley, "Mama wants our Four and hers to meet to discuss how to keep Marisa from doing things she shouldn't."

"Okay. We can use all the help we can get." He smiled at me as we curled up on our brown loveseat.

I *called* Mama with my mind, and Charley *called* Peter and Beth, the other two of our Four.

Mama, Uncle Bay and Aunt Pauli, Charley's parents, and Uncle Gabe, Adam's son, who moved up from the second Four after his father died, made up the first Four.

We all *connected* our minds, and Aunt Pauli *sent*, 'I've been wondering about her. Beth's kids say she knows too much.'

'We can't lock her indoors,' Mama *replied*. 'She has her needs, too.'

'We can control her now,' Uncle Bay *remarked*, 'but for how long?'

'She needs a program where she can learn how to control her Talents and use them properly,' Gabe *sent*.

'But who can do this?' I *asked*. I squeezed Charley's hand.

'Our Four,' Uncle Gabe *sent*. 'We will work on this tonight. Have her meet us tomorrow after class at Aunt Lyn's.'

'Okay.'

'Don't worry, Perri, she'll be all right,' Mama *sent*.

"She's right," Charley said aloud, putting an arm around me.

"Okay, but what about when she reaches puberty?" I asked.

"We'll worry about that later. Let's just see how things work out now." I let Charley pull me into his arms. "We've got a handful, don't we," he murmured.

"Charley, I'm scared. You didn't hear those women today. I've never heard Bramite women sound like that. They were about as angry as they can get."

17

"Maybe we should move up north."

"Mama won't like that, and what if the Bramites up there don't either?"

North Point was a secondary community, mostly populated by people of my generation, mainly Bramites and their offspring. Charley and I had stayed in River Point to be close to Mama. In spite of all the childcare I'd practiced, I had no idea how to raise this child.

"Let's go to bed," Charley said, moving me toward the bedroom.

***

I don't know what Mama's Four did to Marisa next day, but there were no more problems for a while. A few tendays later, at crop-planting time, Uncle Bay was teaching Marisa, Will, Susan, and a few others how to plant the seedlings. It was Peter's turn to watch her, but a bug distracted him.

"Look," a Bramite boy near her said. Peter jumped up and *clamped down* on her mind so she couldn't use it, with others of the four *coming in* after him. One of the Bramite women working in the next row stood up.

"Get her out of here," the woman demanded.

I trotted over to my daughter. "What have you been doing now?"

Marisa shook her head and her lip quivered. The seedlings she planted with her mind looked just like the ones done by hand.

With arms crossed, I stared at her.. "Get back to work," I said, "using your hands."

I looked around. "Peter, where are you?" I snapped.

"Sorry, sis, I got distracted." He looked away.

"When you're looking after her, we can't afford to have you distracted. This is too important. If you can't do it, I'll get Mama to get someone else."

"Okay, okay. I won't get so distracted again. Don't worry, it's all right now, Perri."

Marisa picked up a seedling, dug a little hole with her finger, set the plant in it.

However it wasn't all right. A group of Bramite women began talking about getting Marisa and her family to go live somewhere else. I sensed Marisa's fear and confusion, and tried to soothe her. As mad as I was at her, she was still my little girl.

CHAPTER 3 – PERRI

Mama, Papa Larry, and Gan, the Bramites' leader, called a general council meeting one evening after supper. All of us Terrans attended, plus Gan and a few of his Bramite counselors. The tan walls of the meeting hall were decorated with drawings and other artwork done by the children and some of the adults, including Aunt Maria.

We discussed upcoming maintenance on the buildings and the continuing crop planting, when several Bramite women stormed in, led by Treesa, one of the people who went through the tunnels on Brama with Mama and Papa Larry.

"We want the Council to get rid of these unnatural children of the Terrans," Treesa demanded. "Send them away."

"To where?" Uncle Bay asked. "North Point?"

"No. Some of us have children up there."

"Where, then?"

"Back in the mountain forests." Treesa pounded her fist into her other hand

"That's where the Wati live."

"Let them fight it out."

"No, we can't do that to our children," Mama cried.

"Well, they can't stay here," Treesa snapped.

I *felt* Marisa's fear echoing my own as she sat in the back of the room with the other Terran children.

The meeting rapidly descended into a shouting match. Finally Papa Larry yelled for silence.

"Calm down, people. Gan, as leader of your people, what do you have to say?"

"Some say you have gone too far," the young man said, flipping his yellow braid back over his shoulder.

"In what way?"

"When you first came, we took you in. Father believed you were the answer to prophet Bram's prophecy, so he and the elders revered you. But then you took us out of our comfortable cavern, out through long tunnels to the outside. First, things went well. Then, after you left, things went bad. The mountain erupted and destroyed the upper valley and all who were in it. Then there was the plague that killed all the new babies."

"We came back and rescued you," Mama pointed out.

Gan nodded. "But we would have been safe in our cavern."

"No, that whole world was destroyed, and your people would have been destroyed with it," Papa said.

"My father may have believed that, but I don't. We don't."

"You were only a small child when we picked up your father and your people. You wouldn't remember. Your father does. Ask him."

"He wants nothing to do with you people," Gan snarled. "You brought back the aliens who took some of our people."

"Not on purpose," Mama said. "We lost one of ours, too."

"Okay, okay," Papa Larry held his palms out. "It may be best if we find another place for the younger generation, but let's do it in an orderly manner. First, we will send Allen and his explorers out to see what is east of here, to find a suitable place. Then we will have to decide who will go and who will stay here."

"No. All go." Gan insisted.

"If Art and his son go, who will fix your machines when they break down? If we older women go, who will teach your children, heal your sick and hurt? Think about it," Mama said.

Gan didn't answer, just look down at his feet.

"Okay. What else do we need to discuss?" Papa Larry asked. We went over a few minor items, and he called the Council closed. "Peter, Perri, I want to see you," he added, as people began to leave.

"What," Peter said.

"Yes, Papa?"

"When you two were coming home from the mountain gate, did you see any possible areas for any settlement? It'll have to be near the river."

"Not really," I said. "I was paying more attention to my leg and the trail." I'd fallen and hurt my knee badly.

"There was a wide area up above the last camp before home, but I don't remember details," Peter added.

"Don't we want trees?" I asked.

"Yes," Papa said, "but you will need open areas for crops."

"Oh. Are you and Mama coming?"

"We'll have to talk about that. Come on, let's go."

As we passed Uncle Art, he glared at me and muttered, "Now see what you've done."

Papa stopped. "Get over it, Art." We continued on.

***

Four tendays later, we Terrans milled about the plaza preparing to move. Since Gan kept insisting that all Terrans go, we agreed that all of us would move into our new place, Freedom.

"We'll see how they do without us," Mama said. She told me, she and Papa would go back later, and had asked Noa and Kareth to keep an eye on the Terrans' homes

Now, the younger children ran around yelling, until we adults told him to save their energy for the trip. It would take us at least two days. Uncle Allen had found us a place farther upriver, with scattered trees for our homes and open fields for our crops.

Charley and I had been up once to see the place, and I was very pleased with it. I knew Mama was unhappy to be apart from us the mind link was never enough when it came to grandmothers and grandchildren.

Finally, we began herding people up the trail. Everyone carried something. Even the little ones who could walk had a toy in his or her hand, Papa Larry and Charley lugged our possessions, and the others carried belongings and supplies. Marisa swung a bag of her clothes and toys.

At the top of the trail, we stopped to rest. From there, we could see the crop fields in the distance, with forest behind. Uncle Allen, Art Junior and a couple other young men picked up packs from some of the children who kept falling behind, and went on up to the camp.

"We'll be back." Uncle Allen said. "We'll meet you on the way."

Papa Larry wanted to go with them, but they wouldn't let him.

"This is for young men," Uncle Allen said as they left. Uncle Bay and Uncle Art were already up at Freedom, waiting for us. They'd laid out house sites, crop fields, and begun to work on the mill.

Papa Larry had us stop early to camp for the night. The young ones were having trouble keeping up, and no one could carry them.

"Where are Uncle Allen and the others?" I asked.

"They're coming," Marisa said. "They thought we were going to the big camp."

"How do you know?" I demanded.

"I see them." She ran off to her friend, Susan.

"Marisa," I yelled, but as usual, she ignored me.

A little later, the men showed up. Everyone found places to put

21

their blankets along the stream and under the trees.

***

The next day, the sun high in the sky, Marisa complained as she trudged along beside me. "I wish we had something to carry us." Charley was right behind us, with the boys. He stayed close, he was my ears.

"That would be nice," I said. I thought of the large animals that Mama and Uncle Bay had ridden back on Home Earth. There was nothing like them on Harmony, and they had not been able to bring any from Earth.

Later, Papa Larry stopped us at another little stream. "The younger guys can do it in two days, but a lot of us can't. We'll camp here and get there tomorrow." After supper, some of the young men went on to Freedom. We were not that far away, but the older adults of Mama's generation, and the little kids needed to rest.

As I was getting Marisa settled for the night, she asked, "Why is old Art so mean?"

"Why do you say that?"

"He said you and me were nothing but trouble. He said you let his wife die."

"Why the so-and-so." I clenched my fists and slammed the bed. "Sorry," I said, controlling myself. "I did not 'let' her go through the Gate to the other world. I couldn't stop her." I closed my eyes and pushed pain away. "He's always sad because he still misses her. Be nice to him if you can."

"Okay."

***

In the morning, we were up before the sun, eager to reach our destination. By the time the sun had climbed halfway up the sky, the trail curved away from the river. We slowed down as we climbed into the hills. Uncle Allen and several others met us and more of the children's backpacks.

Finally, we reached the top of the hill and saw Freedom spread out below.

A wide, tree-spattered place between a small river and the hills lay before us. I heaved a sigh of relief. House sites had been laid out along the trees, the plaza and surrounding buildings had been marked out nearby. To the right, the crop fields were lines of bare dirt. Mountains rose in the distance.

Charley took the children's packs. "You guys head on down," he told them. Marisa bolted away and the boys followed. We *reached* back to Gabe to let him know we'd arrived. Since his mother was Bramite, he'd been allowed to stay at in River Point. He was our link to the other settlements. Uncle Chad and Aunt Maria and their family had stayed up in North Point, our contact there. Their grandchildren had not yet shown any signs of talent beside beyond basic mind link.

***

We all gathered in the plaza area. "Welcome to our new home," Uncle Allen greeted us. "Bay is working on schedules and such. We have three cabins ready, one for Bay and Pauli, one for Aunt Lyn and Uncle Larry, and one for Perri and the kids."

"Sorry, Peter, you'll have to build your own," Uncle Bay said, grinning. Aunt Pauli hugged him.

"Let's see what you've got here," Papa Larry said.

"First, the outhouses." Uncle Bay led us to a hollow away from our river and well above the big river. Three small shacks sat in a row in the center. "I suggest we get a crew going to build more."

"Right," Papa Larry agreed.

I went to check out our new home. It was even smaller than the one in River Point. Three tiny bedrooms, each with barely enough room for a pair of narrow beds and storage boxes. Even worse was the so-called kitchen. A narrow counter shorter than my arm span attached to the wall, a shelf above, and a box underneath. We were definitely going to have to do some remodeling.

Mama's wasn't any better. "That's what you get when you let men do something without letting the women check it out first," she said. I sighed.

Back at my cabin, I collected the children. "Okay, kids, listen up. Marisa, you can have the back bedroom in the corner, you boys will have the middle one. Get your things in your rooms. We'll eat in a little while.

"At least mine has got two windows," Marisa said later, as she helped me prepare food in the communal cooking area. Too long logs split in half, the level surfaces used as counters and tables, sat in the center of the place, with a few rough boxes nearby.

"It'll do for now," Mama said.

After supper, Mama drew Marisa and me together. "Marisa, you've done very well lately. I think it's time we start teaching you how to use your Talents properly. Yours are appearing at a much earlier age than ours did. It does take time to get used to them."

"The first time I discovered my moving talent, before I knew I had it, it scared me silly," I said. "A toddler was falling off of a boulder, and I caught him and set him down by his mother. I was a long way above them on the trail." Mama nodded. "It took me quite a while to learn to control it."

"Oh," Marisa said, wide-eyed.

"Our Talents are to be used when we need them," Mama said. "They are not toys to be played with. If there is something that is to be done, and we cannot do it by ourselves, then we can use Talent to call for help, or to move something that is hurting someone or something. Mindlink is to be used when you need to talk to someone who is not nearby."

I wish I could've explained it that well.

"Now, we know that you can see hidden people, and move things without touching them," Mama continued. "What else can you do?"

"Um, I don't know," Marisa mumbled.

"You're hiding something," I said, as I realized part of her mind had shut down against me. I looked at Mama.

"Yes," she said. 'Why, Marisa?"

"I don't know."

I *felt* her fear, confusion, and alienation. "You don't know how to say it?" I asked gently.

Marisa nodded.

I *saw* that she wasn't aware of that nonhuman entity within her.

"Okay," Mama said. "The most important thing is to start using your talent in tiny ways until you get used to handling them. Do not try anything on any person unless you have asked them, and they said it was okay. If something new happens, let your mama or me know right away."

"Okay, Granlyn." Marisa nodded.

I sensed something new about my daughter, something way beyond what Charley and I had. Something that would change our colony forever.

A change in my daughter.

A difference.

An otherness.

CHAPTER 4 – MARISA

"No, I'm not going to mate with you, Freddie," I snapped, stomping my foot. "Now go away." The trees around the clearing danced in the breeze as if responding to my agitation.

"But, Marisa, you're seventeen already. You have to be mated." Brown curls dangled around his face.

Freddie, just turned sixteen, had come down from North Point to Freedom to choose a mate.

"I don't have to do anything and I don't want to mate." I stomped off, slashing branches and bushes with my Talent.

"But I want you," Freddie called after me. I *sensed* that he didn't have enough nerve to go to Granlyn to officially choose me without me with him.

Why couldn't Will have picked me like he was supposed to? Why didn't Granlyn make him pick me? Why did he have to pick mousy little Ruthie? Why do I have to be so different? Why do I keep feeling like I don't belong here? The thoughts scrambled through my mind as I marched through the forest.

I never should have let Freddie drag me along to see one of his finds. He did come up with some interesting plants and things, though. Grampa Bay says Freddie is just like his great-uncle, Grandpa Bay's brother.

Aware of so much more than the others, even my brothers and cousins of my generation, sometimes they seemed like stangers. I loved Mama and Granlyn but often it was too hard to deal with them, I felt like I was so far beyond them. Why did I have to have this other, alien thing within me?

I needed a mate, one on my level. Also, I *sensed* a need I couldn't even articulate. Sometimes I felt like I was outside of everything, detached from my clan, observing someone else's life. Either it was all mine or I had nothing.

When I slammed in through the front door, Mama took one look at me and said, "You turned him down."

"Mama, why do I have to have a mate and go through all that stuff?" I flopped down on the moss-stuffed long seat, tossing my wrap aside.

"It's the rule," Mama said, retrieving my shawl and hanging it up. "As long as we need to keep growing our population, everyone must mate and produce children."

"I'm not ready for children," I pouted.

"I understand," Mama said, sitting beside me. "I wasn't ready for you, either."

"Anyway, there's nobody here for me, and don't say Freddie, he's a creep."

"Marisa! He is what he is, and unless you want to wait for one of the younger boys to grow up…"

"Oh, Mama." I stormed into my room. Why couldn't she understand? I needed to find someone outside of our group, not Bramite, but I had no idea how to find him. I knew that we Terrans, the Bramites, and the Wati were the only people on this world. Mama had told me about the Gates to other worlds, but the Rock Gate, on the beach between River Point and North Point had been shut down. There was a Mountain Gate way up in the highlands, and although it had been one way when Mama and Uncle Peter had come through, that could have changed.

That night, I dreamed of a man like Papa, but my age, and our several children, as we ruled a new land of our people.

"No," I cried as I woke. "I'm no ruler." I was shaking. Was this a vision of my future? And where was this new world?

The more I thought about it the next few days, the more I realized I would have to go up to the Gate, find a way through, find someone like Papa. But when I got through, how would I know which world to go to? How would I get there? How would I find my mate?

I couldn't talk to anyone about it, no one here could understand. When Mama went through the Rock Gate to find Uncle Peter, she had her link with him. What do I have? Who could I link with?

***

Next free day, Susan and I hiked as far upriver as we dared. She was Art Junior's daughter, my age, and my best friend. But although I tried to tell her what I really wanted, she couldn't understand how I felt.

Up on a hill, I turned to the direction I thought the Gate was and reached. There was something-the Gate?

"Susan, we've got to go up there and find out," I exclaimed. "If I can go through, I can find him."

I'd confided to her the part of my dream of finding a mate elsewhere.

"We?" she said. "You know we're not allowed to go past the boundary until we're mated, and even then with at least two other adults."

"Spoilsport," I said, starting back down. "I'll find someone."

"Your folks let you go without being mated?"

I shrugged. Although Susan was the logical one, and always tried to talk me out of doing things, we were as close as sisters. She had a point. Mama would understand, she'd gone through the Rock Gate to find Uncle Peter. Papa? No way. Not after what he went through when Mama was gone. I'd heard all about it many times.

We were almost home when we met Papa and Mike.

"Where have you two been?" Papa demanded.

"Up river to the boundary," I said. "We're okay."

"Your mama is looking for you." Mike took Susan's arm. "Said she couldn't find you. She was in a real tizzy fit. You better go find her as soon as you can."

"She worries too much," Susan muttered. "But I'll *call* her now."

That night, Mama and Papa kept a close watch on me.

I started to plan my escape. I would go by myself if I had to.

CHAPTER 5

Two tendays later, I was in a deep sulk. The only ones who were at all interested in going with me were Freddie, who was the last person I wanted, and my brothers. Laurie might do, he was fourteen and large for his age. Susan refused, she was a stickler for following the rule.

Problem was, there were not enough people here in Freedom. Because there were more girls than boys, most of the girls would have to wait and choose someone younger.

My sulk was compounded by my four grandparents and Uncle Art going back to River Point. Uncle Allen went with them and would be coming back with more supplies. Both Mama and Granlyn wept as Granlyn prepared to leave. I would miss Granlyn. Although she said we would have to be careful communicating with one another, I still didn't get why the Bramites hated us so much.

The day after they left, at breakfast, Mama said, "It's time for Susan to take over your job teaching the little ones their letters and numbers. You will teach the ones a little older about plants. The plants we brought and the ones that belong to this world, how they grow."

"Okay." I didn't mind teaching the little ones, they were all so eager to learn.

We went down to the school house, and Mama checked out the cupboards. Inside the building, there were rows of benches and tables all around. I hung a few more pictures on the wall while Mama pulled out the lists of plants. I loved this place, but could't wait to get away from it.

Granlyn had figured out a long time ago how to make a sort of paper from certain sized loovah leaves. Loovah was our universal plant that the Bramites had brought from their original home world. It grew everywhere, under every sort of conditions, and provided food from the small inner leaves, fruit, and roots. The larger, outer leaves were used for cloth, and the stems for rope.

"Sit down," Mama said. "We'll go over these before they come."

"Why do I have to do this?"

"It's one of your responsibilities now. Over time, you'll work your way up to where I am. Marisa, you know this is the way things work here." Mama looked at me. "Also its time for you to have a daughter."

"Oh, Mama." I couldn't find the words to tell her I wasn't ready to mess with babies yet. I wanted a mate with whom I could spend time to plan our future and settle somewhere where we could live peacefully. I wanted out of this place where I felt so alone.

"Now, Marisa." Mama looked at me with a quizzical expression. "I know there's something about you beyond your papa and me, but you have to learn to cope with it. I really wish Granlyn was here."

"So do I."

***

The next day, Will and Ruthie met up with me in the plaza. They had been mated for over half a year. My pain was tucked away in a dark corner deep within me. I knew why she hadn't conceived. She was deliberately avoiding it because she wasn't ready for a baby. She knew I knew, but she couldn't do anything about it.

"I hear you want to go exploring," Will said. "We'll go with you to the Gate."

"Okay." I looked at Ruthie. She shook her head. "Good," I said.

Will was one of the leaders of my generation. Grandpa Larry said he reminded him of Will's grandfather, Adam, who was one of the first leaders.

I couldn't shake Freddie, and Susan decided to come. She wanted to have an adventure before she and Mike settled down. We met to make plans. When to go, what to take, who to tell.

***

One night at supper, I took a deep breath. "Mama, I have to get away. I can't shut out the people here any more, even though they are my friends and relatives. You know how Grandpa Bay always stays on the outside of the group,? It's like that, only much worse for me."

"I was afraid of that," Papa said. "I guess it skipped me."

"Where are you going? Who's going with you? You can't go by yourself." Mama picked up a muffin and put it down.

"Up to the Mountain Gate. Will said he and Ruthie will go."

"At least, both Will and Freddie are big and strong," Papa said. "Susan is clever, but I don't know about Ruthie."

"We'll make sure she pulls her weight." I fiddled with a spoon.

"How many days did it take you to get back from the Gate, Mama?"

She looked at Papa. "It took me six or seven days, but I had that bad knee. Do you think they could do it in five?"

"Depends on how much they carry," Papa said.

"Just to the Gate and back. We can't afford to lose your labor for too long," Mama added.

CHAPTER 6

Early one summer morning, Will and Ruthie, Susan and I met at the Plaza.

"I thought Freddie was coming," Will said.

"Let's go before he gets here," I said, looking around.

Will shook his head. We settled our backpacks and started off.

"Hey," came a voice from behind us. "Wait for me." Freddie caught up with us, panting. "How dare you leave without me."

I turn to glare at him. "We couldn't wait forever." I moved off.

We were almost to the big river when I heard another voice.

"Hey, sis, wait up."

"Laurie, what are you doing here?" I demanded.

"I wasn't going to let you go by yourself."

"I'm not alone," I snapped. Inside, I was glad he had come. "Come on, then." I held up my hand and *called* Mama. When I told her that Laurie had snuck out and joined us, she *sent*, 'You don't need to bring him back, Marisa. I'll tell your Papa.'

I promised Mama that we keep in touch. Uncle Allen had brought Granlyn back to be with Ricky and Mama. Ricky was becoming a troublemaker. At twelve, his talent was expanding and he was having trouble controlling it. Granlyn said he reminded her a lot of Uncle Allen at that age.

The path down to the big river was lined with tall, waving grasses, and a few fluffs of white clouds dotted the sky. I only felt a little guilty about how I was hurting Mama and Papa. At least, Mama understood what I was going through; she'd been there herself with Uncle Peter. With this small group, I was able to focus on the journey and ignore their thoughts.

It wasn't long before we warmed up and removed our cloaks. "Are you sure we should be doing this?" Susan asked as we packed away the garments. "I mean, this trip."

"You didn't have to come." I kicked a stone.

"I know, but I couldn't let you go off on your own."

"Why not?"

"You might not come back. Anyway, we may not get much

farther. Mama is going to send half the clan after me."

I looked at her. How did she know? I hadn't thought about not returning, but when she said that, it occurred to me I had a choice of whether I came back or not. If I found the right mate. I would return, of course.

Excitement with an undertone of apprehension enveloped me. I knew I had to do it, but I sensed serious troubles ahead. The long hours of walking, carrying a backpack of supplies, dampened the enthusiasm and deepened the sense of danger.

At first night camp, under a trio of trees with folded leaves, we sat around the campfire, ate, and sang songs. Susan and Ruthie even made up some of their own. Only Laurie didn't sing, his voice was jumping up and down octaves.

Will yawned. "I'm tired. We're going to bed now." He and Ruthie rose and slipped away.

I couldn't help wincing.

"Come on," Susan said. We laid our sleeping blankets side-by-side, and Freddie and Laurie went off behind the trees. Susan and I talked into the night.

***

Laurie shook me awake in the morning. "Get up, sis, everyone else is up."

I dragged myself out of my blankets and shrugged on my tunic. The others were packing up. Even Susan seemed cheerful, but then she always was a morning person. They saved me a bit of breakfast. I gobbled it down and threw my things together. We started out in a happy mood.

Late morning, we found a place where the river widened into a pool. Tall trees with long leaves surrounded the water, and tiny blue flowers lined the banks. Will and Ruthie pulled off their clothes and jumped in.

"Hey," Freddie said. "We're supposed to be going somewhere, not lolling around in the water."

Susan and I looked at each other, undressed, and joined them. Laurie was right behind us. The water was cool, but not too cold to be uncomfortable.

"All right." Freddie followed us into the water.

We splashed around for a while, and Will and Ruthie disappeared.

"Three guesses what they're doing, and the first two don't count,"

Freddie smirked.

I ignored him and pushed away the pain at the thought of them together, crushing the hidden memories. Somehow, I was thankful it worked out this way. Will would have wanted me to get pregnant right away. But the thought that Will had broken the rule and picked someone else, gnawed at me.

I felt time passing and climbed out. "Let's get going," I said, drying off with a blanket and dressing. Susan, Laurie, and Freddie followed.

"Hey, Will and Ruthie, we're leaving," Freddie yelled.

By the time we were packed and ready to leave, the two splashed out of the river.

"You conceived yet, Ruthie?" I asked.

"Maybe," she said, not looking at me. They quickly dressed and packed up, and we were on our way. The rest of the day passed uneventfully.

***

The next day we had to go inland away from the rocky mess around the waterfalls and couldn't find the river again.

"Come on, Marisa, can't you sense it?" Laurie asked.

"Don't you think I've tried?" I snapped. I hated it when my Talent wouldn't work right.

"Let's all *look,*" Will said. "Everybody, in a circle, facing outward. Focus now."

I *reached* and felt the others. We should be making our own Four. Will and Mike and Susan and me. We linked arms, focused together, and slowly turned.

"There," I pointed, *sensing* water. We broke apart, picked up our packs, and started in that direction. After a short time, we heard the river, and then saw it. We were above the falls.

"Thank Oneness," Will said. Ruthie clung to him. "Well, let's go," he added.

That evening we came to the place where the river curved south, and we had to turn east. Uncle Allen had made us a map with Grandpa Bay's and Uncle Peter's help. As we sat around our campfire, we studied it carefully. At least Will and Laurie did. "Shouldn't be a problem," Will said.

In the morning, we filled our water pouches and headed away from the river. Up to now the slope had not been too bad, but climbing this ridge was a lot harder. We had to stop and rest more often. On the other side, downhill was much easier until we started feeling the burn in our calves. When we stopped to camp by the stream in the valley, I was ready to sit. A row of wide trees lined the river bank.

As we were eating supper, I heard Ruthie ask Will, "How much farther do we have to go?"

"Another couple days." Will wiped his lips on his sleeve.

I thought he was being optimistic, from what I'd heard about the trip from Mama and Uncle Peter. I also hoped he was right.

That night, curled up in my blankets, I *sensed* the Gate, felt its pull, and knew this trip was what I needed to do. The Gate held a key to my destiny.

***

The next day, we followed the map over the next ridge to the river that had fish in it. Laurie, using Uncle Peter's method, caught a couple. We split each fish three ways. They were very tasty.

We'd never seen any in our little river. "Do you think there's fish in the big river?" I asked.

"I don't think so," Laurie said. "Just out in the sea."

This valley, like the other, was full of green grass and small bushes, some with red and white flowers. The hills sprouted larger bushes and tall, thin trees, in clumps. Although it was hot in the valley, we found cooling breezes high on the ridge. The only sound, other than us, was the whisper of the trees and the gurgle of the water.

***

The following day, it took us longer to climb the next ridge. It was higher, for one thing. Ruthie began complaining that it was too hard. "I told you there would be a lot of climbing," Will said. "Talking only wastes your breath." There was an annoyed edge to his voice, which pleased me, although I wasn't sure why.

At the top, we turned and looked back at the distant gleam of the sea. A sudden yearning to sit on the beach and watch the eternal nibbling at the shore came over me. But I couldn't go back now.

As we started down, I *reached*. This time there was something in the distance, behind the next ridge, something large and alive. No, several of them. I didn't *sense* danger, I just wondered what this was going to do to my trip.

"Hey guys, there's something out there," I said. "Just beyond the next ridge."

"What?" Will asked.

"I can't tell, but there are several of them, and they are big."

"What do you suggest we do?" Susan looked at me.

"Keep going and keep an eye out for them. I'll check often."

"What do the rest of you think?" Will asked.

"I thought there weren't any big animals on this world." Laurie waved his hand around.

"I'll do whatever the rest of you want," Susan added.

"I want to go home," Ruthie muttered.

"I think we should at least go far enough to where we can see them, so we know what we are dealing with."

"I agree," Will said. "So let's go on, and keep our eyes open."

We continued on down the hillside to the valley. This one had more trees, mostly along the river, and low bushes spotting the hills. As we set up camp, I *reached* again. "Still back there," I said. "I think they're settling down for the night."

"Okay. Let's move back away from the river. They're on the other side, so they would have to cross it to get to us." Will picked up his pack and walked away from the river.

"And that should wake us up and give us time to get out of the way," Susan added.

During the evening, we kept an eye on the ridge and, just before we called it a night, I *reached* again. "Still in the same place," I reported.

"Good. Come, Ruthie." He led her away from the rest of us.

***

In the morning, we ate and packed up without seeing anything. "They're still there," I said.

We headed south along the tree-lined river until we found a place shallow enough to ford it. I went across first and kept an eye on the ridge. Laurie, Freddie, and Susan made it across in fine shape.

Will, overburdened with both his and Ruthie's packs, followed Ruthie across. Halfway over, she slipped and fell. He tried to catch her, missed, and barely stayed on his feet. Laurie ran back to take Wills packs. Will splashed in and caught Ruthie as a current pulled her along. Finally we got her out, soaked to the skin from head to toe. Will was pretty wet, too. After they got into dry clothes, the wet ones hanging off their packs, we turned to start up the hill.

'I wouldn't have fallen in,' I sent to Will. 'Even with my pack' His back stiffened, but he didn't turn around. I looked up the hill in front of us. A row of large, four-legged animals with long heads stood silhouetted along the top of the ridge. The one at the left end, the largest, reared up on its hind legs.

"There they are," I said, *reaching*. I *sensed* interest and curiosity in them, but found no indication of danger. My heart pounded. Here was something utterly new on our world, and I had found them. I, Marisa, had discovered a new creature.

Stop that, I told myself, looking around at the others. Will and Laurie stared with open mouths. Freddie was moving backwards, eyes large.

"Ooh," Susan cried softly, as Ruthie buried her face in Will's chest.

While we watched, two others, smaller, ducked down behind the ridge. The other three began winding their way through the low bushes. Pointed ears topped their brown heads, and their sides showed the same brown. Tails of long hairs switched.

"Six against six." Freddie was still backing away.

"They are so big," Ruthie whimpered.

"I haven't *felt* any sign that they want to hurt us." A sense of awe of these creatures filled me, and I felt a connection with the alienness within me.

"How did they get here?" Laurie asked, staring at them.

"Possibly through the Gate," Susan said. "The poor things are lost."

I felt drawn to them somehow, and began to walk slowly up the hill, my mind open. I thought Susan was probably right.

The one who had reared followed the first three. Soon the others poked their heads up over the ridge, crept to the top, and started down after their fellows.

I moved slowly, keeping to their pace, as we approached each other on the middle of the slope. I felt the sun on my shoulders, the load on my back, and that sense of awe.

Their leader turned its head and appeared to be saying something to one of its cohorts.

The creatures are intelligent, I thought, and tried to *touch* the leader.

She jerked, looked at me, and *sent* a question. Somehow I knew the animal was female, and that somehow we could connect with each other.

I stopped and held my hands out to my side and in front of me, palms out, quivering inside. I *sensed* a name in my mind. *Quine.*

"Quine?" I said aloud. We were about two house-lengths apart.

She made an *ah* sound that I took to mean 'yes'.

In Standard I asked, "Did you come through the Gate?" I *sent* a picture of a door opening onto a grassy hillside.

She produced the sound again.

I *received* a garbled picture of a small, black four-limbed creature with hands like ours, riding on their backs. Did they want us to ride them? But we were apparently much larger.

The quine approached and looked at me with great green eyes. My friends had backed away. An aroma of a combination of grass and Papa tickled my nose. I *felt* a sense of inquisitiveness and wonder from her. She knelt down, and I sensed that the quine wanted me to climb up on her back. When I hesitated, she turned her head and wuffled at me. I climbed up onto her smooth, soft shoulder and back, and she rose to her feet.

I hung onto the long pale hair growing down the back of her neck as she walked around. The ground lay far below, but I had no fear of falling. I'd fallen longer distances than that and landed safely.

The quine wiggled a bit to adjust my weight, but I *sensed* no discomfort or fear in her. This was fabulous. A way to get around without walking, and as high as a cart. We stopped, and I watched as the largest quine, the one who had reared up, nudged Will. He knelt and Will climbed on.

"Hey, this is great," he said as the stallion walked around. "I propose we take these guys back home."

"What about my trip," I demanded. My quine swished her tail.

"We'll do it later, Marisa. Our people need to know about this." He swung a leg over and hopped off.

The other quines approached our friends, and Will helped the others mount. Soon, everyone except Will was perched on a quine. Sitting on the smallest one, Ruthie's face scrunched up as if she were on the edge of tears. Will told her to hold onto the quine's hair. He remounted, and we all headed downhill, back to Freedom.

We started out at a walk, but the quines soon picked up the pace.

Ruthie screamed. Her quine slowed, and the rest of us waited for her at the river. "Wow," I exclaimed. I'd never experienced anything so amazing.

"Yeah," Laurie added, his eyes glowing. I could tell he was truly excited about the quines.

"Way to go," Will added. Susan just patted her steed's neck.

Sitting up on the quines, we didn't even get wet crossing the river. We started up the hill and, even at a walk, we moved faster than we could have on our feet. The quines' big, flat feet gripped the ground no matter the slant or what was on it. This hill had more rocks and fewer bushes than the other one. I felt on top of the world.

We crested the ridge in the late afternoon and started down. I wondered how to tell my quine to stop. When we came to a small grove of large-leafed trees, she paused, looked at her companions, and lifted her head to taste a leaf. The others followed her example. They knelt to let us get off.

"Oh, I'm stiff and sore," I moaned, staggering around.

"Me, too," Susan echoed. "But it was wonderful to ride instead of walking."

"I'd rather walk," Ruthie muttered. "I'm afraid of falling off of that big, ugly thing."

"No, they are beautiful animals," I said as I looked at my quine. Munching on grass, sleek brown sides covered strong muscles. The line of her head, neck, and back, her long face with the great eyes showed me her beauty. No, more than just an animal.

Her pale yellow tail swished gently.

We made camp and set out our food. As we sat and ate, the quines wandered around, grazing on grass and munching on tree leaves.

"This is what our colony needs," Will said, wiping his hands on his pants. "A faster way than walking to get from place to place."

I remembered what I'd said about wanting to ride, back when we moved to Freedom. Did the Oneness have anything to do with this?

"And they can carry more stuff," Laurie added. He could hardly take his eyes off his quine.

Uncle Bill would love them, I thought. He had been an animal healer back on Home Earth, but the only animals we had on Harmony were the chickens we'd brought as eggs, the little brown chitterers, and the fish in the sea.

As we curled into our blankets for the night, I noticed the quines settling down on folded legs. I felt that they would become important to us.

CHAPTER 7

In the morning, I awoke with a head full of knowledge about the quines. The one I rode called herself Qione, the stallion was Kiong, and the others were their offspring. On their world, they communicated by mindlink and let the little black mooks be their hands. The quines controlled them with their minds.

Apparently the little creatures they called mooks, with round bodies and heads, were clever with their long-fingered hands, and willingly served the quines as long as they received food they liked and a certain stimulant.

Qione's group had found a Gate accidently and had been chased through by the one beast who threatened them, the huge, black barss. The quines could outrun the barss, but the latter had more endurance. Qione had sensed us humans almost as soon as I had sensed them.

When I was up and dressed, I looked for Qione. At her side, I could see the intelligence in her eyes and said, "Thank you, Qione."

She nodded her head and made an agreeing sound. I patted her neck, and she leaned into me. A feeling of belonging to each other wove its way deep into us, and we were permanently linked.

Now I had a partner, but I still needed a mate.

As we headed back, more used to riding these creatures, the quines picked up the pace. I loved the feeling of flying through the air, and enjoyed the idea that she and I were partners.

We returned to Freedom in what seemed like half the time it took us to walk out. Everyone scattered as we rode up to the plaza, stopped and waited.

People came out of the buildings and stared. Mama and Granlyn approached me.

"Where did you find horses?" Granlyn asked, eyes wide.

"These are quines," I said, "and they came through the Mountain Gate. This one is Qione." I patted her neck.

Granlyn touched her gently. "What a beautiful girl you are."

The quine nosed Granlyn's hair delicately.

Uncle Bay appeared. "How wonderful." He examined each one in turn. "Yes, I see they're not horses, but similar. The legs are thicker and the body not as long. Welcome to our home," he said to the quines, who nodded. Qione made the 'ah' sound.

Everyone crowded around, looking at the quines. After a short time, Qione snorted and pushed through the crowd over to an area between two groves of trees, in the hills in back of the settlement, where we dismounted. That area became the quines' territory.

I was glad to be home, but disappointed I hadn't found my mate.

Will asked Grampa Bay to call a meeting, since Grampa Larry had gone back to River Point with Uncle Art and his son, Junior.

"People, Will has something to say," Grampa Bay announced when we all met a little later in the meeting hall.

Will nodded and spoke. "You have seen the animals we rode home. They are quines, and they each have their own name. The big one I rode is Kiong, Marisa's is Qione." He paused and looked around. "We do not own them, they are an intelligent species in their own right. They came through the Mountain Gate and have come here to live with us as partners. On their home world, the quines lived with child-sized creatures who had hands like ours. We will be their hands now."

People nodded and murmured.

Will continued. "The point I am making is that they are not animals to be taken care of, they can take care of themselves. They are simply another people, like the Wati are another people, so treat them with respect. If they want you to leave them alone, they'll let you know."

"Can we ride them?" Ricky piped up.

"Maybe."

***

Mama and Granlyn spread the word through Uncle Art at River Point to Aunt Maria and Uncle Chad at North Point. "This will make it a lot easier to get from one place to another," Granlyn said. "We won't feel so far apart."

We all returned to our duties. The crops were growing nicely. Susan began training as a healer under Aunt Anne.

Qione and I 'talked' from time to time. She understood what I said, and somehow I heard her in my mind. She was pleased with this area, lots of good grass and leaves, with the little river nearby.

She and Kiong roamed up and down the river and into the forest, but they always came back. One day, Qione told me, *my young ones are ready to have the small humans ride them for a short while.*

We marked off an area for the rides, and the children began lining up right after breakfast.

The quines were definitely in charge. Qione gave each quine direction on which person to put on his or her back, and where and how to walk around with the rider.

Kiong stood to the side and watched. Younger children hesitated, and a parent had to walk with them, holding them on. Older children squealed and wanted to go faster and farther, but the quines refused.

After the rides were over, Kiong let Uncle Bay ride him. I'd never seen such a big grin on Uncle Bay's face.

Qione moved over to Granlyn and nudged her. "She wants you to ride her," I said. I helped her on, and she also wore a grin.

After that, it was hard to concentrate on our tasks. People kept peeking over to the quines' territory, including me.

When Granlyn wanted to return to River Point and Grampa Larry, we decided to let her ride. Mama wouldn't let me get near those people down there, so Papa, Will, and Granli went with her. Qione let Granlyn ride her, she wanted to see more of this world, and I missed both of them.

The two smallest quines stayed behind, huddled together under the trees. I visited them several times a day to talk to and pet them.

Granlyn stayed linked with us, and told us the Bramites wouldn't let the animals get anywhere near them. She had to keep them up at their house. Grampa Larry was quite impressed, and Kiong let him ride him. Granlyn said it only took them one day to get there.

By the time Granli on Qione, Papa and Will returned, I was ready to leave home again. There people here were my family and friends, and I loved them dearly, but part of me demanded to get out and find my real life. The alien thing within in me urged me on.

I spent as much time as I could with Qione, and together we learned to communicate. We had a mental link, unlike the link I had with my family. I couldn't describe it, but I understood what she wanted me to know, and she understood my speech. Eventually, the rest of the quines learned to understand us.

She told me how their brains had developed, how they saw how the world worked, and learned to cope without the hands to do things. Then they found the little mooks whose hands they could control. So now we were their mooks, except we were a lot smarter.

Kiong was already communicating with Will and Art Junior about ideas he had. They were working on a platform for us to use to mount the quines, so they wouldn't have to keep kneeling down. The quines let people ride them when the critters felt like it.

I told Qione the history of my people, and how we had animals similar to them, but ours were not nearly as smart.

I also told her how I wanted to find another world so I could find my mate. We talked about going back to the Gate. Immensely pleased as I was with the quines, my need to find my new life overwhelmed my desire to stay here with them and my people.

As nice as this is, I need to return to my world, she told me.

Wonderful, I thought. She and I can travel together.

We started to plan our getaway. She wanted it to be just us two, but I thought we should have another person, on Kiong, preferably. Not Will; as Uncle Gabe and Aunt Beth's oldest, he was the leader of our generation. I thought of Uncle Allen, but he was old. Almost as old as Granli, who was his older sister. Art Junior was too busy here, keeping things going.

Laurie would love to go, but Mama would never let him. The only one left was Freddie, and there was no way I'd let him come. Finally, we decided it would be us and Kiong. Qione told the oldest of the rest of the quines about our plans, and ordered them to stay with our settlement until she got back.

***

The next day, as we were returning home from the schoolhouse, Mama said, "Marisa, you're spending too much time with that animal. You need to spend more time and attention on your tasks. You're making too many mistakes."

"She's not an animal," I snapped. "She's a person like you and me, just a different shape." I picked up a rock and threw it into the bushes.

"Marisa." Mama paused. "I know what she is, but your tasks come first. With or without your Talent. You will stay home tonight and catch up on your mending."

"Oh, Mama." I had to get away, and soon.

***

I made a mess of the mending, sent a brief message to Qione when I went to the latrine, and crawled into bed early. I kept seeing all the other worlds Mama had *shown* me; the ones she'd actually been to, and the ones the Gates had shown her.

Will also was watching me. We were supposed to have been mated to each other, but I was aware that he was afraid he couldn't control me. So he chose Ruthie, whom he could control, and there was nothing the others or I could do about it.

Once chosen, a couple was bonded for life. That was the Rule.

One day he took me aside, and said, "I know you're planning to leave soon, but we need to make our Four before you go."

I looked at him and nodded. "You're right. I've been thinking about that. It would make it easier for me to stay in touch with you. When can we do it?"

"I'll talk to Mike and Susan and let you know."

***

Two days later, the four of us gathered at Will's house while Ruthie was over at child care. We sat in a circle in the middle of the main room, on Ruthie's handwoven blue and tan rug, just touching hands.

Will began the ceremony by saying, "Grampa Bay started the first Four back on Home Earth. Beside him, it included Granlyn, Granli, and Uncle Adam, Granlyn's half-brother. When Uncle Adam died, before we were born (as I was born, I thought), his son Gabe moved up from the second Four. That was Uncle Peter, Aunt Perri, Uncle Charley and Gabe until he moved up. Gabe's brother, Han, took his place."

I felt the beginning of the drawing together.

"Now we will become the third generation Four." He looked around at us. "Close your eyes and open your minds."

I felt drawn in to the others as the outer world faded away; sensing Susan's sweetness, Mike's strength, and Will's need for me, but nothing else. I managed to keep the kernel of pain hidden.

Enfolded in otherness, we drew together and merged into our Four. I felt that alienness within me, somewhere deep down, that one day I would be able to draw out and use to help my people. Right now, if it weren't for the trance, it would have terrified me.

As the trance faded and we embraced, I knew I must leave this world and find another for my people, so that we should continue to thrive.

"Someday," I said to Will, "Someday you will give me a daughter.

But not for a long time yet." His jaw dropped. I strode off, surprised that I'd said that.

***

We reached the slow period when all the crops were planted and growing nicely. The water supply for the crops had been set up, it would be long before harvest. Qione told me it was time to go. I began making preparations.

"What are you doing?" Ricky asked me one day when I was repairing my travel bag.

"None of your business, brat."

"I'm going to tell Mama." He danced away from my swatting hand.

"Tell her what?"

"That you're going on a trip." He ran off.

"She already knows," I called after him. She knew I was up to something, but I kept my plans in a part of my mind that she couldn't reach. In a way, I wanted to tell her, but I knew what her reaction would be. I felt a little guilty about hiding it from her, but I couldn't afford to be stopped again.

I asked Qione if she ever traveled at night.

I can, but I don't care to, why? You shouldn't be out at night.

"It's the only way I can get out of here without Mama and Papa stopping me," I explained.

I'll talk to Kiong.

CHAPTER 8

Two nights later, I woke myself a couple hours before dawn. As I collected my cloak, bag of food and personal items, and a water pouch, a sense of excitement flowed over me. I crept out of the house and trotted up to the quines. The stars were bright enough to silhouette the trees. Qione wuffled as I approached.

I mounted her, and with Kiong following behind, we headed straight for the big river, away from the settlement. As we galloped through the night, the wind in my face, a great feeling of freedom washed over me. For the past couple of years, I'd fought a feeling of being tied down, always having to do what the rules of the community dictated. I had no desire to be trapped by a mate and children. I knew I was supposed to have daughters to carry on the line, but at this point in my life that was not important to me.

We were well up the river when the sky ahead of us grew light. The quines had slowed to a walk and were looking for a suitable place to graze and drink, when I *received* a blast from Mama.

'Marisa, what do you think you're doing? Come home at once.'

'Sorry, Mama, this is something I have to do. Qione told the other quines to do whatever you ask of them. I'll keep in touch.'

'Where are you going?' Papa asked, a pleading note in his voice.

'Qione wants to find the way back to her world, to bring more of her kind through to live with us. And I need to find a mate.'

We had stopped, and I dismounted. 'I'll be all right, Papa.' I cut the connection. I knew they'd talk about coming after us, but the other quines weren't as fast as Qione and Kiong, and we had too big of a head start on them.

After a quick breakfast, we took off again. I had Uncle Allen's map from Mama's trip bringing Uncle Peter home, and the quines knew the way. We alternated between galloping and walking. Although the weather was clear and hot here, once we got farther up into the hills, we found cooling breezes.

The lush greens of the valleys we had seen on the previous trip were fading with touches of brown up on the hillsides.

I made camp, and the quines moved off a little. I sat with my back against a tree, my arms around my legs and my chin on my knees.

The quiet consumed me. My mind emptied out. I closed my eyes and let the world melt away. I could feel the tree against my back and the ground under my bottom. A faint grassy aroma tickled my nose. And that was all I sensed.

I felt the world around me, a dim entity stretching forever. I felt my body and all the processes within. I reached outward and felt the universe. For once, I was at peace.

Curling down into my blankets, I slept.

***

The next day, we came to the river with the fish, but I didn't try to catch one. I still had plenty of food. It was almost dark when we stopped to camp. In the morning, I was up before sunrise, and later we came to the fruit trees that Mama and Uncle Peter had mentioned, but the fruits were not quite ripe yet.

***

Late afternoon on the third day, a small stream led us up to an open area fringed with low, round hills. I could see dark mountain peaks beyond them to the east. Qione paused at a small group of wide-spread trees and let me off. She and Kiong walked over to one of the hillocks and stopped, communicating between themselves. I could not understand how they did it or what they said, no matter how hard I tried.

Qione touched the hillside with her broad flat foot. Nothing happened. She said something to Kiong, and they trotted back to me. *The Gate is in there*, the quine told me, *but we will have to wait for it to open.*

"Okay." I stretched and walked around, disappointed and annoyed. I wanted to go through now. I kicked at a clump of grass. A few wisps of cloud drifted into the eastern sky.

I dutifully *called* Mama and told her we were at the Gate and everything was fine. I also told her that I would *call* her just before we left.

We stayed there all day and the night. I was glad to rest but, impatient to move on. I couldn't sit still and kept pacing around.

Relax, Qione told me. *Pacing around won't make the time go any faster.*

That would be nice, I thought, if I could make time go faster. But no way that could happen. I shrugged and reached for my Four. Susan caught me up on events back home. I showed her the Gate and the area around it. Finally we unlinked, and I managed to get some sleep.

47

***

In the morning, I had eaten, packed up, and was pacing around, when Qione trotted over to the hill and touched the grass on it.

A vertical crack appeared as she backed off, and the opening widened to a doorway. She turned to us and knelt down so I could mount her. We and Kiong trotted though into a long, narrow room. Tables, chairs, and beds lined the sides, but I didn't take in any details, I was so anxious to get to the Gate.

Since the pathway through the room was not very wide, we went in single file, Kiong on our heels. His breath had a grassy aroma. At the end of the room, we passed through a long, gray corridor and into a large round room with several doors.

"Now what?" I said.

Qione trotted around and nosed at each one, until she found the door she wanted. We entered the portal, and I passed out. A moment later I came to, dizzy, still on Qione's back. In front of me, a wide expanse of tall, blue-green grass stretched to a turquoise sky. In the distance were tall trees with long, bluish fronds hanging from their tops. It was warm here, and very quiet. I had to take deep breaths to get enough air. The quines didn't have any trouble, though.

A *frisson* of pleasure passed over me as I bounced on Qione's back. At last, I was on another world, even though this was the quines' world, not my new one. It was different in a way I had not expected, and I meant to enjoy every minute I was here.

Kiong and Qione gulped down great mouthfuls of the grass and bellowed. I grabbed my ears. The bellow had a ringing tone to it that went on and on. Soon, to our left, one, then several quine heads popped up out of the field and answered. We started in the direction of the other quines, through grass as high as Qione's shoulders. A narrow trail led through the grass, but still the two quines had to continually push overgrowth out of their way. It made a rustling sound, like rattling loovah leaves.

Seated up on Qione's back, I could see jagged peaks in the distance, and large groves of round green trees. As we met the other group of quines in an open area around a grove, I could see more coming in the distance. Quine talk flowed around me. I sensed welcoming, and curiosity about me.

For the first time in my life I felt small. I huddled down on Qione's back, my cheek against her neck, and listened.

Several small black creatures jumped down from the trees onto the other quines' backs.

The closest ones stared at me, then broke into high pitched wails.

Quiet, I heard Qione bellow.

The mooks, for that's what I figured they were, shut up.

Kiong marched down a narrow side path, returned carrying a large folded leaf with his teeth, and tossed it to the nearest mook. This led to a scramble by the little creatures over the contents.

Their happy seeds, Qione told me, as the mooks jumped back up into the trees, squabbling over their treasures.

The quines talked and talked and talked. I think Qione even forgot about me. One of the others nosed my pack, and Qione jerked and looked around. She snorted, jiggled, and told me, *I knew you were there all along.*

A little more quine talk, then most of them left, scattering down the different trails through the grass.

What do you want to do? Qione asked me.

By this time, I breathed easier. "Go back to the Gate and find another world for me."

Rest. We will go in the morning. She let me off.

I found a cozy space between a couple trees and curled up in my blankets. As I dozed off, the quines who hadn't left were still talking.

***

In the morning, I mounted Qione and we headed back to the Gate. She told me, *Kiong will take some more of our people back to your world.*

As we traveled back the way we'd come, a tall, narrow cliff, like a headland, loomed up from where we'd arrived on this world. Although different from anything I'd seem on our world, I didn't pay much attention, I was so anxious to find my world.

At the wall, Qione tapped her front foot, and a slit appeared, widened, and we entered. She trotted across the round room to another door. This led into a much larger place with many doors.

"How am I supposed to know which one to go through?" I asked, taking a deep breath.

She took me over to a large screen with a line of letters on it, attached to a center post.

Touch it, she told me.

I reached out and tapped it. Although cold like metal, the screen had a skin-like give to it. A picture came up of deep forest. This took three quarters of the screen. Along the side were several small pictures. The top one showed a man-like creature in heavy fur. The next three displayed an assortment of beasts and flying creatures.

One showed a small bright sun, another showed a map, a globe that turned, showing only two small seas in the great mass of land.

"No, I don't think so," I said aloud, and touched the screen again. This one was a water world with only one large island and several smaller ones. I tried a third time and found a barren world with only a few small bodies of water.

I tapped until my finger hurt. None of them felt right. The only thing they had in common was some combination of land and water. I had no idea there were so many worlds out there.

Finally I found one, about half land and half water. The person in the top picture looked like a young human male, wearing pants and a long sleeved shirt. There were several small, furry animals. As I looked at it, something inside me indicated that this was the one.

This is it," I said. Qione pushed a flat green disc at the side with her nose, and something pinged. As we turned, a door behind us opened. She trotted over, and we passed through.

CHAPTER 9

A moment of blackness, and I found myself sitting on a wide, brown-sand beach. Shaking the dizziness out of my head, I saw Qione getting to her feet.

This not like our Gate, she told me. *Are you all right?*

"I think so." I managed to stand up and stretch my neck, turning my head this way and that.

Large breakers pounded on the shore like thunder, so different from the small slaps of the sea on Harmony. Gray-brown cliffs blocked off the ends of the beach. Behind us were tall bushes with huge dark green leaves and dinner-plate sized red flowers. The air smelled sweet and was easy to breathe.

I trotted along the beach, while Qione sampled the leaves. This place felt welcoming, as if what I was searching for was here. A sense of freedom, of beginning a new part of my life, swept over me. The excitement of another world tickled me.

But first I had to find a way off this beach.

I turned and ran the other way, past her. At the very end, beside the cliff, I found a trail.

"Here," I called, beckoning. Qione trotted over, I mounted, and we marched onto the trail. Trees brushed the cliff overhead, but there was plenty of room for Qione to walk with her head held high. Soon the path sloped upward, and presently we came out in a little meadow in a setback in the cliff. This grass was more to her liking. Tiny yellow flowers grew in bunches here and there.

Only the whispering of the trees and our breathing broke the silence. I hadn't realized how quietly Qione walked. I couldn't hear her footsteps at all.

Here, I could see bits of the beach and the sea down through the tree tops below. At the other end of the meadow, a trail led up the side of the cliff above.

After Qione finished eating, we took to the trail, which curved around, up through a long, narrow valley, and out onto a wide plateau. Here there were grassy fields, groves of wide trees laden with red and yellow fruit, with little white houses here and there.

We followed the trail back between two fields and past an orchard with long yellow fruit, to a line of houses along the road parallel to the cliff edge. In these little buildings, white with dark flat roofs, each front door was a different bright color.

A man with white hair emerged from the first one, which had a yellow door, and stared at us. He made some kind of yodel call, and heads popped out of other houses. The old man made high, squeaky noises at me that I could not understand.

I said, "Hello."

He made louder noises, echoed by some of the other heads, and made a shooing motion back toward from where we'd come. I shook my head, and, as if we'd had the same thought, Qione trotted down the road. The people backed into their houses. Their noises didn't threaten us, and I didn't see any evidence of further menace.

At the end of the row of houses, the road curved inland. As we trotted around the corner, down the road, I saw another person mounted on an animal larger than Qione. The quine made a strange, keening sound in her throat and stopped.

The man, dressed in brown shirt, vest and pants, was huge, larger than even Papa Charley. Shaggy gray hair hung down below his shoulders. He sat on a beast, also huge, that was dark brown, almost black, with a round head and ears, beady little eyes, and a long snout. The man and beast approached.

Qione growled, and the creature stopped about a quine-length away. I felt her stiffen, but she did not back up. The two steeds sniffed at each other from a distance.

Meanwhile, the man stared at me. "Where you from?" he asked in passable Standard.

Qione issued a strangled snort.

My jaw dropped. How could he possibly know that? "Through the Gate at the beach," I said, pointing back down the road.

"Other world," he said.

I nodded.

"Come." He turned his beast and retraced his path. Qione followed as if drawn by a string.

We passed through a short stretch of woods, and the trail ended at a large open area from which several trails led off in different directions. In the center of the area sat a huge, gray stone building three times as tall as our house. Doors and narrow windows were all different shapes and sizes, some slanted this way and that.

"My house," the man said. He led us to a sizable patch of green near one of the off kilter half circle doors. We dismounted and let the steeds enjoy the grass.

"In."

Be careful, Qione told me, and began munching.

"I will," I muttered as I *checked*, and could *sense* no immediate danger, but I kept my alertness on high.

As I followed him to the door, I caught a whiff of his body odor. I couldn't describe it, but it made me feel uncomfortable. The little room we entered, lit by something in the ceiling, had red walls. The only thing in the room was a large bucket containing some long, dark brown sticks leaning together.

The next room was larger, with floors and walls of dark brown wood, and a few ornate old chairs stood about. Way too old to sit in. With doors in each wall, a woody aroma pervaded the space.

Through a doorway on our right, we entered a cozy room with dark red couches and chairs in a semicircle facing a huge fireplace. Each chair had an attendant table. The place had the same hidden light as the other rooms, and the fire sent out a spicy scent.

"Sit," he said, and went to a large cupboard on one wall. I could tell from his thumping footsteps he was as least as old as Grampa.

I dropped into one of the chairs. It was much more comfortable than the ones we had back home. What was he going to do with me, I wondered. I could not *reach* his mind at all, yet I felt no danger.

The man brought me a flat bowl of green mush, with a straw about a half inch in diameter. "Eat," he said, setting it on the table by me.

I was hungry, but not that hungry. I pushed it away.

He pushed it back. "Must eat."

I smelled the mush. Sort of a leafy, flat odor. I could not find anything in it that would harm me, but there were few nutrients my body could use. I tasted it. Not bad, it reminded me of Mama's vegetable soup. I took another taste and ate the rest, sucking it up though the straw.

The man made what I think was a smile through his beard. "My son be back from inspection in few days," he said.

"Inspection of what?" I asked.

"My land." He took the bowl and put it back in the cupboard. "Come."

"Aren't you going to wash it?" I asked, shocked.

"Servants will do. Come."

After Granlyn and Mama's adventures, I couldn't very well pass this up. He'd made no threatening actions, and I had ways to take care of myself.

I followed him through another door to a stairway, a series of steps, each one set above and behind the one before, which curled around itself. I clung to a dark rail along the open side, round and smooth. At the top, we came to a long hallway lined with doors. The walls were a light sandy color with designs in the same color that I couldn't quite make out.

The old man stopped at a door with a knob, turned it, and ushered me in.

I entered a large room with bluish gray walls and one tall narrow window. The place held a bed, a long table, and a shelf on the wall with hooks underneath.

"Yours." He waved his hand around the room. The old man pointed to a door in the wall opposite the bed. "Yours," he repeated. "I return next day." He walked out, closing the door behind him.

"Well," I muttered. I tried the door, remembering Mama's stories of locked rooms, but this one opened. I stepped out and saw a narrow window slanting across one end of the hall, and the top of the steps at the other. So I was free to move around.

Back in the room, I tossed my bag on the floor under the shelf and opened the other door. Inside, I found an outhouse seat on a box, and a shelf with a basin and pitcher of water. The room didn't smell like an outhouse, though. I wondered how they did that.

I sat on the bed and pondered. I felt safe here, but this was not the place I needed to be. Since I had no way of knowing what lay beyond this community, I knew I must stay and learn about this world. A tangled picture of my future began to grow in my mind. A future involving travels and dangers and another man.

I thought of Qione, and said aloud, "Are you all right?"

I am. How long do we stay here?

"I don't know. A couple of days, maybe," I replied. She gave a huff and went quiet.

She'll be all right, I thought.

There was something exciting about all these unknowns, especially since I could *sense* no danger to us. Then I had a thought. I couldn't *sense* the man; what if I couldn't *sense* danger either? But that was different. I always knew what related to me.

I thought of Mama and Papa and Granlyn. If only there was some way I could send a message. I wandered to the window and peered out. A deep overhang blocked my view of the sky. Down below, I watched as several men in rough brown clothes approached the house from fields. Their shadows stretched long. It couldn't be that late, I thought. I'd just had lunch.

However, it quickly grew dark. I was wide awake. Peeking out my door, I saw that the hall was unlit, except for a dim light at the top of the steps. I searched my room for a candle or some kind of light, and found none. Was I going to have to sit here in the dark for half the night?

Suddenly I heard Qione in my nind. *What is this darkness*, she demanded.

"I think that on this world, it's night now," I said aloud. "It's dark in here, so I'm staying in my room. Can you see anything out there?"

A little. The sky is bright.

"Well, we can't do anything until the morning."

Be careful.

I decided to *reach* inside the building. I found the old man in another room on this floor, on the other side of the building. Apparently these people went to bed at dark and rose at first light. There were three or four other people on the top floor. I *reached* through the place room by room, and there seemed to be a lot of empty ones. Had there been many people living here at one time, or had whoever built it expected there to be a lot of people in times to come? I couldn't image building a house with more rooms than was needed.

The place was old, creaky, and nearly empty. And cold. I wrapped my cloak about me.

I settled on the bed and *reached* farther out. There were the workmen and their families in their little houses, there were the people in their homes along the trail, there were more villages with their folk deep in sleep. I *sensed* Qione and the man's beast, as well as small critters in cozy burrows.

Staring out the window at the few stars I could see near the horizon, I wondered which one was Harmony's sun.

Returning to my bed, I thought of Mama and my brothers. Would I ever see them again? I wished Susan was here, I needed someone to talk to, someone I knew.

Will – no, I pushed that memory back where it belonged, out of sight, and drifted into sleep.

CHAPTER 10

The next morning, I awoke to a pounding on my door. I shook my head to clear away the dreams and sat up. Daylight streamed into the room. I shrugged on my tunic and *reached*.

"Who's there?" I called, although I knew who it was.

The old man pushed the door open. "Come," he said.

"Just a minute." I used the facilities and tried to get my hair in order. Then he took me down to a brown room with a long table and showed me where to sit. This time I had a bowl of brown mush that tasted like mushrooms, and a large roll of dark bread. After the meal, I wandered out to see Qione.

We went for a ride across the dirt and stones to a larger grassy area. After loping around several times, Qione stopped under a tree, tasted the leaves, and spit them out.

Nothing on this world good.

"We're waiting for his son to come home," I said.

You mate.

"I don't think so. I haven't even met him."

You need mate.

"Eventually," I said. "I'm not ready for one now."

Qione snorted. We continued on.

Later, hungry, I returned to the house and found more mush and bread on the table. The old man was nowhere around. I sat and ate, listening. I heard people moving about, but no one entered the room where I sat. The place was clean, so someone took care of this house.

I found my way up to my room. I'd left my bed covers in a mess, but when I returned, the bed was made and everything tidy. More water in the pouch, my clothes hung on hooks, my pack and things on the shelf.

"How dare they," I said aloud. How dare they touch my things. I checked it all and found no damage.

Although I felt safe outside, it didn't seem right to wander about this house without the old man's permission.

Since I had no idea where to find him, I went out to find Qione.

***

That evening, the old man appeared with the food, more green mush, and a much too sweet pudding.

"Why you come here?" he asked me.

I shrugged. I didn't know how to answer.

"You too young to go by yourself." He slurped more mush.

"I can take care of myself."

"My son comes tomorrow. He needs mate. You will do. What is your beast?"

Oh no, I thought, as I tried to explain about Qione. I wasn't sure he understood. Finally the meal was over, and I went up to my room.

I decided to see what the son was like, and if he wasn't the one, Qione and I would leave, pick a trail and head inland. I didn't want to stay here any longer.

I couldn't sleep. I tossed and turned, then got up and wandered up and down the halls. Back in my room, I lay down on my bed, closed my eyes, and wished it were morning.

Sinking into a doze, at some point, something inside me shifted. I opened my eyes to see dawn light coming in the window. I sat up. How did I make it morning?

As I stared at the window, I felt that my body was out of joint. I knew I hadn't slept all those hours. I rose and went to the window. The sun was definitely rising in the east, and men were making their way out into the fields. How did I do that, I wondered again. Time was time, one step after another. There was no way to change that. Was there?

I flopped down on my bed. I'd never really sat down and thought about my Talents, I just accepted them. I'd always been able to communicate with Mama and the others by mindlink. That was just what life was all about for me. I could move objects since I was about three. I remembered bringing Granlyn a ball I didn't want to chase after, so I mentally brought it back. I hadn't thought about moving the ball with my mind, I just did it.

Everyone had mindlink, that was normal, and I just accepted that I could move things like Mama and Uncle Peter and the others did. But now...

I dozed, waking with the sun high. Remembering my thoughts, panic hit. What else could my Talent do, could I do?

Through the terror, I realized that was why I hesitated to mate and have children. What would they be like?

"Calm down, girl," I told myself. I looked within my mind and tamped down the terror. I have to exist in this world for now, find a way off, find another Gate. There was none in this place other than the one I'd come through. I'd already *searched* for one.

Ok, this is what I'll do, I told myself. I would wait until the man's son came back, then Qione and I would take off and head east, to the rest of the continent. There must be something better than this on this world. And we still had to find the other Gate. Somehow, I knew that I couldn't go back through the one I'd come through to this world. There were always two on a world. I would not worry about a mate now. I had plenty of time to produce a daughter.

The son was supposed to arrive today. I thought about him as I dressed. Was he like his father? Would he greet me and disappear too? That would make it easier for me to make my getaway. Or would he be garrulous, or go after me? I'd gotten the idea, from the few things he had said, that the old man was looking for a mate for his son. Did he mean me?

I hadn't thought so much in years. I shook my head and went down to breakfast. After the tasteless meal, I went out to visit with Qione. We rode around and stayed in the area because I didn't know exactly when the son was going to show up.

At one point Qione stopped, stared to the east, and flicked her ears. *Someone on a beast comes,* she told me.

I peered in that direction but all I could hear was the sighing of the trees. "I don't see or hear anything."

My far-hearing tells me a person comes. Your hearing is woefully inadequate.

"I have hands," I retorted.

My people had hands eons ago. We will get them back in time.

"What?" This quine was much more complicated than I had first thought.

Qione moved over to a tree near the compound gate and munched. After a mouthful of leaves, she added, *I may tell you sometime.*

Just before supper, still down with Qione, I saw a rider in the distance, coming from the east. His cloak covered his shape, so I didn't really see him until he pulled up at the entrance to the compound and dismounted.

His beast was deep black, and even larger than his father's. Qione huffed and backed away.

"Ho, who be you?" the young man demanded of me in Standard. "What you do here? What that beast?" He pointed to Qione.

"We came up through the Gate on the beach." I nodded in that direction.

"Huh." He took his beast into the compound, as the old man shuffled out of the house and down to us.

"Ho, Roroy," the old man said to the young man. "How is all?"

"Usual," Roroy replied. "Doggers complain as always. Stick Creek down."

"Good. This woman your mate."

"No," I said, as Roroy took a step back.

"Yea," said the old man. "Time you make son of your own."

"Da, my decision." The young man spun on his heel and marched to the house. Tall and dark, brown hair straggling down past his wide shoulders, he wore a grim twist to his lips.

The old man beckoned to me and followed his son. As I turned to go with him, Qione told me, *We need to get out of here as soon as possible.*

The old man took me to a large brown room with a huge table and benches. An enormous piece of dark wood furniture sat along one long wall. It contained a row of cabinets with a counter on top, and several wide shelves above. These held dishes and pots, boxes and baskets I couldn't see into, and large pottery pots.

Three places were set at the table, with grey, cracked plates, wooden spoons that had seen better days, and lopsided mugs full of a dark and nasty smelling beverage. A large misshapen loaf of what appeared to be bread sat on another plate, with a long knife on it.

We settled ourselves, and a scarecrow of an old woman brought in a large bowl that leaked on one side. We served ourselves. As the old man and I ate the thin, tasteless stuff, Roroy took the place across from me. He glanced at me briefly, and devoted his attention to his soup. Neither man said a word.

After the soup, the scarecrow brought in a platter holding a roasted small animal, burnt on one side. I took a small serving and pushed it around on my plate. I couldn't stand the silence any longer and asked the son, "Are you glad to be home?"

He glanced at me, then picked up a roasted leg and started gnawing on it.

For dessert, the old woman brought us a lopsided cake, dry and tasteless, covered with pink sweet stuff. I hoped the color wasn't from somebody's blood. One bite was enough for me.

Finished eating, the old man left us. Roroy was still spooning soup unto his mouth. Finally he looked up and said, "Your hair too short."

"It's the way it grows," I said, touching my curls.

"You big. Make many sons."

"Not with you." Tall and big boned, like Papa, I towered over Mama and Granlyn. I pushed back my chair.

"No go. Not done."

I stood. Roroy stood. "Sit," he ordered.

I continued to stand. I couldn't *reach* him either.

Slowly, he sat down, staring at me thoughtfully with his large brown eyes. Then he said, "Go. Leave this place tonight."

I blinked. "Go where?"

"That way. Into rising sun."

"Why?" I had a suspicion, but wasn't going to say it out loud.

"Go." He banged his spoon on the table.

I turned and left.

Back in the room with the blue-gray walls, I stared out the tall, narrow window. An overhang outside blocked most of the sky. I had *felt* dissatisfaction and anger at his father in Roroy. If I left, would his father want him to go after me? Would he go on his own?

I decided to leave. This was my plan, anyhow. I went down to Qione to tell her.

I will be ready.

Returning to my room, I saw the old man coming down the hall toward me. I backed into a handy alcove, and he walked right by, eyes on the floor. I packed quickly, and waited for the others to retire.

When I sensed that they were asleep, I put on my cloak, slung my bag over my shoulder, and headed for the stairs. Qione waited for me at the gate to the compound. The beasts were over on the far side. I let her out and mounted. We took the trail to the east.

We galloped off, ecstatic in our freedom.

CHAPTER 11

The sky was brightening in the east when we crested a hill and saw a grassy lake. Qione galloped down and stuck her nose in the water. I still had food from home, and ate a bit. When we continued on, we slanted away from a village to my right. I didn't want to have anything to do with these people.

We rode through the day, across the sparse grass, around short, knobby shrubs, and by occasional round trees. Late afternoon, we stopped at a deserted farmhouse and found the well still working. I hauled up a bucket of water for Qione, and had some myself. It was the best thing I tasted since I got there.

As we left, I heard footsteps pounding up to us. It was Roroy on his beast. My heart dropped.

"Ho," he said. "I find you."

"Are you going to take me back?" I asked, clenching my fists.

"No. I go with you. I show you the way. Come."

Okay, so that was how it was going to be. We followed him on his beast until it became too dark to see. I could hardly keep my eyes open on Qione's back.

Roroy found us a large tree to camp under. I fell asleep before I hit the ground.

Qione stood guard over me. She told me the next day that his beast had watched her from beyond his master.

In the morning, we headed south. I wondered what he was doing, but realized he knew this place and I didn't. Presently we came to a trail that wound downward through massive trees. I caught a glimpse of the sea. The steeds walked; the way was narrow and full of stones. We came out at a place overlooking the ocean. A tiny village sat on a wide, flat area behind the beach. Brightly colored little boats lay on the grey sand or bobbed in the water. A line of houses in primary colors lined the boundary between beach and fields.

Yes, I thought, bouncing on Qione's back. She whinnied. We continued on down and stopped at the first house.

A little brown-skinned man came out and spoke to Roroy, who said something reassuring. We continued on, turning east along the beach, away from the village.

Qione trotted down to the water and splashed along in it. I held on and breathed in the sea air. Water splattered my legs, but I didn't care. This was heaven.

We came to a cliff blocking our way. Roroy led us up the hill inland and back down to the farther beach. I saw no sign of people here, only sand dunes stretching to the landward horizon.

'Is desert up there," Roroy said.

"So that's why we're going this way," I said.

He nodded and shrugged. We continued along the beach for several days. He had a large sack of water for the steeds and caught fish from the sea for us and Beast. Qione had to subsist on the sparse grass lining the top of the beach.

I asked Roroy questions. Sometimes he answered and sometimes he didn't. When we stopped, Qione would go out into the water up to the bottom of my pack bags, and I would slide off and swim about for a while. The sea was very flat and quiet along here.

***

One day we came to a little stream. The steeds stuck their faces in and drank. We went upstream and also drank our fill. We camped there, even though the sun was still up.

We sat and watched the steeds munch the grass along the stream. They appeared to get along, although Qione kept a wary eye on Beast.

"This is so nice," I said. "Are you going to go back to your land?"

He looked at me. His face appeared much more relaxed and softer. "I do not think so," he said.

"You weren't happy there, were you?" I shifted my legs.

"Not what I planned. Older brother Tomar to be Father's heir, but he died." He stopped and looked around. "I had other plans."

"To come out here?" I asked.

He nodded.

I listened to the lapping of the sea, the wind in the trees, and felt as close to content as I could get here. I still didn't know what he wanted of me, or why he chose to come.

"Do you have big storms here?" I asked, thinking that this was a possibility for a new home.

"Sometimes, in hot times."

Well, we'd have to build away from the beach anyway, I thought.

At dusk, Qione and I went wading in the sea. "What do you think of Roroy?" I asked her.

Good man. Good for you. He takes care of Beast.

"I don't know him well enough yet to tell if he's the one I want." I watched a round creature with tentacles float by just under the surface of the water. "Are you tired of travelling?"

Some. I need more rests like this. This world not bad, but not the one we want.

"I agree." Something was missing here, something I couldn't pinpoint.

***

We trekked along the beach for many days. Between the needle-leaved bushes along the top of the beach I caught glimpses of sand dunes. When will this ever end, I thought. The beach was pleasant enough, with breezes to cut the heat, but it was getting monotonous. I thought even Qione was getting tired of the sea.

When are we going to get somewhere with decent grass, she demanded one day. I relayed her question to Roroy.

"Soon," he said, not breaking stride.

***

Several days later, we came to a good-sized river. Roroy turned to follow the river bank. "We past desert and mountains," he said. "Now we go inland." The trail along the river, lined with grass Qione approved of, sloped upward, and after a curve, I could see mountain peaks to my left.

"Wow," I said. "I'm glad we didn't have to go over those."

Roroy smiled, lighting up his face.

***

The next day, we came to a wide trail and a wooden bridge across the river. Qione took one step and stopped. *No good.*

"Why not?" I asked. "Haven't you ever seen a bridge?"

Qione shook her head. *Not for my feet.*

"I thought nothing could hurt your feet."

Beast trotted across, and he and Roroy stopped and turned to look at us.

"They're waiting for us," I said. "If Beast can make it across, you can too."

Qione snorted and took a couple steps on the wooden planks.

"Ok?" I patted her side.

She snorted again, and gingerly walked across.

When we camped that night in a grove of small-leaved trees, Roroy said, "Father's brother came this way once, but Father didn't believe what Uncle told us about what he saw."

"But you did." He nodded and smiled.

***

A few days later, I saw something pinkish on the horizon. "What's that?" I asked.

"Trading post. We get more supplies, food there."

"Okay." Good, actually, I was beginning to wonder where we'd get more food.

We continued on along the road accompanied by a small stream. As we approached the large pinkish structure, I saw a scattering of small houses between the road and the stream, which had meandered farther away. The pinkish building had one large door and a line of narrow, horizontal windows along the top.

Roroy led us past the houses to a little park, where we stopped. "You and steeds stay here." He pulled a couple of large sacks out of his kit and patted Beast. "Behave," he told the animal. "Not long," he said to me, and strode off to the pinkish building.

I watched him until he disappeared through the door. The steeds were already munching. Turning in a slow circle, I took in this place. A path wound through the park from the road near the last house, a square gray box with a garden in the back yard. I wandered along, enjoying the feeling of walking. A pond full of glinting fish drew my attention. I squatted and dipped a finger in the water and jerked it out. Although the liquid was cool, it still burned.

My finger in my mouth, I continued on, past bushes with rainbows of colors and bouquets of scents. The park had no real end, it just drifted off into the fields along the stream. A rustic wooden bench drew me. I sat, took a deep breath, and stretched my arms up. The sun sent my long shadow across the fields. Flying creatures made circles in the clear blue sky. A breeze cooled me. I would sit here as long as I could, until Roroy came looking for me.

I savored the solitude. It had been long, before I'd left Harmony, since I had time to myself like this. I *reached*. All around, little clumps of people huddled in their villages. In the far distance, ahead, I sensed something more – a Gate?

The alien thing within me awoke, jerked me to my feet.

I heard myself yelling, "What the hell am I doing here?" It was if I'd suddenly awakened from a long sleep, from a dream about traveling through a strange land with Qione and two companions. But I was still here, an unknown distance from home.

I howled in frustration. Where was my clan, my Four, Susan, Mike, Laurie and Ricky, even Will? Come get me, I cried, fighting the urge to run into the field.

Calm down, my sensible side told me. We have to get to a Gate to get back to Harmony, and that will take many more days. My emotional side wanted it right now. As I tried to reconcile the two I heard Qione bellow.

I turned and broke into a run. Please don't let her be hurt, I prayed. Thoughts about her fluttered through my mind.

When I saw the two of them at the pond, Beast crouched and vomiting, Qione rubbing his back with her big flat foot, I dropped to his other side, thankful it wasn't Qione.

"What happened?" I saw remains of fish. "Oh, no. Those are poison."

I told him not to eat them. Qione shook her head.

I knelt beside Beast, one arm over his back, my head against his shoulder, and *eased* into him.. I calmed myself, *encapsulated* the poison cells seeping into his body, and *returned* them to his stomach, where he heaved them up. After *checking* for any strays, I slumped against him, as he rolled over and laid his head down on the grass.

Please don't let anything happen to him, I prayed to the Oneness. It would destroy Roroy.

A little while later I heard footsteps, a pair of thumps, and felt Roroy on top of us.

"Beast," he cried.

I lifted my head. "He'll be okay. He ate something he shouldn't have, something that didn't agree with him."

Voices interrupted us. Behind Roroy, on the path, three people stood talking. Two wore long tan shifts, the other a dark blue. The latter addressed us.

Roroy looked up and spoke in the local continental language. More people appeared, in tan and green. With her teeth, Qione picked up the bags my friend had dropped and brought them over.

"We must go," Roroy told me, and looked at Beast. "Come, boy." Beast heaved himself up on his haunches and shook his head.

I touched his neck. "He's okay, but I don't think we should go much farther today. He needs water, but not from the pond."

"Stream?" Roroy asked, fishing out a large cup.

"Yes. We've drunk out of it before."

Beast slurped down two bowls of water and struggled to his feet. Before we could move, there was a bang and Beast howled as he jumped.

I jerked around. A person in green held a long pipe aimed at us.

Roroy yelled something, and I *reached out* and *bent* the end of the pipe down. The person dropped it and ran off, followed by most of the rest.

Blue tunic shook his fist at us and yelled something. Roroy yelled back and picked up the bags.

Qione joined in with a bellow as I clung to her.

"We walk," Roroy said. He led the way, followed by Beast, who moved tentatively. I let go of Qione and walked beside Beast, clinging to his side, *sending* healing vibes. Whatever had hit him had not done any real damage, because of his thick fur. Qione brought up the rear.

All I wanted to do was sit and rest, but I had no choice but to keep putting one foot in front of the other.

We followed the path to the fields, stopping every now and then to let me catch my breath and for Beast to drink. Roroy led us diagonally across the field to the road. A little way along, we found a copse of trees and stopped to camp for the night.

Beast and I crumpled to the ground.

***

The next day Beast moved normally, and we were able to ride. The road led us through hill country with many groves of trees. At one stop, he picked round red fruit off a tree and gave me one. "These only grow here," he said. The steeds reached up and nabbed their own.

I took a bite. The fruit was juicy and sweet, almost too sweet for me. I gobbled it down and asked for another. "Can we take some of these with us for later?"

As I ate the second one, Roroy took out an empty bag and proceeded to fill it with the fruits. Our mounts gobbled them down, including some that had fallen on the ground.

"No more," he said to his beast, who raised his head.

"Qione, you'll get sick," I told her. She raised her head and looked around at me. "Don't worry, he's got a bag full, you'll get more later."

She whickered. *I hope so. Best thing I've had since I left home.*

We moved on. I saw mountain peaks ahead.

"Are we going there?" I asked.

"Around."

We rode on in silence. Qione scheduled our rest breaks. When she wanted one, she stopped and refused to budge. Since she was the smaller of the two steeds, we let her have her way.

With the warmer weather, we packed away our cloaks. There were plenty of lakes for water for the four of us. I began to be lulled into a state of languor by the continual soothing motion of the quine and the pleasant days. The urge to move faster, get to the City, get to the Gate, faded.

CHAPTER 12

When I asked where we were going, Roroy just said, "To city."

I understood from Mama that word meant a group of a great many tall buildings, but I could not picture it. However, I figured that sounded like the best place to find a Gate.

Roroy was turning out to be a comfortable companion. He knew where he was going, and how to find things we needed. I could relax with him, and a pleasant rapport grew between us. He didn't talk my ear off as certain brothers of mine were wont to do, and he had never tried to take advantage of me. He treated me as if I were a lady. Whatever that means.

***

One day, the trail led over a hill and down to a place where there was water everywhere, with dark gray trees and bushes growing in it. Qione stopped. "We're not going in that," I said.

"No. Road curves to left. Tell your beast to walk very slow and test each step. Road should be safe, but swamp always changing. Sometimes, there's quicksand."

Swamp, I thought. That name was very fitting. I told Qione, and she nodded her head. We moved on slowly, Beast and Roroy leading the way. Partway around we came to a bridge over a very narrow section of the swamp as it continued up back the way we'd come.

"See, this narrowest part. Starts below end of mountains."

"Okay." I tried to ignore the putrid smell drifting up from the water.

A few steps after Beast left the bridge, his right front foot went down into the muck. Roroy tried to pull him back but the animal continued to fight and soon his right rear leg slipped in. Roroy jumped down and began to pull on his steed.

When Beast's other front leg went in, and Roroy began to slide toward the swamp, I closed my eyes. If we could only go back to the moment before Beast took that step...

Behind my closed eyes, something shifted. A flicker of nothing, dizziness, and another shift.

I opened my eyes as I fell forward onto Qione's neck. She was just stepping off the bridge behind Beast. "To the left," I called without thought. Beast stepped to his left at Roroy's urging, away from the swamp's edge. We continued on safely this time.

I'd done it again, moved in time. How did I do it? Why did it take so much energy out of me? How could I control it? I knew I was special, but this was too much.

"What happen?" Roroy demanded. "What you do?"

"I don't know," I gasped. I couldn't move, I was so totally used up. All I could do was hang on to Qione and watch.

Roroy turned on his steed and looked at me. "Are you well?"

"Must rest." I gulped big breaths.

"Wider up ahead," he said, and lead his beast up the trail. Qione followed. I lay on her neck and held on, feeling her soft, smooth hair under my cheek. A little farther along, the trail widened out and sloped upward away from the swamp. We made our way into a grassy place, with a few small trees.

Roroy alit, patted his beast on the rump and came over to me. Gently, he reached up and lifted me off the quine's back and laid me down in the grass. Then he fetched some water and let me drink. I was beginning to come back to myself. This was not like the man that I left that little kingdom with.

"Food?" he asked.

I shook my head. "Sleep." As I said it, I fell into a deep sleep.

When I awoke it was dark night, not even any stars. A faint glow arose from the swamp below us. I could hear Roroy snoring, and the steeds making sleeping noises.

I crawled away, testing each hand fall, and did my business. When I returned to my blankets, I could not go to sleep.

I thought of Mama and Papa and all the others back home on Harmony. When would I ever see them again? I scratched my stomach. When would we find another body of water so I could bathe again? I closed my eyes and pictured Harmony. First, River Point, then Freedom, Mama's house and my room with the pink streaked walls made from some inedible berries I'd found.

When would I ever see them again?

A cold, wet quine nose woke me up. I saw Roroy sprawled nearby, and Beast placidly munched grass. Qione wuffled into my face and moved away. I sat up.

"How are you?" Roroy asked.

"Much better. That really drained me." I'd never done that heavy a job before.

"You do that? You take us out of swamp?" Roroy pulled at a blade of grass.

"Yes, it's one of my Talents." I stretched, and wondered how he remembered the alternate time. I did, because I experienced both time lines. I guess he did, too.

"You are witch."

"No, I'm just a part of a race of people who can do these things." I was hesitant to tell him anymore.

"Then you are goddess."

"No, not that." I giggled. "I'm just a girl with a few odd Talents."

"You more than that." He rose. "You want food, drink?"

"Yes," I said, realizing that I was starving.

After we finished eating, we mounted our steeds and continued on. The trail led upward at a gentle slope into low hills and valleys sprinkled with small white and purple flowers. Clouds moved in from the west, on a cool wind. When we stopped to camp, under a huge, widespread tree with thick dark green leaves, we dug out our cloaks.

In the night, I woke to rain. Only a few drops got through to us. The pit pat of the rain on the leaves was very soothing, and I drifted back to sleep. When I woke again, it was light and still raining. The steeds were huddled under the tree with us.

"Now what," I said. "How long will it keep raining?" Steady rains like this on Harmony could go on for days.

Roroy shrugged, looked at me. "What you called?"

"Oh." We'd never exchanged names. I knew his, because his father had called him by it. "I'm Marisa."

"I Roroy. Call me Ro," he said. "Nice name, Marisa."

"Nice to meet you, Roroy," I replied.

"Now we eat." He rose and fetched water and bread. We ate in companionable silence. It was nice to have a friend here, for this part of my journey.

Another friend. I went over to Qione, put my arms around her neck and leaned into her. I could hear her big heart beating. "You're my best friend here," I said. She whuffled into my hair.

The rain let off a little while later, so we packed up, mounted, and moved on.

CHAPTER 13

Three days later, we arrived at the great city. We stepped out of the woods we'd been traversing, and a mass of towers stood before us. The city sat on what looked like a mountain sliced off flat in a land of fields and streams. Forest curved around to the north, beyond the city. To the east, the land ended, dropping off into the sea.

The city itself I could hardly describe. It was silvery with rainbow glints, a mass of towers growing to points. Small round trees circled around the outside up on the plateau. It was the most gorgeous thing I'd ever seen. After I caught my breath, we continued on.

"Is beautiful," Roroy said. The trail took us to the base of the plateau and upward, around to the right. It was wide enough for a cart, but we stayed close to the inside by the cliff. A sheer drop off on the other side made Qione and me nervous.

As we came around to the east side, I saw the sea. "Have we come all the way across this continent?" I asked.

"Yes."

We continued on at a slow pace. Once, a cart that moved without anyone pulling it, passed us. We edged over as close to the cliff wall as possible as the cart went by.

"What is that?" I asked. "How does it go?"

Roroy was too busy navigating the road to answer my questions.

Back around on the west side, we came to a tunnel into the cliff. I figured we were about halfway up.

"In here," he said.

I was terribly disappointed. "We're not going up to the city?"

He shrugged and led the way in.

"Come, Beast," he said. "Is all right. You been here before."

Qione shivered and balked. "Come on, girl," I said. "If Ro says it's all right, and Beast is going in, it'll be safe for us." Qione snorted, but took a step forward. "If you don't want to go," I added, "I'll get off and walk, and you can stay here or go back down to the valley." She moved into the tunnel.

Little lights along the roof of the tunnel didn't provide all that much illumination, but we were able to see where we were putting our feet. The place was wider than the trail, so we walked side by side.

"Where are we going?" I asked.

Where is food? Qione asked me.

"Qione wants to know where there's food," I said.

"Not to worry." Roroy patted Beast.

Qione snorted.

We passed two side tunnels and finally came to a vast, brightly lit cavern. Our opening was halfway up the wall. The trail split and curved down each side of the space. Qione and I stopped and stared.

I *sensed* the Gate. "It's here," I said. "The Gate is in here somewhere." I reached and quickly drew back. Something had tried to pull me in.

Down and around the cavern, as far as I could see, rows of little houses lined the walls. I wondered what they were for, until I saw a tiny woman come out of one. Inside the rows of houses was a great arc of green, and more buildings beyond. They grew taller as they neared the center, where one tower reached nearly to the ceiling.

I followed the tower down with my senses and sure enough, the Gate was in its base.

"Come," Roroy said. We took the right-hand branch down. Another trail without a barrier along the drop. Again, Qione hugged the wall. At the bottom there was an open way between the ranks of houses, and we passed through. Why do all these people live in here, I wondered, instead of up in the city or out in the valley.

Qione saw the green and trotted toward it. She snuffled and moaned. *Not real grass*, she told me.

"Come," Roroy said again, turning to his right along the fake green grass. A little farther on was a wide place with real grass and two trees at each end. Beast moved in and began to graze. Qione followed, tasted the grass and munched in earnest.

"People here have small beasts, so this for them. But plenty for ours, too."

Across the green, I saw streets going in between the buildings. "We need to go in there to get to the Gate," I said.

"Not yet. I show you the city first." We dismounted and left our steeds there.

"Good," I said. I followed him around to a large opening in the outer wall and into it. After a short distance along a tunnel that curved down and below the main cavern, we came to a cave about a quarter of the size of the one above. In the center, on a low, flat surface, sat a replica of the city above, twice as tall as I was. I walked around it and marveled. The tiny windows and doors revealed tiny rooms with tiny furnishings.

"This is real city," Roroy said. "What you see up there is copy. I not know how they do it. It been here forever."

"But why?" I was disappointed again. I'd wanted to walk among those silvery buildings.

"No one knows."

It didn't make sense. But if there was a Gate, there had to be Gatekeepers. Maybe they lived up there, hidden by the projection.

"Well, if there's no real city, let's go find the Gate," I said. "I want to get back home." I looked at him. "Will you come?"

"I must think. Will you return to this world?"

"Perhaps."

He turned and headed out. I followed. Back in the main cavern, we found a little house not much bigger than an outhouse on the green. On one side was a map of the cavern. Grampa Larry had taught us about maps. This one showed several circles, one within another, the outer one being the cavern wall. In the center, there was a solid black circle. The cross streets, the ones going from the outside circle in to the black center one, did not go straight through. At every circle street where the cross street ended, we would have to go one way or the other to find a cross street that went in to the next inner circle way.

"Come," Roroy said. We collected the steeds, mounted, and headed into the nearest street. These buildings were all gray; the gray doors closed, and the narrow windows covered inside. It didn't take long to reach the first wide cross street that curved in either direction.

We turned right, and a brown cart came out of a way between buildings. I remembered the other one I'd seen outside. Again, there was no driver.

A rectangular cart, on two sets of wheels, carried piles of boxes, but nothing pulled or pushed it.

"How does that work?" I asked.

Roroy smiled. "I not know. Maybe magic."

I looked at him. "You've been here before, haven't you."

He nodded. "On my man journey, before brother died."

How many 'man journeys' had he made? He seemed to know the

village and this place well.

We turned into the next inward road and continued on. Not until we arrived at the third ring road did I see any color. On this road, the doors were painted different colors, red, blue, yellow. Some upper windows had colorful window sills. How could people live here with all this gray and no sky? There was just an indeterminate brightness overhead.

Finally we reached the inner circle. On the corner of the building at our road and the inner circle road, hung a long banner of yellows and greens in a pattern I couldn't make out. Inside the circle, a great grey wall as high as Roroy's house blocked our way. We walked around it looking for a way in. A narrower wall rose up from the center of it, up to the top of the cavern.

It wasn't until I saw the banner again that I realized we'd gone all the way around it. "Ro, how are we going to get in? I know the Gate's in there."

Roroy pounded on the wall in several places. Nothing happened. He pounded again.

"That's not going to work," I said. I *reached* for the Gate and felt its pull. For a moment my mind was inside, and backing away from the center, through different rooms, finding several beings, but no way out.

I shook my head and found myself outside with my friends.

"Must be way in," Roroy said. "Must be way to Gate."

"So why this?" I gestured at the wall.

"Maybe only certain persons have key." He reined in Beast, who was dancing around.

I squeezed my hands in frustration. We had to get in there, but how?

Qione and I trotted around the inner circle, stopping to look around every so often. *No connection to any building on outside of street,* she told me. *No windows high up.*

"Maybe underground, like cellar," Roroy said.

"How do we find that?" I asked.

What was 'underground'? A hole like kids dug? That wouldn't be nearly enough room for an adult.

"Cellar is room below main floor," Roroy said. "We must go in building."

Qione trotted over to the nearest door and pushed it. I tried pulling, but the door did not budge. Nor did any other.

Roroy shrugged, turned Beast, and headed back to the outer circle.

"Hey," I said, as Qione followed them.

Not good in here, she told me.

I sat and fumed. Not only was I furious because we couldn't reach the Gate, I was scared because I hadn't been able to do anything with my Talents.

When we caught up with Roroy and Beast at the grassy area, Roroy said, "We must talk."

"Okay, talk." I jumped down and paced around.

"We either go back to Beach Gate or try more here." Roroy dismounted.

"We can't go back," I exploded.

Roroy nodded. "Would be hard to avoid my people." He looked at me. "Marisa, you saw inside. Can you see where entry is from inside?"

"Oh." I stopped and turned to him. "No, I didn't, but I wasn't really looking. If I could find that, we'd at least know where it is."

"Your magic could get us in." Roroy fished bread out of his pack. "First, let's eat. I hunger."

I was too upset to be hungry, but I knew he needed his food, so I let him eat and stalked over to Qione.

"How are you doing?" I asked.

I miss my family. Will this be much longer here?

"I hope not." I stroked her soft neck.

This food here not much good. I need good grass. She shook her head.

"You're not starving, are you?"

No, but it is affecting me.

Roroy began packing up the remains of lunch. "You sure you don't want any food?" he asked.

"Well," I turned and grabbed a hunk of bread. "Thanks."

As Roroy finished packing, he added, "We go back and see if you can see entry from inside."

"Okay. Come on, Qione."

We mounted and headed back to the inner circle. The gray wall looked as blank as ever. Roroy on Beast trotted around it.

"Still no opening," he reported.

"Okay. Let me see what I can do." I closed my eyes and *projected* my mind inside the walls. It didn't take me long to *find* the large arch filled with gray blankness.

I was unable to *touch* it or *budge* the grayness. I asked Qione to go around to where it was. There was no sign on the outside. "It's here on the inside."

"Can you open it?" Roroy asked. He and Beast had followed us.

"I don't think so." I could not sense the arch at all from this side.

Roroy took out his pocket knife and tried to scratch the surface of the wall. He looked at his knife, then tried again. "No mark at all."

CHAPTER 14

So close and so far, I thought. "Come on, there must be a way."

Qione had been looking around. *This building outside is taller than wall. You climb it,* she told me.

"What?" I repeated her words to Roroy and looked up at the building. It had deep windows, ornamental crevasses, and protuberances all over it. I guess Qione thought that since we had arms and legs like mooks, we could climb like mooks. "Can you climb it, Ro?"

"No. I do not climb things. You do. You see inside wall, if way in from top."

I sighed. I'd climbed a lot of trees when I was younger, but never a building. "Okay, I'll do it. I just hope no one opens a window at the wrong time." I could just levitate, but that would take too much out of me. I needed to save my strength for later.

Qione maneuvered herself as close to the building as she could, and ordered Beast to stand next to her. *If you fall, we will catch you. Stand on my back.*

"Thanks." I grabbed a protruding stone and pulled myself to my feet. Using a combination of climbing and teleporting, I made my way up to the roof. Turning, I looked across at the circular wall, from about a story above it. Halfway in, the narrower tower reached upward, the same featureless gray. There was no visible roof, but it could be lower down. However, I saw something else.

"Qione," I said, leaning over the edge. "There's a walkway inside the top of the gray building and there must be a way down from there. I'm going to teleport over."

Be careful. Call me, I may be able to hear you from inside.

"Okay." Going to the edge closest to the gray tower, I took a deep breath and visualized the walkway. Closed my eyes and moved. I landed with a thump on my knees and rolled over into the inside wall. Pulling myself up to a sitting position, I peered over the edge, rubbing my legs. A flat blackness about a body length below blocked further view.

I crawled over to the outside edge, pulled myself up and waved to

Roroy and the steeds. Roroy waved back and Qione tossed her head.

Rest. I took a little water from my water pouch and curled up into a ball and dozed. When I woke, I climbed to my feet and trod around the walkway. The others followed me below on the street. Halfway around, I came to a wall that pushed in like a curtain, showing stairs beyond.

"Qione," I said, looking down at my friends. "There are stairs here. I'm going down."

She nodded her head. *Be careful.*

I waved and pushed through the curtain. It didn't feel like cloth, heavier and smoother. Light high up in the walls illuminated the staircase. This one only curved a little. I made my way down, clinging to the rail on the wall.

Presently, I came to a brighter place where the inside wall ended. Ahead, beyond the bottom of the staircase, a narrow corridor continued in the same direction. To my left, a well-lit open area with no furniture held a group of creatures that looked like overgrown stick bugs doing some intricate movements.

Suddenly they stopped and issued shrill squeaks. I ran down the rest of the stairs and across into the corridor. The creatures did not follow me, and I slowed down to catch my breath. At the next bright place, I stopped and peered around the corner. A wide way led to a blank, gray wall. That must be the inner tower, I thought. There were openings along this hallway.

The outside corridor continued beyond this place, slanting downward, so I proceeded to follow it. There must be more stairs down to a lower level. I figured I was almost all the way around when I finally came to another staircase. My insides started to jitter. What was I getting myself into?

It led me down to a tiny room with a door. I pushed it open a crack and saw a gray place with gray tables and chairs. A counter lined the end of the area, holding odd round objects. Seeing no beings in the room, I passed through and tiptoed across to the further door. Before I opened it, I *reached.* Several people moved around out there, but none were very close to the doorway.

I slipped out and stood with my back to the wall, heart hammering. This was a very large open area between the inner and outer walls, filled with long tables bearing machines. Some people were working at them, others walking around.

They all appeared humanoid, like Roroy and me.

Almost dead ahead, around the curve of the outer wall, I saw the large arch. Its inner area was the same gray as the walls. As I watched, a tall person in green approached it and passed through.

"Qione, can you hear me?" I said. "Did a tall person just come out the entrance?"

I hear you, came faintly. *No, no one came out.*

So where did he go? Now I was really scared. How was I going to get out of this trap? I couldn't go through the Gate without my friends. I couldn't go back, the door to the staircase wouldn't open. Terror began to knot up in my gut.

Noticing a couple people in gray robes looking at me, I moved over to the outer wall and along it toward the arch, the only way out. All I had to do was get there without being caught and figure out how to get through the entrance. I moved slowly, head down as if pondering something.

When I saw the bottom of the arch, I looked up. More people, these in gray-blue robes, were watching me, but made no move toward me. I faced the arch, visualized my friends and the yellow banner, and closed my eyes. I want to be there, I thought. A jolt, and I stumbled into Roroy's arms.

Qione whinnied, and Beast licked my ear.

Still shaking, I drank them in.

"How did you do that?" Roroy asked. Qione nuzzled my shoulder.

"The usual," I said. "Maybe it will work the other way. Let's see if it works from this side."

Roroy and I mounted our steeds and put their noses at the grey wall. I visualized a large, square table just inside and murmured, "We are there." An instant of blackness, a pop, and we were inside.

As we stood and recovered ourselves, a short round man in green approached.

"Why are you here?' he asked in Standard.

"We wish to go through Gate," Roroy said.

"Who are you? Where is your entry chit?"

"I am son of a king and this is princess," Roroy announced. "Her magic let us through."

The man in green turned away and spoke into a square object on his arm. Turning back, he said, "Come."

The steeds followed him around and back to the inner gray wall. Here, we found a green door.

Beside it, a round woman with a round face sat behind a long table piled with papers and a large machine with markings on the keys. Unlike the Bramites, her eyes were close together in the middle of her face.

"These people and their beasts want to go through Gate to another world," the rotund man announced.

"How ever did they get those things through the portal?" the round woman asked in a squeaky voice.

"He said magic."

The woman shuddered. "A moment," she said, and began punching buttons on the machine. After a bit, a slip of paper popped out of the bottom of the machine. She read it and looked up. "You have been scheduled for the fifteenth hour."

Before I could ask what hour it was now, Roroy demanded, "Where can we wait?"

"Through here." The rotund man opened the green door to a roundish waiting area. One third had a fenced in area with grass and bushes. Several big lights glared down on us. Several people sat in seats and at tables. walled off areas contained beds and washrooms.

We dismountd, shooed the steeds into the grassy area, and found seats for ourselves.

"So how long do we have to wait?" I asked.

Roroy smiled. "Three of their hours. Be patient."

Papa was always saying that. "So we just sit here?" I said, grimacing.

"No. There is food if you wish. There is entertainment. You can walk around."

"Where's the food?" I asked.

"This way." At the outside wall there was a booth that served food. We each got a plate of beans and green vegetables.

"Sit here," he said, and began to eat.

Later, I went over to visit Qione and tell her what was going on. *This grass no taste but is real. Leaves no good at all,* she told me.

"Why don't you sit down and rest? We don't have any idea what we'll find out there," I said. Harmony, I hope. I returned to my seat and dozed.

Finally, Roroy said, "Is our turn, now."

We collected our steeds and followed the guide to an opening on the far side of the room. The guide gave us blindfolds to put on, even Qione and Beast.

She fought it. I said, "Calm down, this is necessary, be a good girl." She did. Beast growled, but allowed Roroy to put the blindfold on him.

The round man took my hand and Roroy's. We each held on to the neckhair of our steeds with our other hands. "All right, girl, it's all right," I kept saying to Qione. We walked through a place that smelled of machinery and sounded wide open. Qione muttered and Beast growled. It grew warm and stuffy.

Then we passed out of the machine area into a cooler, smaller place. After a turn to the right and one to the left, we stopped. The rotund man let us take off our blindfolds. We were in a large room that I couldn't quite tell whether it was round or many sided. One moment it looked one way, the next, the other. The walls were a pale green with blue streaks. In the center was a round stage with a round structure filling most of it, the same color as the outer wall.

Even before we'd put the blindfolds on, I'd felt the pull of the Gate. As we went through the door, I shut my mind to everything except for what I needed to walk. Now the pull was almost irresistible. Roroy held me tightly as Qione pushed me into him, so I wouldn't be pulled away from them.

The guide stepped aside, and we started for the ramp, wide enough for all of us to walk abreast. As we reached the top, the structure on it began to spin slowly. When a wide door appeared, the structure stopped. We went in. On one side were stalls for the steeds, with wide cloth ropes that wrapped around them. On the other side large soft chairs waited for us, that wrapped arms around us as we sat in them.

A part of me wondered why this one was so different from the other Gates.

"Harmony," I said. The light dimmed until we couldn't see. The place shimmied. I couldn't breathe.

CHAPTER 15

After a moment, the light returned. The pull of the Gate was gone. I *reached*. "We're in a different place, but I don't think it's Harmony," I said as the chairs released us. Roroy hopped up and went to the animals. The big door opened.

A corridor between blank walls led the way led to an arched opening, which opened onto a vast expanse of desert. Sand and tall green poles of plants, and little bits of ground plants, as far as I could see. The hot air was thin and difficult to breathe.

"This is definitely not Harmony," I gasped. I turned around and trotted back into the Gate room. The others followed me. Roroy had not made a sound. I looked at him. He was ashy pale.

I searched for a screen like we'd seen at the first gate, and found it. I punched one button after another until I came to one where the map looked like what I could remember of Harmony's map that Grandpa Larry had showed us several years ago. They had made it from the ship before they landed.

"We'll try this one," I said. "Go on, get in." After the others were in, I punched the button, ran in and flopped into a chair. Again the shimmering and loss of air.

The next world was much better, green and lush. Large droopy trees, fat bushes with red and purple flowers, low plants covering the ground, and vines with little yellow flowers covering everything. Too lush for Harmony, I thought.

The steeds bounded out and started to munch on the greenery. Qione always knew what was good for her and what wasn't.

"This isn't Harmony, either," I said. "Do you want to try again?" I asked Roroy.

"We can't," he said. "Look."

I turned around. The archway in the wall was gone. The wall disappeared into the jungle at each end.

On this side, there was only a semicircular paved place on which we stood, and a trail into the jungle. I understood Mama's pain when she and Uncle Peter had found themselves on a world that wasn't Harmony, where they had expected to be.

"No," I whispered. Were we going to have to walk across another continent to find another Gate? And was there any guarantee the next Gate would take us to Harmony? The knot in my gut was back.

Good here, Qione told me.

"We have to go on to find the other Gate," I said. "Come over here so I can ride," I told Qione.

"Beast, here," Roroy said. His beast obeyed. Qione moved off.

"Get over here," I demanded of Qione. She sidled away.

Roroy, on Beast, circled around the quine and herded her over to me. I mounted and slapped her side.

"Now behave. I'm sure there'll be a lot more of this." I waved my hand around as we started off. Hot and muggy, the jungle was full of flowery and dank aromas. Little buzzing things we couldn't see followed us. The trail wound around and in between the trees. The farther we went, the worse it got.

I don't like this, Qione told me, swishing her tail.

"I know, I don't either." I *reached* and found nothing except the jungle beasts. We plodded on.

Finally we came to a wider place with a bubbling spring. Thank Oneness, I thought, as we stopped and slid off our mounts. Here by the spring, it was slightly cooler, and the buzzers left us. I stretched and walked around. I wondered if I was ever going to get home. At least I wasn't alone.

As we sat and ate, Roroy said, "This not what I expected. I thought we go straight to your world."

"So did I," wiping my chin. "Grampa Larry told me, you can't ever depend on the Gates to get you where you want to go."

"Tell me about your people," Roroy said. It was the first time he'd ever asked about anything to do with me.

"Well, Grampa Larry and Granlyn, Grampa Bay and Granli, and the others, were the first to settle Harmony. They had lived with the Bramites, people who became our colonists, for a couple of years until they were rescued by the brown, furry Wati, tree people.

"The Wati leader, Judee, and Granlyn became friends, and Judee brought my grandparents to Harmony. The Wati have their colony north of us in the forest."

"Go on." He leaned back on his forearms.

"Granlyn had Perri, my mother, and her twin Peter. Mama mated with Papa Charley. His parents are Grampa Bay and Granli. Granli is

Granlyn's sister's daughter. It's all very complicated because while Granlyn and Grampa Larry were out running around on other worlds for about three of their years, all the others were living out twenty years on Home Earth."

"How did you find your world?" Roroy asked.

"I'm not sure. I think they had a list, and went looking until they found a good one."

Roroy nodded. "My people not native to world we met on," he said. "A very long time ago, my ancestors came to believe differently than rest of people on their world. The strong ones made them leave, sent them through Gate, and they came in on the beach like you. They made their home on plateau where you found us. That first group warn us if anyone come up from beach."

"Did you ever go down there?" I asked, wrapping up the remainder of the food.

"Sometimes, to get away from everyone." He stretched. "I wasn't meant to take over after Father dies, but older brother got killed. I was meant to explore world and find other friends. Tomor was to have wed and produced sons to keep the line going."

"So as the surviving son, you were stuck with the princely duties. I think your father saw me as a mate for you. He talked about you before you came back. Not a lot, but enough that I could tell what he wanted."

"He never talks much."

"What about your mother?" I asked.

"She died when I young, with another baby." He rose and went to the saddlebags he'd taken off Beast. Qione and Beast were enjoying the grass.

As Roroy laid out his sleeping blankets, he asked, "Do you have brothers or sisters?"

"Two younger brothers. Laurie is three years younger than me and almost as tall as me. Ricky is two years younger than Laurie." I followed his example. As I curled up in my blankets, I realized how much I missed them. Laurie would have loved to be here.

***

Two days later we came out of the jungle onto the bank of a great river, several times as wide as our big river back on Harmony.

All four of us stared.

"How on Harmony are we going to cross that?" I asked.

"We're not," Roroy replied. "Look, trail goes along bank."

We trotted along the trail, in and out of trees. In some places, there was a wide swath of low plants, and in others the trees came right to the bank. Streams gurgled out of the forest into the river. The steeds drank and we filled our water pouches. At one pool in a stream, I sat down to take my boots off.

"What you doing?" Roroy asked.

"I'm going to take a bath. I can't stand being dirty like this." I stripped off my tunic and pants, walked into the stream and sat down on the sandy bottom. I splashed myself wet, and used handfuls of sand to scrub my body and my hair. The water was cool and refreshing.

Down at the far end of the pool, I saw Qione dunking her head and flipping water over her back. "I'll wash you when I get done," I called to her. She whinnied. When I finally dragged myself out and donned the least dirty of my clothes, I fetched the largest bowl we had. At Qione's side, I began pouring bowls of water over her as she wriggled with joy. I scrubbed her with sand and poured more water to rinse it off.

She shook water all over Beast, who snorted and danced away.

When I turned around, Roroy was in the water, industriously scrubbing himself. His chest was finely muscled and limned with dark hair. It dawned on me that he would be a good mate. The fact that he was of a different people was not a problem, I knew that I could arrange things so that I could conceive, and he was enough like us physically that the child should look normal.

I turned my back when he made movements to get out of the water. I *sensed* his need for privacy, and waited until he had time to get dressed before I turned around. "I feel much better," I said.

"Me also."

He made no move to leave, so I took out my dirty clothes and scrubbed them in the stream and laid them out in the sun to dry.

"I think we rest here awhile," he said. "Tell me about your beast."

"Qione is a quine. She and five other quines came out of a Gate on Harmony. She said they'd gone through accidently. My brother, Laurie, and I and a few others had gone up looking for the Gate when we met them. They are more intelligent than they look, and she and I can communicate some way other than verbally. I don't know exactly how it works, but it does.

"And we've bonded, she won't let anyone else ride her until I say it's all right. On her world, they had a relationship with small creatures with hands like ours. The quines used the creatures to make things and do things they could not do with their feet."

Roroy leaned back. "Our beasts were wild, but came looking for food. My ancestors train them; they had beasts on their world." He stretched out his legs. "Now, boys and young beasts play together until each find one they bond with. Beast will do what I say, but not obey anyone else." He paused and stared up into the deep blue sky. "He might listen to you, we be together a while."

I picked up a stone from under my leg and tossed it in the stream. "I think Qione and Beast are communicating some way," I said.

"Yes, I have seen this."

We sat in silence for a while. A very comfortable silence. I liked that he didn't talk very much, but when he did it was about something important to him. I was beginning to like him a lot. I moved a twig out of the way of a little red bug.

***

At the end of the third day, the trees began to thin out, and I hadn't seen the flower bushes for a while. We camped, and he asked more questions about my world. I enjoyed telling him about it, but it made me homesick. I had no idea how far away from Harmony we were.

For two more days we climbed into the hills. I felt bone weary, and I knew that Qione did too. We couldn't live here without food, so we had to keep going. When we reached the top of the last hill, we saw more jungle and mountains beyond. The trail continued on straight ahead.

We stopped at a copse of the big round trees, half way down.

"This not what I had in mind," Roroy said, slumping to the ground.

"Me neither." Automatically, I *reached*, and sat up straight. There was something in the jungle below, more than just animals. The jungle itself felt odd. I focused on it, and *sensed* many people and large beasts of burden. Structures that might have been buildings. The jungle was just a façade.

"That's not a real jungle," I told Roroy. "There are people and beasts down there in an open valley. Somehow they are able to make it look like jungle from the outside."

"What?" He looked at me, then down at the jungle. "All I see is trees. How you see other?"

"It's part of my Talent. But I do not sense a Gate down there."

We followed the trail down and stopped a man-length away from the first trees. I could see the community more clearly now. The trail led down to the structures. All of sudden it hit me. What if we were on the wrong trail, one that did not lead to the other Gate? What if we were stranded here? No, there had to be another Gate. My heart did flip flops. I straightened up.

"I'm going to see if I can go through," I announced as I dismounted. "Qione, stay here."

"No," Roroy cried.

I ignored him and walked down the trail, which passed between two large trees. As I proceeded through, the forest faded out, and I saw the valley below. There were three great orchards spaced evenly around the area, and a few trees around the structures in the center. Beside those, a stream ran through open fields.

I turned back and saw the others standing there. Roroy had dismounted and was holding on to Beast. I waved. No response. I returned to them.

"Come on," I said. "It's fine." I put my hand on Qione's shoulder and led her to the trees. "It's all right," I added as I felt her shiver, but she walked with me between the trees and out into the valley. I looked back and saw Roroy with Beast coming through. Even the air felt different here.

"Is good," Roroy said as he looked about. We headed down the trail.

CHAPTER 16

We saw a man and boy in a green field ahead. At first I thought they were farther away, until I realized they were much smaller than we were. They wore draped green garments that hung to their feet, and two sets of arms poked through. There were two larger arms on their sides, and two smaller ones on their fronts at the level of the elbows on the larger arms. The people also wore hoods of green, but I could see noses poking out.

The smaller one turned in our direction, tugged at the taller one who also turned. They hopped to the edge of the field where the trail went by and waited. As we approached, I noticed they each had a pair of large, round eyes, and a long round nose with what appeared to be nostrils above.

Qione muttered. "Easy girl," I said, and patted her neck. We stopped several paces away.

The little one, who only came up to my hips, squeaked. The other tapped him and stared at us. I *felt* something in my mind and said, "Hello." He jerked out, and stared at me. I *sensed* questions.

I *touched* his mind. It was so alien I wasn't sure I could communicate with him. 'What place is this?' I asked.

I *sensed* something about falling from the sky. I *sent* a picture of us coming in on the trail and going on through to the other side. And *received* a picture of a wall across the trail.

"Oh, no," I said aloud.

"What is happening?" Roroy asked. The steeds shifted and wuffled.

"They won't let us through," I said, trying to figure out what that meant.

The larger one slapped the young one softly, and the young one took off bouncing to the village.

"Uh oh," I said. "We're in trouble now."

"We go back?" Roroy asked.

Qione snorted.

"To where?" I asked. He shrugged. We moved on. The man, whom I called Biggs, waved, and something stopped me, in the lead. I couldn't see anything, but when I put my hand out I felt something rubbery blocking my way.

"Oh, crud," I said, and explained it to Roroy. He came up and felt around it, as Qione nosed it.

I don't like this, she told me.

"None of us do," I said.

After waiting awhile, a cart came out of the village, with three females and a male in it, the latter driving a pair of pale brown beasts smaller than Qione. They had six legs and small heads. Qione made a noise like a combination snort and snuffle. Beast growled. We could only wait until they arrived.

Biggs turned to them, and I *sensed* he was communicating with them. He waved a large arm at where the trail came into the valley. The cart stopped and the females climbed out. One was taller than the others, almost up to my chin. The others came to about my midchest. They all wore the same type of garment in shades of green, except for the tall woman who wore a pale blue.

The three lined up facing us. I braced my mind for an onslaught, also thinking how quiet it was here. But it was only a gentle probing. I opened the part of my mind that held our travels on this world. I heard Roroy grunt; they were exploring his mind, also. I realized that they didn't use words as such, but communicated in pictographs, sensations and emotions.

I came to understand that they thought we were giants and didn't want us in their land, and that the trail didn't go through but down. That didn't make sense to me, but they couldn't explain it, so I had to accept it. Their names, for themselves and their community were not available, so we made up our own names for them. The first man we called Biggs, and the kid with him, Little One, and the tall female who appeared to be their leader, Tally.

Finally, they removed the barrier and let us through. They led us toward the village, to a place where the trail curved to the right. We followed them around the village. The structures were of a silvery rounded material, long and narrow, but not high enough for even these people, the Minis we called them, to stand up in. Then I saw a piece of one slide open and a ramp sloping down into the ground.

So they were half buried, I thought.

Later, when I told the uncles about it, Uncle Art Junior said maybe they were part of the ship they came in, like the way our people used parts of the ship we rode to Harmony.

Once past the village and approaching the hillside where the fields ended, the Minis turned back and motioned us on. Partway up the hill I saw a dark area in the direction of the trail. I *sent* appreciation, and received no response.

"Need food," Roroy said. We were about out of what we'd brought. Qione and Beast seemed to be able to eat almost any kind of greenery. We walked up the slope, and sure enough, the trail led into the dark area, which was an opening in the hill.

"Not again," I said, peering in.

"Where else we go?" Roroy asked.

"Okay, let's see what's in here." I took three steps in and the walls began to glow pale green. The others followed, Qione nuzzling my back. We came to an area where one side wall had collapsed, narrowing the way to where we had to walk single file. Roroy insisted on going first. I followed, then Qione, and lastly, Beast. The way sloped downward, but stayed lit by the same green glow. And the air remained fresh.

We came to a great cavern, open to the sky and more brightly lit. On the far side lay a great mass of mangled machinery. Must have been what made this place, I thought. Not far in front of it, on a layer of black mossy stuff, lay a giant egg, glowing a pearly pale-pinkish sand color. I stopped, and leaned again Qione.

"What that?" Roroy wondered.

I *reached*, carefully. There was something alive inside it, but I couldn't tell what. Then it occurred to me that the Minis meant us to come here. They could put up a jungle, surely they could make a trail appear to go wherever they wanted it to.

"I think this may be part of the ship they came in," I said. "They want us to do something here, but what?"

"Perhaps the egg thing? What it made of?" He walked over and touched it. "Tingles," he said.

I followed him over. The steeds stayed behind. Qione muttered. I laid my hands on the egg, which was as tall as Roroy. There was a tingle, then something reaching out to me. I focused my mind on it. I *felt* a need from something inside to leave the egg. It sent meaningless instructions to my mind.

"Ro, we need to hatch this egg," I said. It had survived this fall, so it wouldn't be easy.

Roroy hunted around in the wreckage for a piece of metal he

could use to bang on the egg. It didn't even make a dent. Or a scratch.

We banged and poked and stabbed with various hunks of metal until the steeds began complaining, with nary a mark on the egg. Well, I knew it would be difficult.

"Can you use your magic?" Roroy asked.

"Oh." Maybe I could move it. "Get back." I concentrated on the life form. It was about my size, at one end of the egg. With eyes closed I saw myself picking up this being and moving it outside, onto an end of the mossy stuff. I strained and strained, and finally heard a pop. I opened my eyes, saw a limp pink mass on the moss, and passed out.

***

I came to outside on the grassy hillside, Qione sat beside me and nosed me. The sun was just poking over the horizon. As I turned my head, she nuzzled my ear, and chortled.

"Marisa, you awake?" Roroy sat on my other side.

"I guess," I mumbled. I checked all my parts; I felt as if I'd been run through the mill.

He touched my face. "I worry about you. You did it. You got thing out and, not long after, egg broke open. Thing oozed back in, and came out wrapped in cloth like other Minis. So we brought you out here and Supermini too."

Something stepped in front of me, someone wrapped in a dark blue garment.

'Pleasure you back,' I heard in my mind. 'Gratitude. Go people.' Supermini turned and moved down the hill.

I managed to sit up. People were pouring out of the village and up the trail. "I hate my Talent," I said. "It takes so much out of me when I use it."

"You are goddess. Only goddess could do that."

"No I'm not. Do we have any water?" He gave me a pouch and I drank it all down. My stomach growled. He handed me a small piece of bread. "All we have. Not see any small animals I can catch."

I gobbled down the bread and plucked a handful of grass. "My mama ate grass on her trek when they ran out of food," I said, munching on it.

"No," Roroy stood up. "I must find you food. Beast, stay here." He strode down the hill.

My knight in shining armor, I thought. Now where did that come from? He would make a worthy mate. Qione got to her feet and moved away. I turned and saw Beast sitting behind me, his deep black eyes following Roroy.

I watched Roroy meet up with the Minis, keeping his distance. He pantomimed eating. When there was no response, he rubbed his stomach. They stared at him. Finally Supermini turned her head and stared at a woman in the back of the crowd. The woman whirled and rushed into the village.

She returned with a large bowl almost closed at the top, like a gourd. Roroy took it, sniffed it, and brought it to his mouth. After taking a sip, he looked around at me. I could sense nothing poisonous from this distance and beckoned for him to bring it to me.

I took a sip of some kind of a vegetable mash, very tasty. I sucked up as much as I could and let Roroy have the rest. He moved away when a group of Minis led by Supermini, marched up the hill to us. Qione and Beast were munching their way around the hill.

Supermini stopped and bowed, the other females behind her did the same. They began laying out objects they'd been carrying. There was a tent that two of them put together, mattresses which they blew air into, boxes of garments, and other containers. Out of a small box, Supermini pulled out a necklace made out of woven vines with a dark purple-blue pendant that had silver sparkles inside it. She placed it over my head, and I sensed goddess.

'Thank you,' I *sent*, 'but I am not a goddess.' I touched the pendant, and *heard* her more clearly.

She let me know gratitude for releasing her from the egg, and for giving leader back to people. We would live on the hill and take care of her people, and they would provide us with food and whatever we needed. She did not seem to know anything about the Gates. There were others of her people elsewhere, and she wanted us to find them.

'I need rest.'

She seemed to understand that, nodded and took her sisters away down the hill.

"Wow," I said, and told Roroy what I'd learned.

"I told you, you are goddess," Roroy said, sitting beside me. "I think you are my goddess." He pulled me back against him.

"No I'm not. I'm just Marisa, daughter of Perri, granddaughter of Lyn, of the Harlan clan."

I couldn't say more, my mind wanted to shut down. The long sleep had helped, but I needed at least a couple more days of rest to recover properly. I fell asleep in his arms.

***

The next morning, I awoke on one of the inflatable beds in the tent thing. I managed to get to my feet and go behind a bush. When I returned, I sat down heavily outside the tent and watched Roroy doing something with a big pot.

"I found some little creatures," he said. "You need meat."

"The Minis won't like that," I said, twiddling a blade of grass.

"They won't know."

Ha, I thought. "Tomorrow, I'll be ready to move on. We need to find that Gate, and it's not here."

"How? Where we go? Trail ends here." He dipped something out of the pot into a bowl he'd made by cutting the top off one of the gourd like things. "Here, eat."

I ate a lot, and hoped I had left him enough.

"I've been thinking about that," I said between bites. "If these people could make us think their village was a jungle, surely they could make us think the trail came up this hill. I bet, if you go down and look, you'll find the real trail curving around this hill."

After we finished eating and he packed up the remains, he went down to look, taking a curving route away from the village.

I tried a *search*, but could only *sense* him. I wanted to get going, but I didn't want to leave until my Talent was complete again.

When Roroy returned, he said, "Yes, there is trail around hill. But how we just leave them?"

"They wanted us to find the rest of their people," I said. "I'll tell them that's where we're going."

"All right. I go ride Beast. He needs exercise. You rest."

CHAPTER 17

The next morning I felt much better, and walked around, stretching my legs. Qione told me it was time to go. We were packing up what we could when Supermini and her sisters marched up the hill to us, full of questions.

I answered them as best I could, about who we were, where we'd come from, our steeds. I let her know we were going to go look for her people. She seemed satisfied. They gave us more gourds of food and left. After we finished packing, Roroy led the way down to the trail.

I *reached*, first to Minis to renew my impression of them, and then in other directions, but could not detect any others.

The steeds walked briskly. I was glad to be able to ride. It was another clear, warm day. Around the hill and upward we went, until we came out into a small valley.

Something glinted in the sunshine, not far off the trail. It looked like part of another egg. Roroy tapped it. The thing sounded hollow. I could not *sense* anything inside the egg. Roroy pushed at it and rolled it over. We peered into a large opening on the newly exposed side. The egg was empty, except for a skeleton huddled up at the end.

"Oh, no," I said. "This one didn't make it."

Roroy nodded. "We not do anything here. We go."

We mounted and rode on. At a rise at the end of the valley, I reached again. This time, I felt something to our right. "We have to go that way," I said, pointing.

"But trail goes other way."

"Not anymore." I pointed. "Look." The trail was bending itself around to the right, leading us up into the higher hills. A little later we came to another valley, which appeared to be empty, but I *sensed* more Minis there.

We entered, and when we were about a quarter of the way across, the world blinked and the Mini village appeared.

Also appearing were three Minis in the same garb as the others.

We stopped but did not dismount. I *sent* them greetings in the manner of their people, a map of where the others were, and about the broken egg. Silence reigned as the Minis communicated among themselves, then they asked me to show the map again. I did, and felt gratitude from them.

Passing around their village, we continued on.

The trail led up into the mountains. A large beast followed us for a while, always in the trees, just out of sight. I saw needle leaved trees like the ones in the pictures Grampa Larry had brought from Home Earth. We did not have any like that on our world. They produced a very refreshing aroma, their dropped needle leaves made a comfortable bed.

One day we came out around a bend to an open area, where we stopped for a break. We could see almost half way around us. Beast and Qione began snuffling around the ground cover. Roroy and I walked to the edge. Below us spread a wide valley divided by a broad river. The open area extended across to the heavy forest at the edge of our vision. To our right, were rows and rows of hills. To our left rose mountain peaks, one after another.

"Wow," Roroy said.

"We're not going to climb those, are we?" I asked.

"We go where trail goes."

I decided that this would be a good place to do a *reach*. I positioned myself facing the hills and, using my Talent, I *scanned*, turning slowly to my left. I was almost all the way around when I *sensed* something. Something that could be a Gate. The knot in my gut loosened.

"That way," I said, pointing.

"All right."

We mounted and moved out. Later, when we were looking for a place to camp, I noticed Qione huffing.

"Are you all right, girl?" I asked.

Hard to breathe, here.

I realized I was gasping, too.

"Air is thinner up here," Roroy said. "My father's brother who went to mountain told us that."

"I remember. Grampa Larry told us young ones that it had been hard to breathe up in the mountains when they returned to Home Earth. How much higher can we go?"

"I know not, but we walk now."

We were all panting when we reached the top of a rise. The trail curled down and around a cylindrical opening in the hills below.

"The Gate's down there," I said, peering at the hole. A sense of relief spread through me. Surely, this time we would get back to Harmony.

We had to walk quite slowly because of the curve of the narrow trail and to conserve our air. It was impossible to see the bottom of the opening. We circled down, passed through an invisible barrier, and suddenly found it easier to breathe.

As we continued on down, it grew dim as the walls blocked out the sunlight Then we came to an opening in the wall. Qione sniffed it and shook her head. We continued downward until we could barely see, past several of the openings. The next one we came to, we decided to camp there.

The beasts nibbled at plants growing on the wall. Roroy and I slept sitting up, our backs to the wall just inside the opening. It was not very comfortable after the air bed.

***

When we woke, there was light. Not very bright, but much more than we had the night before. I went out and looked up. Nothing but a glowing circle above. Down below, not too far, I saw something glittering within a mist.

"Hey, Roroy," I called.

"What?" He came out, shaking his head. "Goodness."

We ate and proceeded on down. Presently we came to a place where the trail led into the wall of the cliff. Light inside, it soon became wider than the trail. We reached a cross tunnel and I *felt* the trail turning right, so Qione and I turned right also.

This tunnel curved gently, and there were doors on the right. One opened to reveal a medium sized room with tables and chairs around large cylindrical metal machines, but no people. Eventually we came to a place where our tunnel split into three tunnels. In one I sensed the Gate, the second went straight ahead, and to the left I felt the continuation of the trail.

Qione led the way into the one that led to the Gate. We came to a door with writing on it, but neither of us could read it. I looked for something, a handle that would open it, but it was a flat gray slab of some hard material. There was nothing on the walls beside it.

I said, "Hello." Then we both shouted it. No response. Finally Qione turned around and kicked it with her hind foot. The door rang like a bell. We pounded on it, and Qione kicked again.

A deep voice spoke, but neither of us could understand it.

"We don't understand," I yelled.

Something above us slid open, and a small device on a wire dropped down between us and the door. The thing turned itself around slowly, then moved around us. Beast tried to reach up and bite the device, but it rose into the ceiling and the opening closed.

"Well," I said.

Beast growled. Qione shook her head.

Presently the slab in front of us slid aside far enough for us to move through. We entered a large place with machinery. A living entity inside a large, slightly oval ball with moving colors of greens, blues and purples stood before us.

I *touched* it gently.

'Follow,' I understood from the being.

"Come on," I said, and started off after the entity. We walked after it, down a hall and turned right into a small room. The steeds stayed outside. As Roroy and I stood in this empty, dark blue room with silver sparkles on the walls, floor and ceiling, I felt prepared for anything. Roroy grabbed my hand, and suddenly I felt as if we were hanging amidst the stars.

The air went away and we crumpled to the floor.

***

I awoke on a soft silver couch, surrounded by stars. Roroy slept on another nearby. We seemed to be floating in space, in air fresh and cool. Or maybe the couches were floating.

Something entered my mind, and after it left, I found instructions. We were to go to another world and find something or someone. With my Talents, Roroy's strength, and the beasts' power, we could accomplish something no one else had done before.

"No," I cried. "We need to get back to my world, Harmony."

'When you accomplish your task.' Once again, I couldn't breathe.

CHAPTER 18

When I came to, I found myself in a hammock on an open porch overlooking a great sea. Huge waves broke on the beach. At one side I saw a long pier sticking out into the water. Two Gates in a row. I felt as if something had punched me in the gut. How were we ever going to get back to Harmony? How was I going to find my world?

At the end of the pier, beyond the breakers, a boat bobbed. From where I was, I couldn't tell how big it was, but it seemed larger than the ones we had on Harmony. Those had been crafted from sleeping bunks salvaged from the Emprisa before the Wati leader, Judee, took her down into the sea as she died.

The purple horizon met a pale blue sky, where a few puffy pink clouds sailed. I took a deep breath of the sea air. It wasn't much more than fresh air over the river. I put my hand to my pendant and gasped. Shrunken and gray, with an unpleasant odor, I yanked it off. I guess it only worked on the Minis' world.

Roroy stirred and sat up in his hammock.

"Where are we now?" he asked.

"At the seaside," I said. I passed on the instructions I had been given.

He looked around at the cedar-planked porch and then out to the sea. "Where do we go, goddess?"

"Stop that," I snapped. "I am no more a goddess than you are." I stomped to the door at the back of the porch.

"Where's Beast?" Roroy pushed me aside and barreled through the doorway. I followed, into a glade in a tropical forest. "Beast," Roroy yelled, running around the place.

"Qione," I called, also *reaching* for her. *I'm sorry, girl, for getting* you *into this.*

Nothing.

"What did they do to my Beast," Roroy yelled, running around the glade.

Something told me they were safe and would wait for us. "Safe, I hope." I kept listening for her. "They couldn't go in the boat anyway."

"Boat?"

"Out there at the end of the pier. Come on, let's go." I returned through the door and found a trail at the side of the porch that wound down to the beach. The roar of the breakers was deafening. A narrow path led between where the waves splashed and the massive wall of plant growth at the back of the beach. Huge, deep green, double leaves papered the wall.

Presently we came to the foot of the pier. Made of solid black planks, with guard rails of the same material, it stretched out as far as we could see.

"Okay, here we go." I stepped onto the first of the planks on the upward slope. Roroy followed. As we walked above the breakers, some sent spray up into our faces. Beyond them, there were great swells. It was refreshing out here, away from trees and holes in the ground. I missed Qione, but knew she would be safe.

A little farther, Roroy stopped. "I don't like this," he said.

"I know, but we have no choice. Not if you want Beast back."

Roroy mumbled something and continued on. I was getting a little shaky myself, this far out from land. At least the dock was sturdy; it didn't shake at all when the waves pounded against it.

When we reached the end, we were both clinging to the rail. Wooden steps led down to the boat, which was red and white and huge. A long, wide house sat on it, with a large flat space at both the front and the back. I knew there were terms for those areas, but I couldn't remember them.

I led the way down, clutching the rails on both sides of the stairs, and stepped onto a little dock where the boat was moored. This dock rocked up and down with the movement of the sea. I tiptoed over, holding on to the rail that led from the bottom of the stairs to the opening in the side of the boat, and stepped into the vessel. It rocked a little.

Roroy still stood at the bottom of the stairs. "Come on," I said, "or you'll be left behind." Somehow I knew that the boat would only stay here a short while before it left. Finally he lurched across. As soon as he was on the boat, the open panel in the side slid shut. I led the way into the cabin.

After a couple of pops as the ropes let go, the boat began to move. I sat and watched out one of the wide windows. I recalled our little boats back on Harmony. There, we could only sit still in one spot until we reached the other side of the river. Here, we were in a floating house.

Roroy lay down on the long red seat on the other side of the main room and closed his eyes. After the land disappeared, I prowled around the cabin. I found a tiny room with an outhouse seat and a shower, a small kitchen with food and dishes, and a room at the front with a large bed. Long up and down movements as we passed over the swells prompted me to sit down. Shelves above the seats held books and little toys.

I wondered how the boat was going by itself, but I'd seen so many strange things it didn't bother me at all. There was food and a bed – how long was this trip going to take, anyway? The instructions hadn't specified. I wanted to get this done, get Qione and get back to Harmony as soon as possible.

"How are you doing over there?" I asked Roroy.

"How long," he muttered, not opening his eyes.

"I don't know, but there's food, and a big bed in front."

Roroy groaned.

Poor baby, I thought. He's probably never been on a boat. *Sleep*, I *sent* to him. Soon he relaxed.

I found the rhythm of the boat soothing, and fell into a doze.

Sometime later, I awoke to a more severe rocking. We were moving back and forth sideways as well as up and down.

"Make it stop," Roroy said, as he sat up and clutched the edge of the seat. "Is there a place I can relieve myself?"

"Yes." I showed him the little room and how things worked.

After I took my turn and danced in a quick shower, I investigated the kitchen. I had no trouble moving about the vessel, even in the strongest rocking. In fact, I enjoyed the sensation. The freedom of movement was like dancing in air.

In a cupboard in the kitchen, I found bread and a small pot of something that smelled like nectar and tasted smooth and sweetish. I carried the bread and pot over to a small table at the end of the seat, followed by plates and a flat spreader. A tiny cold box yielded a pouch of a sweet liquid. That and a couple of mugs filled the table, which had a rim around it.

All the tables and counters had rims, and I saw why as I watched the dishes slide back and forth with the movement of the boat. Without the rims, everything would be on the floor.

The bread with the spread was wonderful, but I didn't eat as much as I would have liked. "Come and eat," I said, perching on the end of the seat

I didn't know long our journey would be, how long our food would have to last us. I handed a piece to Roroy. "Try it."

He took a bite, just to appease me, I think, and looked up. "This good." He quickly ate the rest. "More?" I gave him another piece, then told him we couldn't eat too much and why.

The food must have helped him, for he sat up and looked around. "All this water," he said. "How do we know where we going and when we get there? This not bad, but I long for solid ground, and Beast beneath me."

"He's all right, and so is Qione. One of my sixth senses tells me that." I sat down across from him.

"What do instructions say?" he asked.

"Only that it would take a few days, depending on the weather and the seas. But it could be more. We're going to an island to look for a particular fruit or something that comes from trees that only grows on that island. The boat is set to take us there. When we find whatever it is we're looking for, and get back on the boat, it will bring us back to the long dock. Then we retrace our steps to the porch and to the star room, and they will send us back to Harmony." I hope.

I assumed they needed me for my Talent to select the correct fruit.

"All right." He sighed. "I know not what my trek with you lead to, eggs and boats and all."

"Do you regret coming?"

"No. Is much better than home land. I not miss it if I never see it again."

"But your family." I twitched.

"Only father left and he old. Don't remember mother, brother dead. Sister ran off with visiting troubadour and never heard from her again. First trek was to look for her, but never found any sign of her or the man."

"I'm sorry," I said, leaning toward him.

"Why? Is life." He shrugged. We talked a little bit more. Then he noticed the books, rose and picked one out. "Pictures," he said, turning pages.

I took a book, too. This one had pictures of seashores. I couldn't read the marks under the pictures, which I assumed were words, but the pictures were enough.

When I couldn't stop yawning, I crawled into the big bed.

CHAPTER 19

Two days later, I went out on deck for some fresh air. The swells had lessened to almost nothing. When the boat turned a little to the north, I saw a green blob on the horizon. I watched it grow for a while, to be sure I wasn't seeing things, then hollered, "Land ho."

I trotted back to the cabin. "I saw the island. We're almost there."

Roroy jumped up and hurried to the door. I pointed. "How long?" he asked.

"I don't know." As we watched, it seemed to take forever before we could see the individual trees, the beach, and a dock.

Just as the sun was setting behind us, we arrived at the island. The boat pulled up to the dock. I heard hissing and cachunks as the ropes reeled out and wrapped themselves around the poles. Roroy rushed off as soon as the boat was secured.

"Ah. Solid land," he said, stretching and grinning. "Now where we go?"

I looked around. There was a path up from the beach through the sand dunes. "This way," I said. We waded through the loose sand to the boardwalk that led into the dunes. The boards were gray and splintered, and the walkway wide enough we could walk side by side.

When we reached the first dune summit, I could see trees in the distance, a long way off. Our narrow shadows stretched before us.

I sighed. I wanted to go on, but I was hungry and knew we should get a good night's rest before we went any farther.

"Are you hungry, Ro?" I asked.

"Yes. We go back and eat?"

"Yes," I said, "and sleep. We need to be fresh for this trip."

"True." He turned and started back.

The food I'd brought from the boat was welcome, but I had a hard time getting to sleep. I hadn't wanted to go back on board in case the boat thought we were done and took off.

I was getting a bad feeling about this endeavor.

If we went back without what they wanted, they'd either send us back here or to some other place, not Harmony. Whoever they were.

I still wasn't sure what we were supposed to find. I didn't want to be here, I wanted to go home. Why did they say the beasts would be useful when they didn't even come with us? I could just see them huddled in the corners of the cabin. And we'd have to clean up after them. Maybe out on deck.

And why us? As far as I could see, anyone could do this. My thoughts grew fragmented, and I slipped into sleep.

***

In the morning, we rushed through breakfast and hurried up to the dunes. The sun was high in the sky when we hiked up a hill and saw a number of paths going out in several directions through groves of different kinds of trees. All about the same height, they had dark green smallish leaves and were studded with a rainbow of fruit.

"Now what?" I asked. A picture of a red-orange oval fruit came into my mind. "About time," I muttered.

"Do you know what this fruit looks like?" Roroy asked.

"Somewhere between red and orange."

"Those orange," he said, pointing to the first grove on our right.

"Okay," I said. "Let's check them out and work our way around."

These weren't the ones, the smell didn't match what the aliens put in my mind. The next grove had yellow fruit, and the third, green. Following that we found an orchard of red fruits, and an orange grove, neither of which was the right one. It was pleasant walking through the groves, but it wasn't getting me anywhere. The fruits all looked delicious, but I had been told not to eat any of them.

I had a thought. Did I tell Roroy that? I turned. He had just taken a bite of a yellow fruit.

"No," I cried.

"What?" he mumbled. As he started to take another bite, I ran over and knocked the fruit out of his hand.

"Don't eat them, they're poison," I cried, as he bent to pick it up.

"Oh," he said, straightening.

Maybe only one bite, I thought, then saw his face turning red. "No," I said, and moved him back in time to before he took a bite, and swatted it out of his hand. "These fruits are all poisonous to us," I told him, and sat down hard.

The trees spun around me, and I closed my eyes.

"What happened," Roroy squatted beside me. "What wrong?"

Somewhere in the back of my brain I realized that what he'd seen was me walking along and then all of a sudden falling to the ground.

"I don't know," I lied. He didn't need to know that I had saved him again. "Let me sit here for a moment." A wind gathered in the tops of the trees. Something dropped in front of me. I picked it up.

It was the fruit we sought. I tucked it in a pocket. If I showed it to Roroy, he'd want to leave right now, and I wasn't ready to do any more walking for a while. Only he saw it anyway.

"What's that?" he asked.

"Nothing."

"Don't lie to me, woman." He reached for my hand, still in the pocket, and yanked it out.

"Don't squash it," I cried.

"Is this the fruit we seek?"

"Yes," I muttered. "But I need to rest."

"Why? You just sit down." A speculative look came into his eyes. "You not use your Talent?"

I looked down. I could not keep anything from this man. Is this what I wanted in a mate?

"We have fruit, we go." He turned and strode off.

"No, wait," I called. At least he could have helped me up, I thought bitterly. I crawled to the nearest tree and hauled myself up. My legs were too shaky to walk. I dropped and crawled to the next tree. He would get on the boat and it would leave. I would be stranded on an island full of food I couldn't eat. I collapsed into a ball of tears and tried to fight my way out of it.

Maybe I could *reach* whatever was running the boat. 'Don't leave,' I *sent*. 'Stay until I get there.' I repeated it a couple of times, then crawled after the man to the next tree. This time I could stand long enough to take three steps to the following tree. The tree after that was the last, and I had to crawl across the top of the hill to the boardwalk and haul myself up by the handrail.

I tottered along, stopping to catch my breath every little bit, and finally reached the beach. The boat was still there, and I could hear Roroy yelling at it. I sat on the bottom step of the boardwalk and screamed at him.

He didn't hear me. I *sent* my scream directly to his mind, and he looked up and at me.

I stood up, holding onto the end of the rail, took three steps into the sand and collapsed.

He watched from the deck of the boat.

I crawed toward him. He did not move.

All right, you bastard, if you won't come help me I'll crawl all the way, I thought. I wondered if there was some way I could have him sent to another world than Harmony.

When I was a few paces away, he stepped down, helped me up, and onto the boat. I collapsed on one of the seats.

"You did use your Talent," he said. "Why?" Then he put one and three together. "I start to eat fruit, yes?"

I could only nod.

"One thing I cannot stand is someone lying to me or hiding something from me," he said sternly. "Now rest." He stalked off to the front room.

How was I supposed to know, I thought. I was doing it for his own good. I curled up and dropped into sleep.

When I woke, we were on the high seas. Roroy sat on the other seat and watched me. "Good morning," he said.

I glared at him, remembering my crawl, and sat up. I looked out the window at the overcast sky. No way was I going to ask the time of day. I stalked off to the little room.

When I returned, Roroy shifted in his seat. "Is midday. How about food? I'm hungry."

"You know where the food is." I plopped down on the red seat and picked up a book.

"Women fix foods."

"Not always, where I come from. My papa and the other men cook fish in the fire pits."

However, I was starving, too. In a cupboard, I found pouches with pictures of foods on them. At least some looked like foods. Rattling through cupboards, I found a large pot. Picking up a pouch that had a picture of what looked like a tomato on it, I tried to figure out how to open it. The pouch wouldn't pull apart, so I tried to bite it open, a strip pulled off and the contents went all over the place, mostly into the pot.

"Oh," I cried, breaking into giggles as I grabbed a rag to wipe myself off.

"What you do?" Roroy asked, coming into the kitchen. "This look good." He picked up a pouch with a large animal on it. Holding it upright, he bit into one end, pulled the strip across, and dumped the contents into the pot. He picked a couple of root-like vegetables and something green. "Put in," he said, and returned to his chair.

I opened them with no problem, dumped them in the pot, stirred together with a big spoon, and put the pot on the cooker.

After we ate, he sat at the table and paged through books. I cleaned up the kitchen, and sprawled on the seat, watching the sea. I was aware that Roroy looked at me every so often.

The next day, he was polite, even solicitous toward me, but still kept his distance. How long was he going to be mad at me, I thought. Could I live with someone like this?

The following afternoon, we arrived back at the long pier. I was my normal self, and glad to see land again. We trudged back along the pier, the fruit tucked into a pocket. At the porch, we settled in, and waited for the Gate to open.

"We have the fruit," I said aloud. It was wrapped and in a special box we'd found on the boat. I held it out.

Soon after that, a chime rang, the door opened and we returned to the star room. The place shut itself around us, and the stars flickered out as the air went away.

***

When I came to, before I could get my senses together, one side of the room slid away and our guide stood there. The blue and green being led us through gray corridors to another, larger room. One with animal stalls. Qione whinnied when I walked in, and Roroy ran over to greet his Beast.

Where have you been, Qione demanded. *How dare you leave us in* this *strange place*. She stomped a front foot.

"It wasn't my idea," I said, patting her.

Roroy and I were escorted to seats and wide arms wrapped themselves around us.

Again, the tingle and loss of air.

CHAPTER 20

When I woke, I found myself in the long hall I'd seen before as we'd left Harmony. At least, it looked like it. Roroy and I mounted our steeds and galloped down the hall to the long room. The door at the end opened, and we dashed out into the real world.

I *reached*. We were on Harmony. "Yippee!" I yelled. Qione let out a long, loud bugle. We galloped away, Beast and Roroy on our heels.

Tears streamed down my cheeks. I was home at last. And with a good man I could trust, if not totally accept. We galloped until Qione tired and had to stop to rest.

In a wide, green valley, I *reached* again and *made contact* with Mama. 'We're back.'

'Thank Oneness,' Mama *sent*. 'Are you all right?'

'Yes. And I have company. You'll meet him when we get there.'

'Him?' Mama *asked*. 'Who is he?'

'Someone I met, who doesn't belong in his home land. He had no kin except an elderly father he doesn't get along with.'

'Okay. Take care on your way home and don't do what I did.'

'I won't. I'm not going to fall and hurt myself. See you soon.'

***

Late the second day after that, we met up with Will on Kiong and Laurie on Quest. Kiong nuzzled Qione as I embraced my brother. He looked older.

"Have you grown taller?" I asked him.

"Yeah. It's been almost a year since you left," he said.

I was bewildered. "But we haven't been gone that long. Oh, excuse my manners. This is Roroy, from the first world I went to. Roroy, this is my brother, Laurie, and this is Will. He's a cousin."

Roroy nodded. "Marisa has been good companion."

"Did you get to use your Talents, sis?" Laurie asked.

Roroy and I looked at each other and broke out laughing.

"I guess that's a yes," Laurie said. "Come on, let's get going. Mama's all in a tizzy."

We got home in record time, met up along the river by members of our clan, some on quines. They shouted and pushed to get close to me. Roroy watched with a bemused expression.

As we barreled into the valley, the rest of the clan were waiting for us near the plaza. The people all looked a little different and there were a few new buildings. I jumped off, and Qione trotted over to the quines' territory. Mama rushed up to hug me, followed by Granlyn and Granli. Then Papa came running up and gave me a big hug. Finally, Ricky pushed his way through to squeeze me. He was definitely taller than I remembered.

I introduced Roroy to my parents, grandparents, and Ricky. The latter thought Beast was cool.

We led Beast over by the quines. He growled. "It's all right, boy," Roroy said, patting him. "Plenty to eat here. This our new home."

Mama and Papa took me into their house, with Granlyn. "Laurie, show Roroy around, would you?" I said as I followed them. The place hadn't changed much. There were a few more of Ricky's bark drawings on the yellow walls, a second shelf by the door held Laurie's wood carved creatures, and the yellow kitchen curtain was new.

Papa stood in the middle of the room with crossed arms. "And what do you have to say for yourself, young lady?" he demanded. I noticed new wrinkles around his eyes.

"Now, Charley," Mama said.

"Don't you 'now Charley' me. I'm sick and tired of my women running off, and it's not going to happen again, if I have anything to say about it. Now, Marisa, where have you been and where did you find that man you brought home?"

"It's a long story." I seethed and felt guilty at the same time.

"So start."

"Qione wanted to go back to her people, bring more of her herd over here. I wanted to get away from here for a while, maybe find a mate. Whether Roroy is the one, I'm not sure yet. We went to Qione's world first, and Kiong brought some of their people here."

I sighed. "Qione and I picked a world that looked a lot like ours. That's where I met Roroy."

"And who exactly is he?" Papa had not moved a muscle.

Mama fussed at her tunic.

"He's the son of a king of a small country on his world," I said, trying to figure what to tell him and what to keep to myself. I'd grown adept at keeping things I didn't want others to know hidden in a special place in my mind. "He wanted to see his world, not be stuck in that little place on the edge of a continent the rest of his life. So he and Beast came with Qione and me, and he showed me how to get past the desert and the mountains, and to the city with the Gate."

I took a breath. "I thought we were going to be sent home to Harmony, but they sent us to a jungle world, and from there to an ocean world. After that, they sent us back here."

"They who?" Papa kept his eyes on me.

I looked at Mama.

"Gatekeepers," she said.

"I guess," I muttered.

"What exactly are these Gates," Papa said, unwinding his arms and dropping into a chair at the table.

"You know. They are ways to get from one world to another," Mama said. "Like the Rock Gate, where I went through to get Peter. They are all different, but basically you are wrapped in some kind of harness and then the air goes away. When you wake up, you're on another world."

"Can you choose where you go?" Papa asked.

"Sometimes," I said. I explained the screens at the Gate after Qione's world.

"What do you know about this young man you brought home?" Papa demanded.

"Roroy is very honest. He can't stand being lied to. He's an outdoors guy, knows a lot about how to do things out camping. He's quiet, and he hardly even touched me, even though I could tell he was physically attracted to me. He's good with animals." I paused, thinking. "He's strong and healthy, and he can open food pouches."

"Hmph," Papa muttered.

"Will you be able to bear his children?" Granlyn asked.

"I believe so." I hated the way they assumed he was to be my mate, because although I saw a lot of good in him, I still wasn't sure whether I was ready to mate, or whether he was the one.

Although if he wasn't, I'd have to go off world again. To change the subject, I asked about the quines.

"They seem to be very happy here," Granlyn said, "but the Bramites don't like them at all. They've never seen anything like the quines before, and the critters scare the kids. The quines know to move slow and easy around them." She shifted in her chair. "Just the other day, the Bramites told us to keep them out of River Point." She sighed.

"Will and Laurie took a couple up to North Point," Mama explained. "The quines loved splashing in the water along the beach, but the Bramites up there didn't like them either, even though Uncle Chad and Aunt Maria wanted to keep them. I don't think the quines cared much for that grass up there."

"So they're back here now?" I asked. It had never occurred to me that the Bramites might have a problem with them.

"No," Granlyn said. "Art has them up in the hills somewhere above River Point. In case anyone needs to get back here fast."

"Otherwise, everything's going well." Mama rose. "I need to go back to my duties, but I'm looking forward to hearing all about your trip tonight." Mama kissed me. She and Papa left.

"You can tell me about it," Granlyn said. "I have no place to go."

"Did they retire you?"

"I do teach a couple of classes every other day, and one for new teachers. Help with feasts and that. My fingers aren't steady enough anymore for sewing. I can still weave baskets and look after babies while their mothers are working."

I felt her sadness and tried to *soothe* it with my Talent.

"Ouch." She jumped.

"Sorry, Granlyn," I said, *jerking out* and moving away. "I guess I'm too strong for you." I turned and looked around the room. "Do you mind waiting 'til tonight, when I can tell both you and Mama and whoever else at the same time, so I don't have to go over it twice?"

"Sure," she said, and relaxed. "Apparently, your Talent is too strong to send it to me direct."

We chatted about what was going on, how the crops were doing, and who had babies.

"Noa is mainly supervising and teaching now," Granlyn said. "Everyone is getting old."

"You're not," I said defensively.

"Oh my dear, I certainly am. After all, I have a grown up granddaughter."

I rose. "I need to find Susan. I didn't see her in the plaza. See you later."

As I approached Susan's house, I *felt* something wrong.

"Hi, Mari, glad to see you back," she said when I walked in. Susan sat on her couch mending a quilt.

"What's going on?" I dropped down beside her.

Her face crumpled. "Oh, Mari, I lost my baby." She burst into tears and I pulled her into my arms, soothing her physically and mentally.

It was rare for one of us to miscarry, and I knew personally of only one other.

"I'm sorry I blubbered all over you," Susan said finally, wiping her face. "I so wished you were here."

"I'm here now. You'll have more."

"No." She gulped. "Anne says things are too messed up in there. I can't have any more."

"I don't believe it. Susan, you're meant to have babies. May I look and see if there's anything I can do?" I squeezed her. "I didn't even know you were pregnant."

"Mike couldn't wait. When I realized I was pregnant, I asked Granlyn to mate us, but she said she couldn't do it until you got back, she needed you for some reason. I was hoping there was something you could do."

"Let's get together first thing day after tomorrow. How did it happen?"

"Mike and I and Megan and her younger three were riding down to the beach. I was on Qietta, Qione's aunt and she got spooked by some birds flying right by in front of her and dumped me off. I rolled the wrong way to get off a rock, and her foot came right down on my stomach."

"Ouch," I said. Then, "Birds?"

"That's what Aunt Maria calls them. They were roosting down by the river. Look at this." She pulled up her tunic to show me a nasty scar on her left side.

I touched it gently. "I'm pretty sure I can help you. But right now, I'm exhausted and need to rest before supper."

"Okay. Come on in here." She took me into the bedroom. We lay on the bed together and talked and dozed.

"Ruthie had a baby boy, named Willie," she told me. "She was in labor two days."

"Poor thing. How's she doing as a mother?"

"Good. She hardly lets him out of her sight. He looks like Will."

That knot of pain bubbled up again.

Thank Oneness she had a boy. My daughter-to-be had to be the first girl born in our generation, to carry on the race, according to Mama and Granlyn.

Later, when I returned to my room to prepare for supper, I hoped my Talent wouldn't be too strong for Susan. Of course, she was of my generation. But the whole idea of going inside another person to heal something was too weird. The feeling of not belonging, of something other, grew more intense and tighter.

That night, my parents, grandparents, Susan, Mike, Will, Uncle Peter, Aunt Anne and their kids, and my brothers made themselves comfortable in Mama's living room, and I told my story.

Roroy was up with his Beast and the quines.

I gave them an edited version of our travels, downplaying the episodes of my using my Talent. The boys were fascinated by the boat. I didn't really want to hash over my trip. I wanted to get away from it for a while and enjoy being home, as much as I could. After I finished, they wanted to talk about it, but I excused myself, saying I was too tired and needed to rest.

When Laurie protested, Mama said, "That's enough. We'll talk about this later."

I went to my room and collapsed. It was strange to be sleeping indoors.

***

The next morning, Roroy and I were assigned duties by Grampa Larry. We worked ourselves back in to the clan, and Roroy became part of the community. It took some of the others a little time to accept him, especially Freddie.

"Where did you get that creep," he sneered as we crossed paths.

"He's a better man than you are." I tossed my head and continued on to the schoolhouse.

***

At supper that evening, I asked Mama if she'd heard from Dela, the Wati leader, lately.

"I haven'd heard anything from them. Chad told me several of the guys went on a trek upriver and found areas where Wati had lived, but there were none there then. They probably moved farther inland, or over to the mountains. Would you like to contact her now?"

"Sure." Dela's mother, Judee, had befriended Granlyn and brought them here to Harmony.

Mama and I sat on the couch and *reached*. '*Dela, do you heard us?*'

114

we *sent*, repeating it several times.

Finally, we *made contact with*, faintly, Suli, Dela's daughter.

'How are your trees?' Mama made the customary greeting.

'Trees are well, but too many clans out on their own,' Suli replied.

'Where?'

'In mountains. Going back to old place at north river. Will contact you then.' She faded out.

Mama and I looked at each other.

"Well. At least they're still there," I said.

"Judee was the only one who could hold them together." Mama stood. "They'll go back to their roots, er, branches, and live the way they always did."

***

In the morning, I met Susan at her house. Mike had built them one because neither set of parents had room for three of them. "I hope I can help," I said, as we went into the bedroom.

"I know you will." Susan pulled her tunic up and her pants down to her hips and lay on the bed.

I laid my hands on her abdomen, closed my eyes, and *eased in*. Her left ovary was a mess, but the right one appeared to be normal, as was the connection to the uterus.

"Have you been having your periods?"

"I had one. It wasn't a lot, but the cramps were bad."

"Okay." I gently *moved* bits and pieces around until the damaged uterus was close to its normal shape. As I *eased out*, I sat back and looked at her. "I can't guarantee anything, but keep trying. I think it may work." I prayed to Oneness that it would.

Susan sat up and hugged me. "You're wonderful, Mari."

"Thank you." If I could do what I'd just tried to do, what else could I do? And would I want to? I shivered and rose. "It's time to get to our tasks."

***

A few days later, Grampa Bay got a *call* from Uncle Art. Uncle Chad's eight-year-old grandson, Jimmy, up in North Point, had seriously injured a Bramite boy, and the other Bramites had given them one day to leave. Art was taking his quines up, and they would come straight here.

"Oh my Oneness," Granlyn said, when he told us. "Now we're really in trouble."

CHAPTER 21

Gan's son, Little Emek, who was not so little anymore, and a couple others, let Uncle Chad, Aunt Maria and their brood get a head start, then came down after them to report to Gan and the council.

I heard all this from Aunt Maria through Granlyn's Four. They stayed linked with Aunt Maria until she and Uncle Chad passed by River Point. I'd never heard her so angry. Normally, she was very quiet and efficient, and kept her kids under control with an iron voice and lots of love.

'The child provoked Jimmy unbearably,' she *sent*. 'Jimmy's been having growth spurts in his Talent, and it was just too much for him, poor baby.'

Uncle Art met up with them, with the quines, shortly after they left North Point. Chad III was also furious. 'They had no right to do that to my son.' Little Emek and the others had tied up Jimmy, gagged him, and locked him into a shed until they were ready to leave.

I *sensed* the Bramites' fear of us overcoming their placid rationality.

'You are so right,' Uncle Art said. 'Let's get packed up and out of here.' He took all the baggage they'd been carrying and put it in the quines' panniers. He set Aunt Maria, wearing a snuggie carrying the youngest baby, and Jimmy, on one quine; her daughter, Barbie, on the other, with her two youngest. Jimmy had totally shut down his Talent, and with it, most of his mind.

Just as Uncle Art's group left, the Bramites caught up with them.

The man whose son had been injured, yelled, picked up a rock and threw it at them.

Jimmy's older brother, Joey, had stumbled and looked back. He stopped the rock in mid-air and let it drop like a feather to the sand.

The man stepped back, open mouthed, as a second man picked up another stone.

'Run,' Uncle Art yelled. He, Uncle Chad, and the rest of the children and grandchildren ran after the bolting quines. 'Down on the wet sand.'

The Bramites ran after them, but in the soft sand, soon fell behind, and turned back.

When the quines saw that they were no longer being chased, they stopped until the people on foot could catch up with them. The runners collapsed on the sand, cooled by a sea breeze.

'How's he doing?' Uncle Art asked Aunt Maria. She just shook her head. 'He'll be all right once we get him back to Freedom,' he added.

'I hope so,' she said.

Joan, Jimmy's mother, lurched over to her son and put a hand on his leg. Aunt Maria patted her hand.

'He'll be okay,' Chad III said. 'He's a tough little guy.'

Uncle Chad's family sat and watched the waves, the forest at their backs. A pair of seabirds sailed by. Uncle Art made sure everyone had a drink of water. As he put his water pouch away, he asked, 'Is everyone ready to continue on?'

The others rose and started walking down the beach. After a couple of hours, Uncle Art decreed they would stop and camp for the night.

'Relax,' he said. 'We're safe now.'

'Do you think we should post a guard?' Uncle Chad asked.

'No. The quines are light sleepers. They'll let us know if anyone comes close to us.'

***

The next day, when Granlyn's Four and I tuned in, most of the people were up and rousting the others. This time, Joan rode and carried Jimmy. The quines kept to a slow pace and stopped every now and then to let the walkers catch up. At the midday stop, the quines and the youngsters splashed in the sea.

Uncle Art and the gang reached the cutoff to the shortcut in back of River Point as the sun was sliding into the sea. They went up the trail a bit, away from the beach, to camp.

***

The following day, Aunt Maria *sent*, 'We'll be all right now. We've just passed River Point on the high trail. See you soon.'

"That's a relief," Granlyn said. "I don't understand what has happened to the Bramites to be like this. But we'll definitely have to keep the kids away from them,"

I agreed, and left to find Roroy, to let him know what was going on. He probably thought I was avoiding him.

***

The group showed up just after supper two days later, along with

Uncle Art's kids, who'd been at River Point.

Art Junior had a huge sack of their scientific gear, and he and his father would ride back early the next morning to get the rest. We met them at the plaza, where Granlyn took Jimmy in her arms, kissed him, and handed him off to his father.

Granlyn led the way to her house. "Come on in," she said to Aunt Maria, Joan, Mama and me. "First thing we need to do is heal him," she added, as Chad III lay the boy down on the couch. He had curled up into a fetal position and refused to respond to anyone, not even his mother, who sat beside him.

"I'll get the Fours," Granlyn added, rubbing the boy's head. The first Four was an entity composed of Granlyn, Granli, Grampa Bay, and Uncle Gabe, who had taken his father's place when Uncle Adam died. The second was Mama, Papa, Uncle Peter, and Han, who'd taken his brother's place.

I couldn't help listening in, although listening wasn't quite the right word. The others had arrived quickly and sat in a circle of chairs, with Joan on a stool in the center, Jimmy held tightly in her arms. The Fours reached out, held hands, and joined mentally. Slowly they *eased* into Jimmy's mind. 'I know you're in there,' Bay *sent*. The others repeated the message. The boy twitched. The Fours *oozed in* farther, and found the nub of his Talent. Gently they *touched* and *massaged* it. Slowly the nub began to unfold. The Fours cupped Jimmy's Talent in a 'hand' and carefully *drew it out*.

'You are well, Jimmy,' Granlyn *sent*. 'Come to your mama, she wants you.' The boy moved. After the others repeated the message, he turned to face Joan and opened his eyes.

Joan began to weep as she held him tightly to her breast.

He pushed away. "Mama?" he said.

"Yes dear, I'm here." She wiped her eyes.

Gradually the Fours *pulled out* of him, dropped hands and sat back. My eyes were wet, too.

Jimmy sat up and looked around. "Where am I?"

"We're in Freedom, with all the rest of the clan," Joan said, wiping her eyes. "We rode on a quine."

"Where is it?" He jumped off her lap and ran to the door.

"We'll take you up to see them in a little while," Grampa Bay said. "Now you need to eat and rest."

Eat maybe, I thought, but rest? He'd been resting the last several days. He needed to get out and run around.

"Are you hungry, Jimmy?" Aunt Maria asked, getting up.

He nodded.

Granlyn climbed to her feet, and she, Joan, and Aunt Maria went to the kitchen. Grampa Bay took Jimmy out to the latrine.

Uncle Gabe stayed. "We need a council meeting today. Now," he annoiunced.

"After duties," Granlyn said from the kitchen.

Uncle Gabe looked at her. "Well, all right. This evening for sure."

Grampa Bay, Granli and Han left with Uncle Gabe.

***

At supper, Grampa Larry called for a full clan meeting right after the meal. As everyone wandered into the big meeting hall, a hint of doom touched me. Uncle Gabe, as the son of the previous leader, Uncle Adam, was the nominal head of the community, but Grampa Larry actually did most of the leading as he was the oldest male. He, Uncle Gabe and Granlyn, the power behind the leader, sat in the center looking outward, with everyone else around them looking inward. The younger children gathered in a group by themselves at the back.

The pale walls were broken by many small windows, and a door at the end led to the communal kitchen. I looked up at the big beams crisscrossing the ceiling and remembered watching the men hoist them up with Uncle Art's pulleys.

"Time," Grampa Larry yelled, on his feet. Everyone quieted down. "You all know what happened to Jimmy. And, as you can see, all of us Terrans are here at Freedom. From the Bramites' reactions, I think it's safe to say we'd better not go back to River Point for a while."

"But," someone began.

"I know," Grampa Larry cut in. "There are some things, such as fish and some fruits that we can only get from them. We'll just have to do without for the time being. But the big question is, can we afford to stay on this world?"

The room erupted with babble. Granlyn and I were probably the only ones not surprised. Maybe Mama, too. I saw people shifting in their chairs, waving arms, looking at each other.

Grampa Larry held his hands up for silence. "We can stay here for a while, but with the Talent increasing with each generation,

119

eventually we won't be able to avoid interacting with the Bramites. The situation with Jimmy shows that we are already beginning to separate from them. So my questions is, how much longer can we afford to stay here in Freedom?"

"Where would we go?" Art Junior asked.

"There is another continent on Harmony, in the southern hemisphere," Grampa Larry said. "I've been looking at the maps we made when we first came. There is a place on this continent that is relatively close to a point on the other one."

"How would we get there?" Art Junior persisted.

"Build carts here to carry our stuff," Grampa Larry replied. "Build them in such a way that when we reach the crossing, we can recycle the carts into boats. We can do that. People on Home Earth sailed clear around the world in wooden boats. We'll have to make sails, large sheets of fabric that will catch the wind and blow us across."

More babble erupted

I projected my voice. "Grampa, that might work for a while, but in two or three more generations, we'll probably be too much for the Bramites even down there. I think we should look for a completely different world with nobody else on it."

Stunned silence filled the room, then Grampa Larry spoke. "That's a pretty large task, Marisa. I know you've found a way to get there, but how do we know that will work?"

Granlyn stood. "I think I agree with Marisa. It's quite likely we'll outgrow this one, and we don't want to impinge on either the Bramites or the Wati. Also, it makes more sense to make one big move, rather than two of them. We'd have to come back here to go through the Gate anyway."

"Okay, okay, hold it." Grampa Larry put up his hands again. "You're right, babe. We don't have to do this right away, but everybody, start thinking about it. We will need carts. We have quines to ride, and, Marisa, if you would, find out whether they would be willing to pull carts. We will need to figure out how to take down this place and put it up on the new world. Let me know any ideas you come up with."

Granlyn added, "Also, watch the children carefully, especially the ones who are approaching puberty. We don't want anyone else hurt."

People relaxed. Grampa Larry took a deep breath. "Now, any old business?"

There were a few uninteresting items, like crops, so I left. I thought I'd come home to a nice, relaxing routine, but no such luck. And now we had to focus on damping down our Talents. So what was the purpose for having Talents if we couldn't use them?

CHAPTER 22

As I walked over to the quines' territory in the trees, I pondered some more. I knew none of the others had my Talent to bend time, but several of the older children in my generation could move objects up to the weight of a small child. They had even invented a game where they had to move pieces the size of large rocks without touching them. Granlyn approved of that; it taught them control.

I also knew that only I had a piece of non-human otherness in me. First Granlyn, then Mama had noticed it. None of us could really describe or identify it, it was just there, No one else, not even Will had that. When I thought of him, or saw him, that little knot of pain deep within me throbbed.

As Qione came to greet me, I pushed it away.

***

Granlyn had me set up a class to teach the others of my generation about our Talents, what we could or could not do with them, and how to control them. "While we stay here, we need to able to keep control of our Talent," she said. "We also need to be more serious about control when the next little ones come. They'll be even stronger than you."

"When will this stop?" I asked.

"When we become Watchers," Granlyn replied, looking away. "My father, your great grandfather, did not want this, but it seems there is nothing we can do about it."

"Maybe there is," I said. A thought had come into my mind, but I couldn't put it into words. I didn't want to become a Watcher, whatever they were.

"What do you mean, dear?" She looked at me.

"I'm not sure. I can't really see it yet."

"Well, when you do, let me know."

"Oh, I will."

***

Life went on. People talked about finding a place on the other side of this world, finding a new world, how to control Talent. As I taught my class, I discovered that many of my pupils did not know the extent of their Talents, especially the young ones. I set up tests, and let each child know exactly where e was.

Roroy worked in the fields with some of the men. He knew a lot about plants and was able to provide some information, which helped make him feel wanted. He and I made time for ourselves in the evenings, and one night he asked, "When is next bonding? I think is time for us to join."

"I don't know. I'll have to ask Granlyn. I know Susan and Mike are ready. Are you sure you want me?"

"I been sure for long time."

"Oh." We were sitting under a tree near the quines, and Beast, who sometimes had to be chased away from our meetings, sat and watched us with his black button eyes. "Well then, I'll talk to Granlyn. I'll be ready." I cared for him a great deal, but still something was missing.

***

Granlyn told me to have Roroy build us a house. I picked out the site and laid out the rooms.

As we worked on our new home, the notion picked at me; what if he couldn't give me a child? Nonsense, I thought, I can do whatever I needed to conceive.

Once our house was finished, Granlyn set a date for the bonding. As the matriarch, she performed the ceremony for Roroy and me, and Mike and Susan. I wore Mama's long white tunic she had put away after her mating, and great grampa's scarf. Aunt Anne, Mike's mother, gave Susan a blue scarf Anne's mother, Betty, had brought from Home Earth. Susan and I helped each other dress, giggling a lot. I was so glad we were being bonded at the same time.

Roroy and I moved into our new house. I was careful not to get pregnant, I wasn't ready for that yet. Roroy had refused to go along with the custom of trying for a baby before mating, which was fine with me.

***

After a few months, I began hearing snatches of talk about why I wasn't pregnant yet, and people wondering whether it was because of Roroy. Granlyn knew I was doing it on purpose.

When it became obvious that we weren't going to become parents in the near future, Granlyn suggested we become world hunters.

"Now is the best time, before they start a family," she told the high council of the First Four and Grampa Larry.

He did not have any Talent, he was Granlyn's cousin on her mother's side.

Later that evening, at Mama's house, we talked about looking for another world. Granlyn and Grampa had gone home.

"Well, we didn't look at all the worlds in that room with the screen," I said. I liked the idea of getting away from all the when-are-you-going-to-get-pregnant looks. "Roroy and I will go. Who else?"

"I'll go," Laurie said.

"No," Mama said. "Not both of you."

"You'll still have Squirt," Laurie smirked.

"How long will you be gone?" Mama asked.

"I have no idea."

"You were gone almost a year before," Laurie said. "So maybe twice that, depending on how many worlds you have to go to." He turned to Papa. "Can I go, please?"

Mama winced. I understood how Granlyn had felt when Mama had gone after Uncle Peter. But this must be done. I'd become more and more positive that we would need our own world. There were so many out there, surely we could find one that met our needs.

"Don't worry, I'll take very good care of him," I said.

Laurie stuck his tongue out at me. "I can take care of myself."

"Can you?" Roroy asked. "I take very good care of both of them."

Mama took Papa off to talk in private.

I sat and waited and twiddled my fingers. Laurie paced the room.

When they returned, Papa said, "Roroy, you're a man of several worlds. Do you think Laurie could handle the journey?"

"Yes. He rides quine well and takes care of it." Roroy paused. "Another person with your Talents be useful. He is strong boy, and we may need muscle power somewhere."

"Like if you fall off your beast and get hurt," I couldn't help saying.

"Marisa!" Papa snapped. Mama gaped.

"Well it could happen," I said, looking down at my feet.

"Things do happen," Roroy added.

"You'll still have Ricky." I smiled.

"Wanna try for another one?" Papa asked, grinning.

"At least you can."

"Marisa," Mama snapped, lifting her hand as if to slap me.

I took a step back. "Sorry." I would never have said that if

Granlyn were there; she and Grampa Larry couldn't have kids. I knew that Uncle Adam was Mama and Uncle Peter's biological father. But it gave me an idea.

"Let him go," Papa said, changing the subject. "You all take care of each other and the quines."

"All right," Mama agreed reluctantly.

We decided to leave in three days.

Grandpa Larry rearranged schedules. Uncle Art and Roroy created panniers for the quines to carry supplies in. Beast already had his. The three of us packed them and our backpacks. Qione chose a quine for Laurie to ride and made sure Quest understood what was expected of him.

As I prepared for another journey, both excitement and sadness swept over me. It would be nice to have a world to ourselves, to develop it the way we wanted. Life would be hard until the crops were ready, and the move would take a lot of planning. But first, I had to find another world. And that wouldn't be easy.

On the down side, I would have to leave my family again. At least, Laurie would be with me. Us.

***

The day before we were to leave, Granlyn and Mama gave me Great Grampa's scarf. "I gave this to Perri when she left on her trek, so we decided this would be a good time to pass it on to you," Granlyn said. "This was the one thing I had of his." She lifted it to her nose and sniffed it. "I can still smell his aroma." Tears came to her eyes.

I *sensed* how much she'd missed him when he was gone, and how she regretted not having her childhood memories of him. I thought of my idea again. She really wasn't that old.

Granlyn handed the scarf to Mama, who also sniffed it. "Grandad is still here," she said. "I wish I'd known him. He's really the father of our new race, right, Mama?"

"My grandfather was the first to show any Talent, but the Watchers started programming our ancestors long before that," Granlyn said. "My father started the two lines, ours and Bay's."

***

In bed, I *reached* to Granlyn, to her body, into her ovaries. Yes, there still were a couple of viable eggs there. Then I *reached* into Grampa Larry, to his sperm. They were still viable. After I *unblocked* a tube and *moved back* into myself, I prayed to Oneness it would work.

***

In the morning, Roroy and Laurie went to fetch the steeds, and I hugged Mama and Papa, Granlyn and Grampa Larry, Susan, and many others. We packed up and mounted. I looked around at this place that had been my home for the last ten years, and wondered if I would ever see it again. For a moment, a *sense* of otherness came over me, a *sense* that this place and these people were strangers I'd never seen before. Then it was gone.

CHAPTER 23

I shook myself and told Qione to lead the way. She took off with a little bounce in her step. Roroy followed, holding Beast back to a slow trot, and after him, Laurie, on Quest. Beyond the first bend, we broke into a gallop.

When we got that out of our systems, Roroy reined us back. "We have long way to go. We must keep the beasts healthy." Our group continued on at a more sedate pace.

Laurie bounced up and down on Quest's back. I told him to calm down, to no avail. He exclaimed over every new sight, and pointed at rocks and trees Roroy and I hadn't bothered to look at. I'd never seen him so excited. Poor kid, he was the middle one, and always got the least attention after Ricky came along.

I enjoyed the sun's warmth and gentle breezes. We passed over rocky ridges and across green valleys, listening to Laurie's chatter. At the river where we'd found fish before, I didn't see any. Had we eaten them all? Or was there some other reason?

We made it to the Gate in three days. The glade welcomed us with lots of shade and whispers of leaves. Roroy and I set up camp.

"Can't we go through now?" Laurie asked.

"No." I lay out my sleeping blankets. "We need to wait 'til morning so we'll be fresh, wherever we go."

***

The next day, when we were ready, Qione placed her foot on the hill, but nothing happened. She tried several other places nearby. Still nothing.

Oh no, I thought, my heart sinking. Would we have to go all the way back and over to the Rock Gate?

"What's the problem?" Laurie asked.

"The Gate is supposed to open when Qione puts her foot in a particular place, only it's not working," I explained. "Qione, are you sure you're in the right place?"

Of course, she snapped, continuing to tap the hillside.

Laurie dismounted and trotted over to her.

He peered at the grass on the side of the hill, and closed his eyes. I *sensed* him looking at the machinery underneath.

"There," he said, pointing to a place a little ways from where she'd been tapping. Qione stepped over and touched the hill there. A vertical slit appeared and slipped open to a doorway. Laurie ran back to Quest, jumped on, and we all went through into the long room. Everything was as it was before.

At the room with the screen, we all dismounted, and I sat down and looked through choices. Roroy's world was no longer listed. I found three possibles. They all had gravity, climate and air similar to ours, mountains and more sea than land. They also had no sentient creatures much larger than our furry twitterers. I made a mental note of them so I could find them later.

"Okay, I've found some. Let's try this one." We mounted, and I pushed a button. A door on the other side of the room opened. We cantered over and through. Down a short hallway that jittered and briefly darkened, we came out onto a narrow beach with high white cliffs behind it.

"A beach," I said, delighted. But then, how do we get off of it?

"You go that way," Roroy said, pointing to one end of the beach, "and we'll go this way."

"What's that line along the bottom of the cliff?" Laurie asked.

"Looks like tide line," Roroy said. He turned and looked out to sea. "I think tide going out. We must hurry."

"Then there must be a moon," I said, looking up. Although Harmony did not have a moon, the grandfathers had taught us all about Home Earth's moon.

"Not up now. We go."

We split up. The sea was quiet here, only small curls onto the shore, and not much wet sand to walk on. Qione didn't mind getting her feet wet at all. In fact, she splashed a little too much, and Quest followed her example. Not Beast, he plowed through the dry sand.

"He hate getting wet," Roroy said.

At the end, the cliffs stretched out into the sea, with large piles of rocks lining them. Qione stopped short. She told me she couldn't swim that far. There was no kind of trail up the cliff that a quine or beast could climb. It was rocky enough in a few places that we people could climb it, but we couldn't leave our steeds there. For one thing, there was no grass or other plants.

When we met the others down toward their end, I just shook my head. The cliffs at this end did not go out so far into the sea, and were not as tall.

"Can you and Quest swim that?" I asked Qione.

If I don't have to carry anything or anybody.

"Here's trail, if we move rock out of way," Roroy said. "We go up this way, and the beasts swim around."

"Let's go up first and see how far they need to swim," I said.

"Good idea."

Then we three people tried to move the boulder blocking the bottom of the trail. It wouldn't budge. Roroy came up with a makeshift harness for Beast and had him pull while we pushed. We dug out the sand on one side, and the rock rolled a little. We looked at each other.

Laurie put his arm around my waist and said, "We'll use our minds while you push." We *reached* together and, with the physical force, moved the boulder enough so that we could get by.

"We need to rest for a moment," I said, as I flopped in the sand. Laurie dropped down beside me, taking deep breaths.

Qione nosed me. "I'll be all right, girl."

After a while, I said, "Okay, let's go. Qione, we'll go up first, then I can show you how far you have to swim." She nodded.

I took my backpack and a bag of food. Roroy and Laurie each took a pannier; Beast kept his. We started up the steep, twisty trail, full of rocks to step over or around. Halfway up, we stopped to rest, clinging to the cliff. Tiny blue flowers that smelled like dead fish poked out of the cliff wall. When we finally reached the top, we collapsed without looking around.

After I caught my breath, I sat up and saw the cliff stretching along the sea far too long for the quines to swim around. Turning, I saw the sand dunes. The land sloped down from in back of the top of the cliffs and, as far as I could see, lines of pinkish-tan sand dunes stretched out to the horizon. Not a tree or blade of grass in sight. Nor body of water. The quines couldn't go that far without water, even if we could wade through the dunes.

"Sorry, guys, this is a no. Qione, go back to the Gate, open it if you can, and hold it open."

Descending was even more difficult. We had to manage our loads and not slip or fall.

At the bottom, Laurie put his panier back on Quest, Roroy carried Qione's, and we headed back to the Gate. Roroy made Laurie ride, but he and I walked.

Qione, bless her heart, had found the Gate.

We went back in to try another world. This door opened into a room that we barely fit into after Roroy and I mounted. The room darkened as it moved upward. What was the word Mama used for it? Oh yes, lift.

After I experienced a spell of dizziness, the room came to a stop. As the light came up, and we waited for the door to open, I thought, now what.

We were in a place of machines, with a pathway lit with red arrows on the floor pointing around to the right. We followed them to a wide archway that opened onto a covered patio with grass around the edges. Several small metal tables and chairs sat along the sides. Large gray paving stones covered the floor. Arrows led to wide stairs that led down into a garden.

Looking out, I saw a mountainside below, and at the bottom, flat green land that stretched to the horizon.

"They don't make these easy, do they," Laurie said.

Qione headed for a nearby patch of grass, Quest following. Beast had found his own food.

As I walked along the railing, I looked down at the garden. Rows of bushes sprouted round pink flowers, with beds of smaller plants around the edges. A path down from the steps circled the garden. I wondered who tended it.

It was strange there were no people here; someone must have built the machines around the gate, and this building it was in. But the screen had indicated there were no people here.

"Dusty," Laurie said, drawing a finger across a table. "Whoever used to live here has been gone for a long time."

"Over here," Roroy called at the far end. We went over to him. A path led down from the porch outside the garden and down switchbacks along the side of the mountain. The steeds could handle this, I thought. But Qione refused.

No way out.

"How can you tell?" I asked her. "There's trees all along the bottom."

Look.

She *showed* me a spot in the trees, which she magnified into a river rushing off the edge of a cliff.

"We have to go back," I said, turning.

"Why?" Laurie asked.

"No way down," I said. Actually, I was glad. It looked like a long and steep trail.

CHAPTER 24

Laurie and I returned to the gate, but the door to the little room was closed. There was no screen, only a small panel of five buttons with no labels. I could not *sense* anything associated with them.

"How do you know which one to press?" Laurie asked.

"I don't." I pushed at the door. Nothing happened.

Roroy showed up. "Come out front," he said. "There must be other Gate. Better that than to trust this thing."

"You're right," I said. "Let's go."

A walkway that hadn't been there before, between the little room and the machinery, led us out onto a wide porch with broad, flat steps leading down to a large grassy area. The steeds trotted down to the grass.

I looked back at the building we'd just left. It stretched a long way to either side. Other large gray edifices lined the sides of the open space. What is this place, and why is there no one here? I *reached* all around and found no people and no direct danger, but something I could not pin down lurked in the background. I didn't like it at all.

"Why are there no people here?" Laurie asked.

"I have no idea," I said. Ahead of us, and beyond the buildings, rose tall black mountains. How are we going to get past those, I thought.

Laurie headed for the nearest building on the right. I followed, to keep an eye on him.

"The door won't open," he said, after pushing and pulling at it.

"They probably locked it up when they left."

A great wide, white walkway led down the center of the grassy area. Roroy dragged Beast away from the grass and headed down the way. Laurie and I continued along the fronts of the buildings, trying each door. They were all locked. None of the windows were low enough to look into, even on quine back.

Occasional tall narrow trees punctuated the grass, and flower beds in front of the buildings held narrow red flowers with no aroma. Under a deep blue and cloudless sky, the air was cool with little wind.

We trotted along the monotonous landscape. Qione soon dropped to a walk. *Harder to move here*, she told me.

The square gray buildings, with one large door and a handful of narrow windows scattered in the walls, sat one after another, all the same. As the small sun sank in the sky to our left, the grass and the buildings ended, although the way continued, narrower and graveled instead of white and hard.

We walked over to where Roroy waited, at the end of the grass.

"Is the gravity stronger here?" I asked.

"Yes," said Roroy. "We go slower."

On either side now, gray barren fields stretched to the far-distant purple mountain peaks. Here and there were small groves of wide, rounded trees. We stopped at one to camp.

Where's water, Qione demanded.

I looked around. "Do you guys see any water?" I asked.

"I don't," Laurie said.

"Don't see any either," Roroy added. "We must use some of our supply for the beasts."

"I hope we find some tomorrow." I patted Qione.

"It must be in ground where tree roots can reach it," Roroy said.

"Do we have to dig a well?" Laurie wanted to know.

"What about the grass?" I asked.

"Maybe it rains much here," Roroy said. "Look." He pointed to clouds piling up in the east. "I dig watering hole." He chose a depression in the ground out from under the trees and unpacked a small shovel. After digging for a while, he got out a large shallow bowl and set it in the bottom of the hole. He put away his shovel just as the first drops began to fall.

Beast and the quines watched with interest as Roroy, Laurie, and I huddled under the nearest tree. Beast stood in the rain for a little bit, then shook violently and came in under the trees. The quines ran and danced and stood with their heads turned up and mouths wide open.

"You're going to choke, you silly beasts," I said, remembering an experience I'd had as a young child doing the same thing.

***

In the morning, the rain had stopped, and the sky clear. The steeds had drunk all the water Roroy had collected.

He took up the bowl, wiped it out, and put it back into his panier. We ate and packed up. The fresh smell of rain faded away.

We continued on, through cloudless days and rain-filled nights under trees. Every evening, Roroy dug a water hole for the steeds, and I collected water for us. I hoped they were getting enough to eat and drink.

It didn't seem like we were getting anywhere, like we'd ever find our new world. This wasn't it. I didn't want someone to have to dig water holes every night. Besides, it just didn't *feel* right.

***

One day, Laurie asked, "Why don't we go over to the peaks? There might be rivers there."

"No, we stay on the way," Roroy said. "Is there for a reason."

Every morning, I *reached* in all directions and found nothing. The background unease grew. A few days later, we came to a crossroad. As I looked in both directions, the mountains appeared larger.

"Do the mountains look bigger to you?" I asked Roroy.

"Closer, yes."

"We've got a road here, can we go look at the mountains?" Laurie asked.

"I don't *feel* any danger down there," I said. "Which way?"

"Away from sun." We turned right. After a while, we came to a great hole in the ground. Qione took one step off the road and quickly pulled her foot back.

Bad, she told me.

Laurie dismounted and put his foot on the ground beside the road. "It feels funny," he said. "Like walking on a bed."

"We go back," Roroy turned Beast around. At the crossroads, the men wanted to try the other side road. We found another huge hole and returned to the main road.

That night, we only found one skimpy tree and got soaked.

***

The next few days, my uneasiness grew as the mountains drew closer. It must be connected with the peaks. No green showed on the mountains, only occasional patches of gray marked the black sides.

On the fourth day, the road led into a large tunnel into the mountain. There was no way to get over the mountains, they were almost straight up to the high passes.

I *reached* into the tunnel. Still no immediate danger.

"Do you *sense* anything?" I asked Laurie.

He *reached*. "No. But there's something I don't like in there."

"So you feel that too." I looked at the men. "Well, we can go on in, or we can go back to the Gate, pick at random, and hope it works."

"It's not that bad," Laurie said. "Let's go on."

"If the Gate does not work, we have to come back here anyway," Roroy added.

So we walked into the tunnel. Qione snorted and Beast growled. Quest shivered.

Although there was light and air, it was difficult to see where the walls ended and the ceiling and floor began. The floor was mostly flat, with a few stones here and there. Qione and Quest walked side by side, almost touching. Laurie and I kept bumping legs. Beast, with Roroy, ahead of us, seemed to shrink into himself.

Presently, we came to a place where the tunnel narrowed, and Qione and I dropped back behind Laurie and Quest. Soon, I felt a presence. Turning, I saw something massive blocking the light of the tunnel behind me. I tried to touch it, but could not. Chills ran up and down my back. What was this thing I couldn't touch?

Qione poked her nose into Quest's behind, pushing him. He ran into Beast, who growled. Roroy looked around and told Beast to go faster. He trotted ahead and we were right behind them. I began to feel something pushing at me. Quest whimpered.

Suddenly we were in a great open area, and the massive something was pushing us to a round green structure in the center. As we trotted up the ramp onto the platform, a cloud of shimmering pale blue hanging above us, a huge, upsidedown bowl-like thing descended down over all of us and the green structure.

"What's going on?" Laurie asked, quivering with fear. I steeled myself to not shake. This was beyond weird. Roroy's face was as pale as snow, as were his hands clutching Beast. All three of the steeds were huddled as close together as they could get, whimpering.

"Hello," I shouted. "What do you want of us?"

A sense of expectancy filled the air. The blue dome darkened slowly, and a deep bell tone tolled.

We waited, holding on to each other. Everything went black.

I struggled to stay awake, as the beasts fell and the men rolled off them. Qione went down on her knees.

I *reached* all around me. Something beyond my understanding was guarding us, but I could not contact it. I slept.

CHAPTER 25

I awoke in a wide, cool glade, with a spring bubbling up into a stream on the other side. Laurie and Roroy lay on the ground next to me. Qione and Quest wobbled around, heading for the water. Beast sat on his haunches, shaking his head. Fine, light green grass pocked with tiny blue flowers surrounded us. Behind me, I saw a flattish tree trunk as wide as my house, with a door outline on it.

That must be the Gate, I thought.

"Now where are we?" Laurie sat up and rubbed his eyes. I remembered how he used to do that when he was little and unsure of himself.

"I don't know," I said. "Let me see." I *reached* all around. Roroy sat and watched me.

The woods around the glade stretched far on three sides, and I *sensed* many animals, some almost as big as the quines. On the fourth side, the woods thinned quickly and the land ended. I thought I *detected* the sea. The stream burbled in that direction.

"That way," I said. We all climbed to our feet. The men wobbled, and the beasts teetered and tottered. I took a step and forced myself to stay steady.

I checked myself and could not find anything wrong or other than it should be. After another step toward the stream without wobbling, I knew I was okay. The others came along behind me. I put my arm around Qione's neck and nuzzled her

"How are you doing? I asked, as the men joined me.

"Better," Laurie said. "What's going on?"

"I think we're on another world. It's easier to walk."

"Yes," Roroy said. "I have my legs back."

After drinking deeply and filling our water pouches, we followed the stream down to the sea. As we walked out on the wide beach, a feeling of homecoming wrapped itself about me.

The dark blue sea stretched out to a row of green islands and beyond to the horizon, to a pale blue-green sky. To our left, the sun, the same size as Harmony's star, hung in the pure, luminescent heavens. Warm breezes brought flowery scents from the red blooms on the bushes at the back of the beach. Far down to the right I saw a rocky prominence sticking out into the sea, but the beach stretched forever the other direction.

"Welcome to Peace." I took a deep breath and exhaled. The air itself was exhilarating. I savored the feeling of having accomplished something great. The first step, anyway.

"You think this is it?" Laurie asked.

"I'm sure." I jumped off Qione, pulled off my boots and ran down to the sea. The water was warm right at the edge

The quines pranced into the sea and splashed around.

"Where do we plant crops and build houses?" Roroy asked.

"Let's go see." I collected my boots and looked both ways. The rocky point drew me, so I started off in that direction. The others followed, the quines splashing along in the water.

"I had no idea you people like the water so much," I said to Qione.

Feels good on our feet.

It was warmer here than on the previous world, which pleased me. I looked out at the sea, at the line of small islands in the dark blue water, and wondered if we could make boats to go out to visit them.

Laurie and I began singing some of our family songs.

By the time the sun hung low in front of us, the point seemed as far away as ever. Tall trees, bushy on top, had crowded out the flower thickets.

We made camp up under the trees, and the sounds of the sea lulled me to sleep.

***

In the morning, the point appeared closer. We continued along the water's edge. The line of islands went on and on. The sand was much softer than what I remembered of my home world's beach and wonderful to walk on.

By afternoon, the trees thinned out, and we saw a great grassy meadow sloping up from the beach. Shortly thereafter, we found a good-sized stream and followed it away from the sea.

Several house lengths from the beach, we stopped and let the steeds drink their fill. We people did, also.

A little farther upstream, we were able to ford the little river at a narrowing with scattered rocks in the water. We stopped and looked around. In front of us, a line of tall trees marched up from the ocean as far as we could see. Between that and the forest behind us, lay open land dotted with groups of wide trees. The quines munched the grass, and Qione told me, *It's the best I've ever tasted.*

"This good land," Roroy said. "Must be river behind trees. Let's go see."

We trotted toward the trees. The sun was touching the top of the the greenery by the time we reached them. We heard the rushing river before we saw it. I *reached* beyond it and found no danger, but a hazy uneasiness I couldn't pinpoint. I would worry about that later.

Laurie and I jumped down and pushed through the trees. The great river was at least three times as wide as the one at River Point.

Roroy joined us. "Much water there," he said.

How are we going to put a mill on that, I thought. First, we'd have to find a way down to it. Something else to do when we were settled.

We turned back through the trees, and I regarded the distant forest on the other side of this vast space.

"This is Freedom Two, on the world of Peace," I proclaimed. "We will move from Freedom One on Harmony to Freedom Two, here on Peace."

"How?" Laurie asked. "How do we know where this is?"

"Good questions, young one." Roroy looked at me.

"Well, I saw what must be the Gate in the glade. We'll just have to go back and see how we came through," I said.

"I will stay here," Roroy announced. "Beast and I."

"Are you sure?" I demanded.

"Yes, Marisa." He smiled at me. "I am home here and do not wish to leave. You have Laurie now."

"What about us?" I wanted to know.

"I will build us a house here." Roroy smiled at me.

"What do you think?" I asked my brother.

"It's okay with me." He shrugged.

"But right now, we need to decide where to place the center of our new community."

"We will find something to eat." Roroy, on Beast, galloped off toward the forest.

Laurie and I remounted and trotted to a long line of trees near the smaller river.

"I think this would be a good place." I felt a sense of belonging, of a fresh start, of fulfillment.

"Yeah, this looks good," Laurie responded. We dismounted and let the quines browse.

"The houses along by the trees, and the plaza buildings over here." I pointed. "Let's get this stuff unpacked." When we had everything laid out, Laurie gathered stones for a fire pit. I found branches to make a lean-to to cover our supplies.

I prowled among the trees and found a long, sweet fruit. With those, we had a half loaf of bread. There was one more full loaf left. I'd leave it with Roroy.

I took inventory of our food. If Roroy could catch things to eat, he'd be okay. Of the food we brought, there was enough to leave some for him and some for our trip back to Freedom One.

Roroy returned with three small animals with long ears. Laurie and I checked them to make sure they would not poison us. They were fine, and even had proteins we could use. Roroy took them away to skin and prepare them for cooking.

"Mari, have I turned fifteen yet?" Laurie asked me as he collected plates and mugs.

"I have no idea." Usually our colony had four birthday parties a year, at the quarterly feasts, for those who had been born in that quarter. But this was different. It occurred to me we would have to figure out the seasons and the length of the year here.

Laurie got a fire going in the fire pit, and Roroy threaded the creatures on long, thin branches over the flames. They smelled heavenly as they cooked, and tasted even better. The only meat I'd ever had was chicken, and that was nothing as compared to these creatures.

We sang songs, and Roroy told us some tales of his youth. Laurie was entranced and kept asking for more. Finally we retired to our various sleeping places.

***

Two days later, Laurie and I left. "Take care," I told Roroy. "I'll be back soon, with some others." Something about leaving him here by himself made me uneasy, but I knew I couldn't change his mind.

We took time to splash in the sea with the quines.

At the glade, I showed Qione the outline of the door, and we pushed on it. The door slid open, and we were back in the Gate room. After we passed through the darkness, I turned around and, using my Talent, made a mark on the door we'd come out of.

"That's the door to our world," I said. Going to the screen, I

139

found Harmony, and we took off for that Gate. We made a fast trip
back to Freedom One.

CHAPTER 26

As we approached Freedom One, I drank in the half circle of log cabins around the plaza and its buildings, the green crop fields, and the hills beyond. It wouldn't be easy to leave this place where I'd grown into a woman. But when I did, maybe I could leave the knot of memories behind.

"Hey, Marisa," Ricky shouted, riding up to us. "Did you find us a world?"

"Yes," I said, jumping off Qione.

"Where's Roroy?" Will asked, right behind him.

"He decided to stay and start working on the new settlement with Beast." The rest of the clan surrounded us.

"So you found a world," Papa said, appearing in front of me. "How do you know it is the right one?"

"I feel it in my bones." I looked around for Mama and Granlyn, but didn't see them. I pushed my way through the crowd to Mama's house.

Mama hugged me. "I'm so glad you're back."

"Where's Granlyn?" I asked.

"At home, come see her." Mama led us over. Granlyn sat on the green couch looking fragile, with Grampa Larry watching her from a chair at the table.

I hugged her, and felt life within.

"I still don't believe it," she said. "I'm pregnant. And it has to be Larry's this time." She beamed at me. "How did you do it?"

I didn't know what to say at first. I was happy for her that my intervention had worked, but a little uncomfortable that she had realized right away that I was responsible for her conception.

"I opened a tube," I said finally.

She closed her eyes. "Thank you, Marisa," she said. "Only this old body is not quite ready for that. Did you have to give me twins?"

"Twins?" I said. Grampa Larry's grin split his face.

"Yes."

"What do you think, Mama?"

"We thought it was a miracle, at first," she said. "Then, after thinking about it, I figured you had something to do with it." She grinned.

"Perri and Peter will have siblings younger than their children," Granlyn added.

"Do you know their gender?"

"One of each. Like before." She smiled.

I thanked Oneness that I was able to do this for her and Grampa Larry.

***

We had feast day early to celebrate our return. Everyone wanted to know about the new world.

"When can we go?" Aunt Maria asked. "I need to get my family as far away from those Bramites as possible."

Uncle Art frowned. "How do you know you can find it again? Do we have to go through all those worlds you went to?" he demanded.

"No. I know which one it is on the screen, and we can go straight there." I crossed my fingers.

After the feast, Granlyn announced, "We need a council meeting. There are several things we need to discuss. This will be a general meeting, right here, in an hour."

In the meeting hall, Grampa Larry officially welcomed Laurie and me home, then gave Uncle Gabe the floor.

"First of all, I have some disquieting news from my sister, Amy, in River Point," Uncle Gabe began. "They are having a lot of problems over there. The crops aren't doing well, except for the loovah, they can't keep the warehouse stocked, and there's a shortage of teachers for the school. She says many of them, including Leader Young Gan, are saying it's because of us."

I knew Amy had a little of her father, Adam's Talent, but could only reach Gabe. He kept track of what was going on back there through her.

"We tried to tell them," Granlyn said.

"I know." He continued, "Amy says there are some who want to bring us back, and others who want us even farther away. She will keep me informed of what's going on over there. So this is another reason to consider moving.

"We have a new opportunity here. A new world all to ourselves. But on the other hand, we will have to plan how to make the move." Uncle Gabe pulled his beard.

"We will have to provide for ourselves. We will have to be

142

responsible for ourselves. Marisa, tell us about this new world."

I stood. "The place we found there is two days from the Gate on that world," I began. "It's a wide open space with a river like ours here, with lots of trees along it. On one side is forest, and on the other, a great river, at least three times as wide as the one in River Point. The new plaza is about a quarter day ride up from the beach. The plain stretches as far to the north as we could see. The weather was like it is here, but we'll have to figure out the length of the year and seasons. It has a moon."

"Wonderful," Granli breathed.

"It has good grass for the quines. There are low hills, with bushes of red and pink flowers, here and there. Roroy says the soil is good." I took a breath. "We made a fire pit near the smaller river, and we can build our houses along by the trees. Any questions?"

"Are there fish in the rivers?" Grampa Larry asked.

"I don't know. Did you see any, Laurie?"

"Not in the little river, but I think there were some in the big river," he replied.

"Are there any animals around there?" Aunt Pauli asked.

"Roroy found some small ones in the forest. He said he didn't see or hear any large ones."

"Forest animals would stay in the forest anyway," Grampa Bay noted.

Grampa Larry asked for the floor. "I propose we send back a small group of people with Marisa to view this new world and see how easy or difficult it is going to be to get there from here. If we agree to go, it will take some planning. Marisa, do you think the quines would pull a cart?"

"I don't know. I'll ask Qione. Why?"

"We have a number of large items, like furniture, and shelving, that are too heavy for the quines to carry. Also, how big are these Gates? Will we be able to fit everything through?"

"I think so. We had the three steeds and us," I said. "There should be room for a cart and a quine, with one or two people on the cart."

"Okay." His eye caught Granlyn's. "Do you think there will any problem with a pregnant woman going through a Gate?"

"No, Papa," Mama said. "I carried Marisa through four or five gates and look at her."

I rolled my eyes.

"Oh, right." Grampa Larry cleared his throat.

I saw Granlyn shake her head.

"Do you know what time of year it is on that world?" he asked.

"It was warm, and flowers were blooming. The trees had green leaves."

"Sounds like summer," Grampa Larry said. "We will have to plan our move after harvest and before planting."

We talked about other items until finally Grampa Larry asked, "Who wants to go back with Marisa?"

Uncle Peter stood up. "I and my family will."

I looked at Aunt Anne, who shook her head.

"Talk to your mate first," Granlyn told Uncle Peter.

"Yes, Mama."

***

People were assigned tasks of gathering, sorting and packing supplies and personal belongings.

Aunt Anne, a healer, agreed to go with her three youngest. Mike would stay here with Susan.

The day-to-day activities still had to continue, and no one was sure when the actual full move would take place. Grampa Larry thought it better if one family at a time went through to the new world.

Doug, Uncle Peter's youngest at ten, was all agog and eager to go, but the girls, Carla and Marti, were not happy. They'd be leaving their friends and all they'd known to go into the unknown. And most importantly, there would be no boys, until the others got there.

"Okay, Petey," I heard Mama tell him. "Just don't get trapped again."

He elbowed her, grinning. "I'm not a carefree kid anymore," he retorted.

Later, I met up with Susan at the plaza for a chat. "How could you do that, go through that Gate who knows where?" she asked.

"I had to. I couldn't not do it. Besides, I couldn't feel any danger." I grinned.

"Do you really think it'll be better over there?" Susan twisted the bottom of her tunic.

"Yes. Lots more room and lots more water. And a real beach not far away."

"At least we won't have to worry about the Bramites sneaking over." She looked out at the crop fields.

"Exactly."

I returned to my regular tasks and gave Mama and Granlyn detailed descriptions of everything I'd seen and done. Mama helped me select foods to take on the next trip, cleaning supplies and cloths, and a few dishes.

**

Four days later, Uncle Peter and his family were packed and ready to go. Furniture would come later on carts. Qione and Kiong refused to be cart quines, but said some of the younger males would. We packed panniers for five quines, Qione plus four for Uncle Peter's family. Doug would ride with his father. I took the bags Mama and I had collected, and a few extra items of clothing.

Ready to leave, we all mounted our quines, Doug, sitting in front of Uncle Peter, bounced up and down. Aunt Anne wore a solemn face, but I *knew* that, underneath, she was excited to be going somewhere. Laurie was staying behind this trip, teaching people how to ride the quines. Twelve-year-old Marti was openly crying, while fourteen-year-old Carla was biting her lip.

Goodbyes said, hugs finished, we took off.

"Yippee," Doug shouted.

"Oh, shut up," Carla snarled.

Qione kept us to a slower pace this trip because Aunt Anne and the girls hadn't had much experience riding. The quines understood this and made sure they had a smooth ride. The girls weren't too happy about camping out, either, but they didn't make a big fuss about it, because their mother took it calmly and in stride. Doug wanted to run around and explore, so Uncle Peter had to keep a close eye on him.

Other than a brief rainstorm on the third day, the trip passed uneventfully. By the time we reached the Gate, the girls had accepted their fate. Qione opened the Gate easily this time, and she and I led the way inside.

Aunt Anne and the girls sat and waited while I played with the screen. Uncle Peter and Doug watched, eyes wide. I found the third world, our world, and showed them the globe map.

"We'll be here," I said, pointing to an area at the south edge of the northern continent. "This river is much bigger than the one at River Point." North of us stretched great wide plains, and forest to the east. To the west, the map showed mainly plains and, far distant, a tall mountain range running from the southern coast to the far north.

"Okay, good," Uncle Peter said. "Let's go."

We mounted, and I touched the button. A door at the side of the room opened, and I led the others in. One of the girls screamed when the room went black, before we all passed out.

***

As I came to in the glade, I released a great sigh of relief and waited for the wooziness to go away. The great trees around us whispered in the wind. All the others were awake and sitting up. "We're here," I announced. I pointed to the springs and stream, where the quines were shoving each other to get to the water.

Aunt Anne shook her head. "Dizzy," she mumbled.

"It'll go away soon." I patted her shoulder. "Down the stream to the beach, down the beach to the river, up the river to our new home, which will be called Freedom when we have all left the old one behind." I rose, tottered over to Qione, and mounted her. The others followed suit.

As we travelled down along the stream, I thought, we'll have to make this trail wider for the carts. At the beach, I stopped and dismounted. "These guys love to splash in the water. If you don't mind getting wet, stay on. If not, walk like I am."

"I'll risk it," Aunt Anne said, but the kids all jumped down and ran into the sea. Uncle Peter also stayed on his steed. I walked along the edge of the light surf, as the quines and the kids splashed along. We stopped to eat at one point.

"I like this beach," Carla said.

"Me too," Marti echoed.

"It's certainly different," Aunt Anne said, wringing out the bottom of her tunic. The warmth of the sun soon dried our clothes. "That blue-green sky."

Later, at the camp we set up for the night, Uncle Peter had to drag Doug out of the water when we were ready to eat. The kids asked me all sorts of questions about the new place, most of which I couldn't answer.

The next day, we all rode and tried not to get too wet. As we approached the end of the thinning trees, Uncle Peter whistled as he saw the wide plain. "We can really settle in here."

When we reached the river, we stopped to look around.

"This air smells wonderful." Aunt Anne took a deep breath.

"This river isn't much bigger than ours," Uncle Peter said.

"Oh, this isn't the big one, that's over there where that line of trees is," I explained.

"Can we build a boat?" Doug asked.

"Not now," Uncle Peter said. "After we all get settled. We'll see."

CHAPTER 27

We turned inland, and found the ford. Roroy had built a log bridge across it, so he could get the logs for building over to the site. The quines wouldn't go on the bridge until I dismounted and walked across. Qione followed me, and Quest followed her.

As we headed north, I saw the cabins in the distance. When we arrived, three small log cabins in a row under the trees along the river, the latrine downriver, and marked out crop lines greeted us.

"Roroy," I yelled. We pulled up at one of the cabins, and the others looked around.

"Roroy," I yelled again.

Beast burst out of the woods, howling, running toward us. He thudded across the bridge and up to me.

"What's the matter, Beast? Where's Roroy?" I asked, rubbing his ear. His muzzle was a bloody mess. My heart clenched. He's hurt, I thought.

Beast made a moaning sound, turned and headed back to the forest. Qione and I followed him at a gallop. "Anne, come with your kit," I called back to her. A short way in, I found Roroy sitting against a tree, a huge tree trunk diagonally across his legs. Three or four stumps surrounded him, with trees and bushes all around. A vine with heart-shaped leaves hung down from another tree, almost hiding him.

Beast pushed at the log but it wouldn't budge. The animal moaned again.

"My goddess," Roroy croaked. I jumped down and offered him my water pouch. He gulped the water down. My heart did cartwheels.

"What happened?" I asked as Aunt Anne pulled up beside us and dismounted. My heart thudded as she poked around his legs.

How could this have happened? I dropped down beside him. Touching his leg above the log, I *reached in* and dampened the pain.

"Tree fell wrong way. My axe?"

I looked around but didn't see it. "Maybe it's under the tree."

"Marisa, look," Aunt Anne said. "If we lift it here, I think we can slide his legs out. I'll *call* Peter."

"Okay." Shaking, I sat beside Roroy and gave him some bread and some more water. I tried not to think about his legs, how bad they must be hurting, how long he had been sitting here like this. "We'll get you out. Did you build those cabins all by yourself?" Stupid question number one.

"No. Beast helped push and pull the logs, and held up ends. He's good friend." Roroy sagged back against the tree.

"Yes he is," I agreed.

Beast, who was standing nearby, pushed his big bloody nose into Roroy's neck. Roroy twisted his fingers in the animal's curly black fur. "Fix Beast, please."

I put my hand on the back of Beast's head, closed my eyes, and *oozed* into him. After dampening the pain, I spent a little time trying to heal the wounds. When he shook his head, I withdrew.

"Better?" Roroy asked him.

Beast nodded and huffed in my ear, as Uncle Peter arrived.

"I left the kids back there," he said. "Carla will handle Douggie. What's up?"

Aunt Anne explained the situation.

Uncle Peter poked around the log and said. "I think we can handle this." He fished a pulley and tackle out of his gear, looped it over a large branch, and pushed the hook underneath the log. "I need Beast over there to pull."

Roroy relayed the instructions, and Beast trotted around the tree to the other side. Uncle Peter tied the rope around Beast like a harness.

"Anne and Marisa, are you ready? When Beast pulls, Marisa, you move his foot toward you, and Anne, you pull his thigh." We nodded, and I grabbed his boot. "Pull."

Beast heaved, Aunt Anne and I eased one leg out. Roroy moaned. I dampened the pain once more. Beast pulled again, and we moved the other leg.

The tree trunk rolled over, and Beast danced back so it wouldn't hit his feet. Everyone gave a sigh of relief.

Roroy's legs were a mess, and began to ooze blood. I sucked in my breath at the sight. I noticed the end of a bone sticking out of one side of a leg, gulped, and turned away.

"I can see you won't be walking for a while," Aunt Anne said, her voice shaking as she began pulling supplies out of her kit.

First on were two tourniquets. "Peter, can you cut his pant legs off right here?" She pointed to a place above his knees.

I undid the rope around Beast, and he shook himself. "Good boy." I patted him. It gave me time to get my emotions under control.

"Sure." Uncle Peter dug out his big knife and began sawing away, only cutting Roroy twice. He removed the pant legs from around the wounds and pulled them off.

"Marisa, help me disinfect this bone," Aunt Anne said. Together, we used our Talent to clean off all foreign matter as she moved the bone back in place. My task, until we returned to Freedom One, was to *go into* his legs periodically and clear out any infection, along with keeping his pain down.

Aunt Anne used clean cloths to dab at the wounds, smeared healing goop on them, and bandaged the open wounds. Uncle Peter found some branches and made splints. I held Roroy to me.

Roroy muttered thanks, and fell asleep in my arms.

"Now how are we going to get him back to the camp?" Aunt Anne asked.

Uncle Peter pondered. "We'll need some kind of low sled to put him on, so we can pull him back. I know I can't lift him high enough to get him on Beast's back, even if he kneels." He picked up Roroy's axe, which had been under the tree. "Let's see what I can do."

"Looks like we'll be here awhile," Aunt Anne said. "Marisa, you did a great job. Have you had any thought of becoming a healer?"

"No." I hadn't, but now I thought it might be a useful profession. The more the merrier, as Granlyn liked to say.

"Think about it," she said. "But right now, I'd like you to go back to the kids. Roroy will probably sleep a long time now."

"Okay." I laid Roroy down, kissed his forehead, and mounted Qione, who had been standing there watching, and left.

The kids sat along the edge of the river dangling their feet in the water. Trees whispered above them. The water mirrored the blue-green sky.

"Hey, guys," I called as we cantered up.

"Where's Mama and Papa?" Carla asked, turning around.

"They're with Roroy. We got the log off his legs, but he's hurt so bad he can't walk. Your papa is making a sled that Beast can pull him on to get him back here. Have you looked in the cabins?"

"They're like doll houses," Marti said. "We'll never get all of us in one of those things."

"That's why there are three. One for your folks, one for you two girls, one for Roroy and Doug."

"What about you?" Marti asked.

"I'll sleep out. I'm used to it."

I dismounted and let Qione head over to the other quines. "Let's go have a look."

The cabins were tiny, with white walls. One room, with two narrow bed shelves on one side wall, one above the other, a small table and benches opposite. Along the back a wide shelf hung with narrower ones above, and a large food box under the wide shelf. A narrow seat ran along the front wall on the table side.

"I suggest you pick one and start moving your stuff in," I said.

I *kept track* of Roroy and the others, *checking in* every so often, as I unpacked the food.

The sun hung at the tops of the trees along the big river when Uncle Peter and Aunt Anne appeared, walking on each side of a low sled on which Roroy lay, still asleep. Beast marched slowly and sturdily, his head held high, pulling his master home. We managed to get Roroy onto the lower bed of the first cabin, and used extra clothing, folded, to prop up his legs.

Uncle Peter fed Beast a special treat, and then we fed ourselves around the fire circle. I was in shock. I'd never seen anything like this before. Oh, we'd had a few broken bones, scrapes and cuts, but no major injuries, nothing like this.

After we finished eating, Uncle Peter said, "This looks like a very good place for our new home. Thank you, Marisa."

"You're welcome."

"Now, this is what we will do," he began. "First, unload everything. Did Marisa tell you girls, two to a cabin?"

"Yes," Marti said, rolling her eyes.

"Dibs on the bottom bed," Carla added.

"All right you two," Uncle Peter said. "Our duties here are to lay out and build more houses, lay out the plaza, site the mill, and plant some seed to see how they grow here," he continued.

"I don't know how long it will take until the next group arrives, but we can figure the time it took us to get here, and for Marisa to go back. We need to have at least three more cabins done by then. After we get more people here we can start building real houses."

He dug out a bundle of loovah seedlings, took them over to the crop site, and planted them. They were the Bramites' all-in-one plant. Inner leaves and fruit for food, outer leaves for cloth and paper, stems for rope, roots for flour for bread. They grew like weeds.

Aunt Anne checked on Roroy. She told me to let him sleep as long as he needed to. "It will help him heal," she added.

Later, I went to sit beside him. His legs were swathed in bandages over splints. He looked so young and peaceful lying there

A sense of relief stole over me. I knew he would heal.

That night, I slept well.

***

In the morning, after glancing in at Roroy, still asleep, I walked a little way from the cabins and *reached*. The uneasiness was still there, in the west. I tried not to worry about it as I went to see Qione.

"How are you all?"

We need rest, but otherwise well, she told me. *Grass is wonderful.*

"Good. Enjoy."

I returned to the camp. At breakfast, Aunt Anne said, "Roroy's still sleeping. I think we should take him back to Freedom as soon as he can travel. We can do a lot more for him there."

"How are we going to get him up on Beast?" I asked.

"Why can't we use the sled?" Aunt Anne picked up a piece of bread and took a bite.

"It would never last the trip," Uncle Peter replied. "It's already starting to come apart. We'll use the wood to build more cabins."

"Okay."

"When will he be able to travel?" I asked.

"As soon as possible." Aunt Anne took a bite of bread. "Peter, can you make some kind of harness for him?"

"Sure." Uncle Peter nodded.

How could they tie Roroy onto Beast without him slipping, I wondered.

When I went in to see him, Roroy opened his eyes and shifted on the narrow bed. One foot hung out, resting on a stool. "Hello, my goddess," he said. "You saved my life."

"Beast and Aunt Anne did a lot more than I did."

"But you found me."

I took his hand. "Beast led us to you. We're going to make a harness on Beast for you to hold on to, so we can take you back to Freedom in a few days and get your legs fixed."

"When will I be able to walk again?"

"I don't know. You'll have to ask Aunt Anne."

Later, per Uncle Peter's request, I took him and his family over to the big river and they oohed and aahed over it.

"That should give us plenty of power if we can figure out how to harness it," Uncle Peter noted.

"You kids stay away from here," Aunt Anne ordered. "Especially you, Doug. If you want to go swimming, go in the little river."

I knew then, we'd have to make some arrangements to keep the boys away from the big river. Maybe escorted trips? I shrugged. Worry about that later.

Back at the camp, Uncle Peter and I dug out ropes, and he and I worked on a harness for Roroy to use on Beast. The animal didn't care for all the ropes and cloths for padding we put on and around him, but I think he understood it was for his master.

The next morning, we took Beast to Roroy's cabin and had him sit with his back to the man. Uncle Peter and I managed to get Roroy up, turned, and laid face down against Beast's back. As the animal stood, Roroy hitched himself up so his face was against Beast's neck.

Uncle Peter looped a rope around Beast's chest and forelegs, then up and around Roroy's middle. A second rope went around Roroy's thighs and under the animal just in front of his rear legs. Two more went from the front ropes to the rear ones. Roroy's knees lay on Beast's rear end with his bandaged lower legs out behind.

Aunt Anne and I used all the extra clothing for padding, and to wrap around Roroy's legs. He had full use of his arms, and could move his hips a little.

Presently Roroy said, "We go now." Beast stood and lumbered out the door.

The rest of us were ready to leave. We walked Beast around for a bit, to make sure nothing would slip.

Finally Uncle Peter was satisfied, we mounted our quines, and walked slowly down the slope toward the beach.

Uncle Peter and I rode on either side of Beast and Roroy. I reached out and held Roroy's hand for a while.

Several times a day, I *checked* his legs for any signs of infection. When I *found* some, I was able to eradicate it using my Talent.

At the beach, Beast stepped very carefully in the sand. He plodded down to the hard sand and kept a slow but steady pace. Uncle Peter and I kept an eye on Roroy, but our harness was working fine.

When we camped that night, I gave Roroy food and water, and Uncle Peter produced a receptacle for him to pee in. We planned to leave Roroy on Beast until we reached Freedom One.

The trek along the beach was pleasant under the blue-green sky. We walked for a while so the quines could splash along in the sea. I ached for Roroy and did what I could to keep his pain under control. This was not how I'd planned the first trip to the new place.

The first part of the trail up to the glade was only wide enough for two, so Qione and I dropped behind. Beast had to pick his way very slowly to avoid joggling Roroy. At the top section, only one rider wide, Uncle Peter, with Doug in front on him on his quine, led the way, with Beast behind him.

CHAPTER 28

As we arrived at the glade, Aunt Anne and I heaved sighs of relief. We crammed into the little room to pass through the Gate. Because we stayed close together, with Beast and Roroy in the middle, everyone was still mounted when we awoke. The trip out to the door to Harmony didn't take long, and I immediately *reached* for Mama.

I *told* her about Roroy, and that it would take a day or two longer than usual to get back.

'Be careful, but don't take any longer than you have to. We've got problems here, and we want you home.'

'What problems?'

'Bramites. We'll talk about it when you get here.'

Oh boy, now what, I thought. I crossed my fingers, muttered a prayer to the Oneness, and told the others. "Let's get going."

The trip took longer than I'd expected. Level areas and small slopes were no trouble, but on the hills, up and down, we had to make a lot of switchbacks so Roroy wouldn't slip back and forth.

Mama, Papa, and the boys met us at an open area upriver from the settlement. We dismounted and hugged, except for Roroy, who waved.

"He's slept most of the journey," I told Mama. I wanted to keep going, but knew we needed rest.

"I wish we could get Noa down here," Mama said. "I know you and Aunt Maria are very good, Anne, but Noa is the most experienced."

"So send someone for her."

"No, Marisa, none of us dare go near River Point now."

"Why not?"

Mama looked at me and sighed. "One of the younger boys went back to River Point, was scared by something they did, and inadvertently used his Talent to dump a bunch of people in the river. No one was killed, but many were hurt, and a special tool was broken.

"A group of men chased and caught him, tied him up and locked him in a shed. They forgot about his Talent. He immediately *called* his father, who organized a group to go get him. Art Junior and his companions were told in no certain terms to get out and stay out. The Bramites gave the boy, still tied up, to Art Junior and chased our guys out of town."

"That doesn't sound like the Bramites at all," I said. "They've always been so quiet and peaceful."

"I know," Mama said.

When we continued on, I told her about the new world.

"I hope it's as good as you say. We need to get away from here. When the next generation comes along, it could be worse. I'm concerned about how much more advanced they'll be."

"I know. I've thought of that, too."

We plodded on until we reached the settlement. I looked at the circle of log cabins and the grey buildings around the plaza and wondered why I didn't feel at home. My house was behind the school and craft buildings, not visible as we approached.

All of us, except the youngsters, led Beast with Roroy to the clinic. Peter and Papa helped Roroy off of Beast and onto a bed in the corner with soothing blue-green walls.

"Thanks," Roroy said. Beast nuzzled his master's shoulder, snuffled into my hair, and we let him out. He trotted over to the quines' territory.

"I'll take care of Roroy now," Aunt Anne said. "Don't go away, Peter. I may need your help moving him."

Mama and I walked to her house, where Granlyn waited for us. After hugs, Mama said, "I told Marisa about our problem. She wanted to know how come the Bramites have changed so much. Since you've known them longer than we have, I thought you might have a way to answer her."

"I think there was always little bit of resentment for us dragging them out of their cavern," Granlyn said. "And then rescuing them from Brama. Also, I think our Talents scare them because they have nothing like that. You, Perri, saving that baby made it worse, and every little thing that happened after that. Then with Marisa's generation so obviously superior, they're waking up to the fact they have to defend themselves. Even Noa seemed a little cautious the last time I talked with her."

"So what do we do?" Mama asked.

"I think it's time to move to our new world."

"But your babies..." I began.

"I'll go soon, before I get much bigger. We'll take Ruthie, too. She's expecting again."

"But, Mama," Mama said.

"No buts. Let's get busy. You, Marisa, go get some rest. We'll eat in a bit."

As I lay on my bed thinking about what Granlyn had said, I wondered if I could *reach* Noa. I knew I could *reach* the Bramites, but could I pick her out? Only way I could find out was to try.

I *reached* carefully and from above. There she was, plodding home. I *touched* her and *sent* the idea that Lyn needed her, and could she come to Freedom. I had no idea whether it worked until Noa and her mate, Karil, walked into the settlement two days later.

***

After supper at Mama's, we sat and discussed the situation.

"We can't all leave at once," Grampa Larry said. "We need a few people at first to get the site ready, start building shelter and get crops going. Plus, there's not enough quines. Marisa, what's the most that can go through the Gate at one time?"

"Six. It was a tight squeeze, but Beast is bigger than the quines. But we could take twice that and go through in sections." *I think.*

"Okay. Marisa, you will need to be the guide. So we need five or eleven." Grampa Larry paused. "How shall we go about determining who shall go when?"

"Let's ask each family," Granlyn said. "We should keep families together as much as possible."

"Good idea, babe. Can you and the gals do that?"

"Sure."

Granlyn and I spent the next day talking to people. No one seemed to want to go first except Uncle Allen. Of course, he was an explorer at heart.

Finally, Aunt Maria told us that she and Uncle Chad would like to go, along with Chad III and his family.

"We haven't been here that long, and I don't want us to get too settled here. I want Jimmy and his family as far away from here as possible."

"I have room for nine," I said. I wanted to do five at a time at first, just to be sure it would work. "You and Uncle Chad, Chad Three and Joan, Joey, Sally and Jimmy makes seven. Uncle Allen wants to go, that's eight."

Uncle Bay returned from a walkabout and agreed to go.

That night, I told Mama, Papa, and Grampa Larry who was going.

"Very good," Grampa Larry said. "Maria's a healer, and Bay can get started on the mill. The Bramites want us off this world as soon as possible. Marisa, is there another place like this area farther up where we can take supplies away from here?"

"Yes, the place where Mama and Papa met us coming in. How many quines do we have now, anyway?" I twiddled with the hem of my tunic.

"Yours brought five others, Kiong brought another six his first trip and five more the second. So we'll still have seven here."

"Good." I nodded my head. "Young children can ride with parents, but other than that, it's one person per quine. Jimmy could ride with his dad, I think, so we would need eight besides mine. I'll bring them back for the next group."

I began collecting items to take on the upcoming trip. Uncle Chad and Chad III packed their furniture in one of the carts the men had built and took it up to the place where we'd met Mama and Papa coming in, now called the staging area.

The next evening, Noa and Karil arrived. Like all Bramites, they wore their long blond hair tied back in a semi-braid. Mama and I greeted them with pleasure at the plaza, and I took them to Granlyn.

"Noa! How did you know to come?" Granlyn exclaimed.

"The thought just came to me, and I knew you needed me. Anyway, I wanted to see you one more time before you people moved on."

Granlyn looked at me, then back at Noa. "It's so good to see you. We never meant any harm to your people."

"I know." Noa's round face, with very widely-spaced eyes, glowed.

"Some of us are very thankful that you and your friends saved our people, and gave us children," Karil said. "I do not approve of some of the things Gan and young Emek are doing."

"How is your brood?" Granlyn asked.

"Wonderful." Noa beamed. "Nell and the other girls have given me sixteen grandchildren. Kai and Vol, three each, and Kai's mate is pregnant. I think Vol's mate is too, although she hasn't told me yet."

"Fantastic. I'm so happy for you. I remember when everyone was having babies except us."

"Ancient history," Noa said.

"How is Kareth doing? Does she miss Adam and Gabe?" Granlyn stroked her belly.

"Not really. I think after we came here, she wished she'd been chosen by someone else. Kareth was fascinated with Adam because he was so different, but I don't think she ever truly cared for him. She's taken charge of the food and education areas."

She sighed, and added, "Amy misses Gabe, I think, but the younger ones don't. Han relishes being the oldest son there now."

"How is our Emek doing?" Granlyn asked, nodding.

"He teaches Gan and Young Emek, and some of the others, everything he can about our history, but he does not go to any meetings." Noa smoothed her tunic. "He never recovered from the loss of some of our people, even though we created a shrine to honor them."

"I know," Granlyn said. "I still miss Betty."

I knew Betty was Uncle Art Senior's wife who had been taken through the Gate with the Bramites when Mama was carrying me. Only Mama was able to stop the alien, because she could not hear the alien's summons.

Noa stared at Granlyn. "I feel something different about you. You can't be pregnant."

"Yes, I am. Twins again." Granlyn grinned. "But enough of this. Marisa, take her over to the clinic. We have a badly injured young man, and Maria and Anne seem a bit overwhelmed."

"Certainly." Noa heaved herself up out of the chair.

As we walked across to the clinic, I pointed out our meeting house, the general kitchen and the child care building. A host of questions buzzed through my head, but I didn't feel comfortable enough with her to ask them.

I knew Noa was Granlyn's best friend among the Bramites, and that she had not been able to have children until the Bramites and Granlyn's group made their way through the tunnels to the outside valley. Noa had been the head healer when they founded the colony of River Point.

We reached the clinic and met the others. "This is wonderful," Aunt Anne said. "We could use some help. Aunt Maria, come see who's here." We took Noa to Roroy, and Aunt Maria joined us.

"Noa, this is Roroy, someone I met off world," I said. "Roroy, this is Noa, the Bramites' head healer. She will help the aunts heal your legs."

"Thank you," Roroy said. "My goddess found you, yes?"

"I'm not a goddess," I said for the nth time, and left them.

The next day, I found Roroy sitting up with clay casts on his legs. He stretched his arms up and out.

"How are you feeling?" I asked.

"Better. Pain not bad. How is Beast?"

"Moping. I'll bring him over in a little while. He can stick his head in the window."

"Good."

I told him about the episode with the boy and our plans to move to the new world. "I will be taking a group in a few days, but I'll come back. You stay here and get well." I leaned over and kissed him.

***

Noa and Karil visited for three days. She held training sessions for some of us who were interested in becoming healers, while Karil surveyed the crops and asked Grampa Larry and others a lot of questions about how we did things. He had brought us a half dozen fruit tree seedlings.

"These are from me and Noa, because you arranged it so we could have children," he told Grampa Larry. Karil also instructed Grampa how to care for the seedlings until we reached our new home and planted them there.

Noa and her mate were fascinated by the quines. "We never got to see them close up," Noa told me. Qione picked quines for them to ride, and when the pair left for River Point, Uncle Allen went with Noa and Karil as they rode back.

***

I *tuned in* on Granlyn's farewell walk with Noa, through trees north of Freedom.

"I regret that it has to be this way," Noa said. "I will miss you and Perri and the child, and all the others."

I'm not a child, I thought, and made a fist.

"I know," Granlyn replied. "We didn't choose to have these Talents, and although they are useful at times, many of us wish we could turn them off once in a while. Enjoy your children and grandchildren."

"Oh I will. I can never thank you enough for bringing us out of the cavern so I could have babies." Noa hugged Granlyn. "Your healers have been well trained and are as proficient as I ever was, but you people keep learning. There's always more to learn."

"We will, and I thank you for training our girls after Alice died."

"She was a wonderful woman. It was unfortunate that she was unable to have her own children."

"I know. Thank you, Noa, for all your help. I will remember you always."

"And I, you. Be well." She turned and ran down the path.

CHAPTER 29

Finally, the day came for my group to leave for Freedom Two. Everyone gathered around the plaza as we packed and mounted the quines. I took a last look around. Pink and purple flowers bloomed along the fronts of the buildings. Grampa Bay had already collected flower seeds to take with him. A few fluffy clouds floated along the treetops behind the settlement.

After many goodbyes, I led off. Uncle Chad had to hold Jimmy tightly as he kept bouncing around. Uncle Allen rode behind me, followed by Joan and Chad Three. After them came the children, with Aunt Maria, and Grampa Bay at the tail end.

Qione kept to a slow pace, as the others hadn't had that much experience riding the quines. Jimmy and his fourteen-year-old brother Joey wanted to go faster, but Qione refused. It took eleven-year-old Sally most of the day to get comfortable riding her quine.

The second day we picked up the pace, but still proceeded at a walk. Aunt Maria and Sally oohed over the different colors of flowers we passed in the valleys. When we arrived at the glade at the top, I announced, "Here we are at the Gate."

"Where?" Joey asked, looking around. "Hey, those trees look like they have fingers." Long, narrow, yellow-green clumps hung from their branches.

"You're right," I said. I tried to remember if they'd been that yellow before. "The Gate's over there in the hill. It's late. Let's camp here, and we'll go in the morning."

The boys wanted to go now, but the rest of us were glad to stop and relax.

I had trouble getting to sleep. Thoughts of my old home mingled with anticipation of my new one. I also felt the responsibility of leading the others through the Gate and to the new place. I knew I could do it, but still...

***

In the morning, we packed up and mounted our steeds. The glade was still in shadow. I told the others what to expect as we crossed to the Gate. Again the hillside opened to Qione. We led the group through the long room to the room with the screen, which was quite crowded with all of us. I pulled up the correct screen, touched the button, and the door opened on the other side of the room.

Grampa Bay led Uncle Chad, Aunt Maria, Joey and Jimmy through. I waited a little while and tapped the button again. A different door opened.

"Oh no," I said. "Don't go in there." Now what, I thought, clenching my fists.

"Maybe you have to wait for it to recharge or something," Uncle Allen said.

We waited until that door closed, and a little longer, and then I tried again. The right door opened this time, and the rest of us passed through into the room that went dark.

***

When I woke in the glade on Peace, the first group was sitting up or wandering around. Uncle Chad peered down the trail, and the quines splashed in the stream.

"Is everyone all right?" I asked as I sat up.

"Oh, my," Aunt Maria said, shaking her head. "My head. I don't know whether I can stand up."

Uncle Chad helped her to her feet. "You'll be okay. Is it always like this?" he asked me.

"It affects people differently." I stood. "Okay, everyone. We're going down a narrow and rocky trail along the stream to the sea. Hold tight on the first part, it's steep. We'll have the rest of the day along the shore, camp there, and tomorrow afternoon we'll reach Freedom Two."

"Is it on the beach?" Aunt Maria asked.

"No. There's a wide open area well above the beach where we'll lay out the settlement."

We rose, mounted, and I led the way. I had Grampa Bay bring up the rear so no one could wander off.

"Oh, yes," Uncle Allen said as we came out onto the beach. The quines practically threw us off so they could run down into the sea. The kids followed them in, and we adults doffed our boots and waded in the shallows.

"Come on, Qione, we need to get going," I said after a while.

This feels so good on my feet. We never had anything like this.

"You can walk along in the water, if you want. But we need to keep moving."

The sea here, a gorgeous dark blue, was a perfect temperature, not too cold, and not too warm, topped by an unbelievable blue-green sky. This beach was bordered by fat bushes with red flowers and taller, thin trees behind. Green islands off-shore paralleled the beach.

"I like this world already," Aunt Maria told me.

"Are there any dangerous creatures in this sea?" Joan asked.

"I don't know, but it looks like it's shallow a long way out, so nothing big could get close to us," I replied.

At camp, I had a hard time getting everyone out of the water and settled down for the night.

***

The next morning, after I told my group we'd get to Freedom Two late that afternoon, nobody dawdled. The children rode their quines in the sea, and we adults walked as our quines splashed along. I still couldn't get over that blue-green sky.

When we stopped at a small stream so the quines could drink, I looked up to where the trickle came out of the trees. A gray, four legged creature with large eyes and a mass of horns on its head stared at me, then bounded away.

"Did you see that?" I exclaimed, turning to the others.

"Looked like a deer with a headache," Uncle Allen said.

"I wanna see it," Jimmy demanded. "Where is it?"

"It's long gone," his papa replied.

"Let's move on." Grampa Bay picked up his pack and marched down the beach.

When we reached the first, smaller river, Uncle Allen said, "I thought you said it was bigger than ours."

"The big one's over there where that line of trees is." I pointed. "This one will be for drinking and washing and crops at first. I think we can put the mill on the big river."

"Okay." Uncle Allen nodded his head and smiled at me. "Looks like you picked a good place."

After we enticed the quines and children out of the water, we trotted up the slope to the bridge, crossed it, and on up to the cabins and fire pit.

"How are we going to get all of us in those little things?" Joan asked.

"We're not. Uncle Chad and Aunt Maria will be in one," I told her. "You and Sally in another, and the boys in the third."

164

"What about you and the other men?"

"We'll camp out. We're used to it."

Grampa Bay took charge. "Let's get everything unloaded and into your cabins. Then you ladies can start on supper."

After we removed the paniers, Qione led the other quinés over to their territory between the two groves of trees. I picked a place to sleep above the cabins and laid my pack there.

The Chads, father and son, made a makeshift table out of the extra lumber, and we women and Sally laid out the food we'd brought on it. Aunt Maria put together a simple vegetable stew. I made a mental note to bring some chickens next time.

As we sat on logs around the fire pit, I breathed deeply. There was no doubt in my mind this was my world. I reached, turning around. It was clear and quiet, except beyond the great river. The pink and purple sunset sky was streaked with dark blue and dark green ribbons that made me vaguely uneasy.

I turned my attention to the children, who couldn't stop talking. They wanted to go exploring right away.

"It's almost dark," their papa said. "We'll go in the morning."

After supper, Grampa Bay announced, "We need to plan what we need to do here. First thing in the morning we men, and that includes you, Joey, will enlarge the latrine. You gals can look around to see where you want your houses.

"The first building we need to build is the meeting hall. We can use it for storage and other things while we build the others." He looked around. "But before any of the buildings, we need to put up more cabins for the next group of people. I planted the fruit tree seedlings over there," he pointed downhill to the southwest, "and in the morning, we can plant the loovah plants and seeds."

"We need to start work on a clinic, too," I said. "In case someone else gets hurt." I thought of Roroy up here, all alone except for Beast, with that tree on his legs, and shivered.

"Yes," Aunt Maria nodded. "And right now, some kind of shelter for our food."

"Okay," Grampa Bay said. "I'll work on that, and the Chads can work on the houses."

"I'll check out the rivers and find the best places to access the water." Uncle Allen stood.

***

In the morning, I woke up chilled, even wrapped in my cloak. It hadn't been this cool when I was here before.

When I mentioned the coolness to Uncle Allen later, he said, "Keep an eye on it. We may be coming into fall here."

"Oh no. What will we do for food?"

"One of the things I'll check at the rivers is to see if there's fish in them. Don't worry, Marisa, we'll survive." He smiled down at me.

"I want to do more than just survive." I turned and stalked away. When I was halfway to the big river, which Grampa Larry later named the Grande after one on Home Earth, I stopped and looked around. The green of the fields didn't look as bright, and I thought I saw a speck of yellow on one of the trees. I *sensed* an unpleasant time ahead. We had no idea how long the seasons lasted here. Ideally, we should have had a few families settle here for several months, to figure out the length of the year and seasons, but we hadn't had time for that.

The men went about their tasks, and we women wandered up and down along the river looking at the place. Some round trees had tiny green fruit on them.

"We'll keep an eye on those," Aunt Maria said. "This area looks good." A feathery plant grew beneath the well-spaced trees.

She bent to look. "They're ferns," she exclaimed.

I must have had a 'huh' expression on my face, for she said, "We had ferns on Earth."

"Are they good to eat?"

"No, they just look beautiful."

"Look at this." Sally ran up with a large cup-like yellow flower.

"Where did you get that?" Aunt Maria demanded.

"Down by the water."

"Show us." Joan took the blossom. The yellow flowers lined the riverbank just above the water line.

"What do you think, Marisa?" Aunt Maria asked.

I took the flower and sniffed it. It had a kind of syrupy smell, and I couldn't sense anything bad about it. "I don't think it's harmful. Maybe later, we can get Uncle Art to look at it and see if there's anything we can use."

Unfortunately, they contained a poison, so we couldn't use any part of them as food.

"Fine," Aunt Maria said. "Let's go back."

166

Uncle Chad had come up with a large piece of waterproof fabric. We piled the food together on the table and put the cloth over it, holding it down with fallen branches. At least, our foods were under cover.

At midday, I visited with Qione, who was grazing with the other quines in their area.

"How are you doing, girl?" I asked, stroking her shoulder.

Good, she told me. *When are we going back?*

"In a couple days. Who do you want to take back?"

I'll let you know. Who's going with us?

"One person. Uncle Allen, I think."

Qione nodded. *We go in three days. We will be ready.*

Fine," I said, and patted her again.

***

Back at camp, there were several split logs near the cabins that the Chads used to start a fourth one. On the second day, they began cutting some trees down along the river, only certain sizes and and not too many together.

"Please keep them safe," I prayed to the Oneness. I couldn't get Roroy and his legs out of my mind.

Work continued on all fronts. We had a real latrine again, and Bay had marked out and laid the foundation for three buildings; clinic, meeting hall, and general kitchen. Aunt Maria and Joan laid out the interiors.

I regularly *searched* and *reached* for anything unusual, on the plain, in the rivers, in the forests beyond. Something out there bothered me, and I couldn't figure out what or why. I'd just have to keep a watch on it. The vivid sunset that night gave me the creeps again.

***

Uncle Allen invited me to walk along the big river. The trees were thick, with prickly bushes between, and it was hard to find places we could push through. When we did find a place, we sat on the edge and watched the water churn by. I felt very comfortable with this uncle I didn't know all that well.

"This would give us a lot of power," he said after a while, "if we can figure out how to harness it. I think I'll stay here and trek upriver, see if I can find a place we can use. Do you mind going back by yourself?"

"No." I did mind, but wasn't going to let him know that.

167

"I'll give you a message to take back to the council in the morning."

"Sure." We returned to camp.

CHAPTER 30

When I told Aunt Maria I was going back alone, she protested. "No way are you going by yourself. You're too young, and we don't know what dangers wait out there."

"Not a problem," I said. "I'll stay linked with you until I get to the Gate, and then link up with Mama when I get through."

She stewed about it for a couple days, while I made my plans to go, and finally agreed, on condition Uncle Allen went with me to the first camp.

***

Qione selected four of her brood to go with us.

I packed up, we hugged all around, and I left. Uncle Allen rode with me down to the beach.

"Take care, Marisa," he said. He reached over and touched my shoulder. "We need you safe. You are the center of the new generation. I'm going to leave you here. I trust you."

"Unhuh," I mumbled. "But there'll be a newer generation soon."

"True. Travel mercies," he said, as he turned and headed back to the settlement.

It was strange riding alone, but always being aware of Aunt Maria. Two of the extra quines trotted on either side of us, and the others behind, which made me feel safe, but since they insisted on going in the water, it also made me very wet.

On the trail up to the glade, one quine went in front and the rest in the rear. It was late afternoon and I decided not to wait until morning to go through the Gate.

'I'm at the Gate,' I *sent* to Aunt Maria. 'We're going through now. See you soon.'

***

I stretched and breathed in Harmony air. For the first time, I noticed there was something missing in it that was in the air of Peace Grampa Larry told me later that it might have been a little more oxygen.

I *reached* and contacted Laurie. We *linked*, and he told the rest I was coming.

We made camp a short distance away from the Gate. Qione had a hard time keeping her brood under control. They wanted to run and explore everywhere.

***

We were halfway home when we were met by Papa and Art Junior.

"How are things?" I asked, when we stopped to eat and rest.

"Not good," Papa said. "Uncle Larry is sick, Anne thinks it may be a stroke. Too many people are trying to be in charge, and some of the young ones keep trying to go back to River Point to get things they left behind, or want."

"Can't you or somebody stop them? What about Uncle Art? He's the oldest."

"He won't have anything to do with it. He does his work and keeps away from everyone else except us kids," Junior said. "I try to. We put a block at the river, but they just go over the hills."

I thought for a moment. "When you catch one, bring him to me."

"Sure will."

***

When we came up off the river trail, the first thing I saw was a row of carts full of everything including the main kitchen sink. "We need to start taking these through," Papa said as we rode over to the quine territory. The other four quines had run on ahead.

After I dismounted, I hurried to our house, to Mama. "They told me about Grampa Larry," I said, as I tumbled into her arms. "How is he and Granlyn doing?" I couldn't imagine him sick.

After a long hug, she let me go. "As well as they can, under the circumstances. Mama wanted me to bring you to them as soon as you got here. She won't leave him."

We trotted next door to Granlyn's house. Grampa Larry, propped up on the couch, grinned as I entered. The wall above him was covered with pictures of Home Earth, mountains, seashores, a valley with a flat-topped mountain and a peak at one side, at valley's end. Granlyn sat in a padded chair nearby. I stopped inside the door, unsure who to go to first.

"Come here," Granlyn said as she rose.

"How is he?" I asked, within her hug.

"I'm fine," Grampa Larry grumbled. "Just can't get around as well as I used to." His voice sounded a little fuzzy.

"He's doing quite well." Granlyn released me. "Sit down." I sat.

170

"He just can't walk very well and tends to forget things."

"We all do, at my age." He moved a pillow around behind his back. "Tell us about your trip, Marisa. How is the new place?"

"It's working out well," I said. 'The area is several times as large as this valley, and with two rivers we'll have plenty of water. Uncle Bay and Uncle Allen planted some seedlings and seeds, to see how they will grow."

"Does the smaller river run into the larger one?" Grampa asked.

"No. It comes out of the forest to the east and bends around. Some hills keep it from going over to the big one."

"Sounds good. Who are you taking next trip?"

"Aunt Maria wanted me to bring Barbi and her family."

"That's seven," Granlyn said. "What about carts? I think they have some ready."

"Next time. Uncle Allen said to get a measuring tape from Uncle Art and measure the room when we went through."

"Good idea." Grampa settled back on his pillow.

"He needs to rest, dear," Granlyn said, rising. Her tummy was round. "Let's go out on the porch." This was a bare area, with a few flowers along the edges, and a couple of wooden stools next to the front door.

I sat and looked about. Several people bustled around the plaza, and a couple of men worked on a cart at one side. "Looks like everything's going well here," I said.

"Oh yes, everyone is being kept busy. I do what I can, but I don't like leaving him for too long."

"So how is he, really?"

"Pauli says it was a stroke. A friend of her father's had one at their house back on Home Earth. Larry can walk slowly far enough to get to the latrine, thank goodness. He can feed and dress himself. His left arm doesn't reach as far as it used to, and that hand doesn't always work as well as it ought. But his mind is clear. He knew what was happening to him and told me what to do."

I reached over and patted her hand. "He'll be all right, Granlyn." I was finally able to relax sitting here with her. "So how are you?"

"Okay." Granlyn smiled. "Only a little morning sickness yet, but I can *sense* them. I will need to go soon. Not this next trip, but maybe the one after."

"I'll put you and Grampa down for that trip."

We chatted for a bit, then I rose. "I need to find Roroy. You take care of yourself and Grampa."

As I checked around for Roroy, I *reached* for Susan. 'I'm back,' I sent. 'How are you doing?'

'Okay. The pain's gone. Come over when you can.'

'I'll be over later.'

I found Roroy down by the river, sitting in a chair with wheels Uncle Art made for him. He had big wooden braces, with joints at the knees, on his legs, over the casts.

"Hello, goddess," he said when he saw me. "Glad you're back."

I put my arm around his shoulders. "How are you doing?" I asked, kissing his cheek.

"Better. I can stand up if holding on to something. Like you." He heaved himself out of his chair, and I went into his arms. We stood there a moment, as I breathed in his essence.

"I missed you," I murmured.

"I miss you, too," he said, lifting my face to kiss me. "Enough. I must sit."

I settled him in his chair. We chatted for a while, watching the river chortle along. Something chirped up in the trees that had large, three pronged leaves.

When he was ready, I helped him wheel himself back to our house.

***

The clan had a communal supper on the plaza. After everyone finished eating, the babbling increased.

Finally Papa and Uncle Art Junior stood up together and yelled. The others quieted down. "It's time for Marisa to speak, to tell us what's going on over there," Papa said.

The people sat down.

I stood up, flitterers in my stomach.

"Hi, everyone. First of all, everything's going splendidly over there. It's a beautiful place, and the work is going well. The trip itself I can do with my eyes closed, practically." I paused to take a breath. "But I see a lot of disorder here. So this is what I am going to do." I twitched my tunic.

"Since I have the strongest Talent, I'm going to play boss." I heard 'no's, 'you're too young', 'you don't know what you're doing', etc. I ignored them.

"Here's what I'm going to do. First thing in the morning, I am going to go around to each family and find out when they want to go. Then I am going to check all the carts, and the warehouse, to see what we need to keep here and what can go first."

I took a deep breath.

"Anyone who thinks he might want to sneak back to River Point will be caught by Officer Art Junior and brought to me."

I took a another breath.

"The culprit will be imprisoned and taken on the next cart that goes through." I looked around. "Anything else?"

People sat in stunned silence. I'd never done anything like that before. Frankly, I was surprised at myself.

Papa stood up and put a hand on my shoulder. "You heard the little lady. She knows more about coming and going than anyone else. So let her play boss for now." He turned me around to face him. "I have a question. Will the carts fit in the Gate?"

"That's one of things that I want to look at," I said. "Are the handles detachable or foldable?"

"They can be. We'll look into that tomorrow."

***

First thing in the morning, Papa took me to look at the carts. "They look awfly big," I said, staring at the nearest one.

"Can you tell me about how much room you have?"

"Well, we had five quines with riders, and they all stood pretty close together. So it's longer than a quine is long, and wider than five side by side, not quite touching, and plenty of room above our heads. Uncle Allen wants me to take a measuring tape first, just to be sure."

"Good idea."

I climbed up and looked inside a cart. They appeared to be pretty well packed. "How'd we get so much stuff?" I asked.

"We brought a lot of parts of the ship down, and we made more out of that and other things. I'll go measure the quines, and you go talk to people."

The first person I talked to was Susan, at her house. "Mike and I want to go. Too much pity here." She rubbed the couch cushion beside her.

"They'll bring it with them."

"Not for a while. Can we go this trip?" She looked at me with wide eyes.

"Sure. How are you doing, really?" I glanced at her abdomen.

"I had one period, like normal, and not much cramps." Susan smiled. "So maybe next time…"

"Good. I'm sure you'll get there." We hugged. "I've got to go talk to people. See you later."

Granli wasn't ready yet. Art Junior said he wanted to take his family soon.

"You'll have to wait a bit. Aunt Maria wants all her family though first, and Granlyn needs to go on the next one," I said. "I'll put you down for the next available one."

Most of the rest weren't sure, but Uncle Art said we needed to start taking carts through to see how they worked, and if they needed any changes.

***

It took me two days to go through everything and talk to everybody. Papa decided the cart would fit, with the quines pulling it.

"But not this time," I said. "I'll measure the room to be sure, then next time we can. And another thing. We need to take some chickens. We need our protein over there."

"Okay. I'll find someone to make up a coop for about half a dozen."

"Thanks, Papa."

Those of us who were going began to pack in earnest. I helped Barbi by watching the little girls and keeping Donnie out of her hair. Ten-year-old Cindy helped her mama, and Jeff went off with his buddies, Sam and Gary. Jeff was the only one who didn't want to go, but I told him the other boys would be over soon.

I packed my backpack with some things I hadn't been able to take before, including great-grandpa's scarf. As I drew it between my hands, I wondered whether I could shake this sense of being an outsider over there. Maybe when we were all at Freedom Two.

CHAPTER 31

Finally, we were ready to go. We had great travelling weather, sunny and warm, with a soft breeze. Cory and Barbi rode behind me. Baby Bonnie rode in a snuggie with her mother, and little Kayla with Cindy. I led off, as usual, and Susan and Mike rode at the rear. The boys wanted to go fast, but Qione put a damper on that. The trip was uneventful, for which I was thankful.

We camped out at the high glade and went through the Gate in the morning, in two groups. After the first group went through, I waited a bit before I hit the button again, and there was our door. I ran in with one end of the tape while Mike held the other end. After we measured the width, we all trotted into the room and waited for the darkness.

***

When I woke in the glade on Peace, I *reached* to Aunt Maria and *told* her we were on our way. "How is everyone?" I asked my group. The children were up and running around.

Mike and Susan held their heads. "You didn't tell me about this," Susan moaned.

"Sorry. I keep forgetting about it until it hits me." I pulled myself to my feet as Mike helped Susan stand.

Cory and Barbi sat up. "At least it doesn't affect the children," Barbi said, hands on her temples.

"Okay, let's get going." I'd hoped that the Gate would start bothering me less, the more I went through it. I wondered how it would affect Granlyn. We mounted and picked our way down the trail to the beach. As usual, quines and children bolted for the sea.

I noticed there were fewer red flowers on the bushes above the sand, and the sharp green of the islands seemed a little off. I loved walking this beach. It produced a sense of euphoria, a feeling that this was my world, for sure.

We reached the camp by sunset, and Susan and I helped Barbi corral her children.

"I love this place already," Susan told me as we prepared supper. "That blue-green sky is something else."

"Isn't it? I knew this was the place as soon as I stepped on the beach." I dumped some cut up squash into a bowl.

"I'm hoping maybe tonight..." Susan stared into space.

"Good luck."

We settled down for the night after supper was cleaned up, and everyone was eager to go first thing in the morning.

***

When we approached the little river the next day, I saw two quines splashing in the water. Uncle Allen and Uncle Chad sat on the beach pitching tiny stones into the sea. They must have heard us, for they jumped up and waited for us.

"Welcome, all," Uncle Allen said, patting my shoulder. Cory's family gravitated to Uncle Chad. "Let's collect the beasts and get going," Uncle Allen added.

We followed them up to the settlement, to the plaza surrounded on three sides by buildings in various stages of construction. I noticed more log cabins beyond. Just about everyone was there to greet us.

"How was the trip?" Aunt Maria asked.

"Fine," I said. "You'll have to watch that the boys don't sneak off down to the beach."

"They liked it that much?"

"We had to practically drag them out. It might not be a bad idea to set a regular day to go down there. Anything new here?"

"The loovah plants are growing, and most of the seeds have sprouted. As you can see, there are more cabins. We did have a rainstorm one day, but it didn't hurt anything and we could use it."

"Good. We need rain every once in a while."

I helped the newcomers get settled and sorted out what we'd brought. Everyone was happy with the place and unhappy with the cabins.

"We need to start building real houses," I told Grampa Bay.

"We've just started one, over here." He led me to a semicircle of round trees just upriver from the settlement. The foundation was laid and rooms marked off. "Who do you think we should allot this house to?"

"Granlyn and Grampa Larry," I said. "They're the oldest. Don't tell anyone, but she's pregnant."

"Lyn?" he exclaimed.

I nodded. "She's the matriarch, and pregnant. I think she should have the first house. Imagine Grampa climbing onto the top bunk."

Grampa Bay chuckled. "Well, I agree with you. When are they coming?"

"The next trip. She requested it."

"Good. I'll be looking forward to seeing Lyn again."

We sat on a handy log and listened to the river burbling through the trees.

"Did Lyn ever tell you how we connected?" he asked after a while.

"Yes. She *reached* and found you *reaching* for her."

Grampa Bay nodded. "I knew she was coming long before that. Gran Dalia had told me about the family, and how Lyn and Larry had disappeared to other worlds, but she always expected they would come back."

"Granlyn told me about that trip. She thinks they went back to a different Earth, in a parallel universe, one not too different from hers."

"Larry thought the same thing." Grampa Bay rose. "Well, I need to get back to work, and probably you do too."

I left him rolling logs into place and wandered farther up river. Another grove of trees caught my eye. Here was my place. I picked up a fallen branch, stuck it upright in the middle of the open area, bent a twig into an 'm' shape and stuck it on top of the branch.

When I returned to the settlement, Aunt Maria pounced on me. "I need you to sit with the babies. Barbi can't get anything done with those two under her feet."

"Sure. Where are they?"

I sat the two little girls down in the play area, with their rag dollies. Jimmy and Donnie played nearby with wooden quines. "Your mama has work to do," I explained to them. "I'll stay here with you."

I relaxed and watched the Chads, father and son, working on the clinic. Joey and Cory, Barbi's mate, were finishing up a cabin, and Joan and Barbi were helping their mother set up the kitchen.

A soft breeze touched my face, and with it, a hint of that otherness I'd felt before. Other, but not dangerous. This place, this world, was ours, the one I had sought, but it was not perfect. Of course, nothing is perfect. Even so, I still felt like I didn't truly belong, there was something I had to do here, first. But I had no idea what it was.

At supper, I suggested, "I think it's time to set up a child care center and schedule of caregivers. I can do it for now, but I'm going to be going back in a few days." I twiddled a spoon. "I'll be bringing Granlyn and Grampa Larry. Who else shall I bring?"

Aunt Maria stopped to think. "Dick and Mindy and their family. Mindy will have her papa here." She was Grampa Bay's daughter.

"Okay. But Ruthie's pregnant, and I may have to bring her, too."

"I thought she was. That's good, she'll be with her family." Aunt Maria picked up a piece of bread.

***

The day before I was to leave, Uncle Allen approached me and said, "I'd like to go back with you, if you don't mind."

"Why? I thought you liked it here."

"I want to collect some things I left behind and see how it's going back there."

"Okay." It would be nice to have some company.

***

That night, as I lay in my blankets trying to find sleep, I thought about Uncle Allen. He'd always been just one of the older uncles, the head explorer. He was Granli's younger brother, he'd been a child when Granlyn and the group came to Harmony. He and his brother Bill took after their father, long face, medium brown curly hair.

I realized that he'd never mated, nor had his brother. Oh wait, yes, Bill had been mated to a Bramite girl, but they never had any kids, so she left him and mated with a Bramite widower. But Uncle Allen had been in between generations, so there wasn't anyone for him. Then.

This was going to be an interesting trip, finding out about him.

CHAPTER 32

The next morning, we packed up. Qione chose the quines who would return with us.

As we left, everyone came down with us to the beach. We said our goodbyes and trotted off, leaving the rest of them to enjoy a morning at the seaside.

Qione and the other quines splashed along in the water and chattered among themselves. I heard them in my mind, but couldn't tell what they were saying.

"These critters are something else," Uncle Allen said.

"Yes, they are. We need to let them use their brains more."

"True."

After that, he said very little. I sensed there was something he wanted to say, but was afraid to. I also realized that he was an empath. No wonder he was gone so much. Suddenly, I found him very intriguing.

We rode together in a peaceful silence. At camp, after we finished eating, he asked me, "Did anyone ever tell you how we left Home Earth?"

"Granlyn told me they had to run up a mountain with people chasing them."

"Well, yeah. Bay came over to pick up Bill and Pauli and me, but Dad didn't want us to go. Bay picked Bill and me up at a ballgame, but Pauli was stuck at home, and we had to sneak her out. I didn't really understand what was going on, the urgency of the situation, just enjoyed the excitement.

"Dad saw and followed us up the mountain to Grampa Pete's cabin, but we got there first and started up the trail with Uncle Larry and Uncle Adam. We caught up with Aunt Lyn and the others, but when we got to the top, we had to wait for the spaceship to come and get us."

"Where were the other cousins?"

"They had met at Grandma's and already gone up."

This was fascinating. Granlyn had never talked much about their return to Home Earth.

I knew it was because she'd hoped to get her memories back, but little had returned, even with the family. Granli wouldn't talk about it because she'd been scared stiff on the trip up, afraid her father would catch them.

"Tell me more," I said, stirring the sand at my side.

"Okay, but remember, I was only twelve at the time, and some things just went right over my head." He squirmed to a more comfortable position on the other side of the fire pit. Little critters made chittering noises in the trees behind us.

"One day, near the end of the school year, Mom picked me up after school and took me, the twins, and Bobby over to Grandma's. Mom said Aunt Lyn and Uncle Larry were coming home. I knew who they were, of course, and that they'd gone off world. So they came, and there was Uncle Adam with them. Because of the way things were in the world then, which I didn't totally understand, I wasn't allowed to talk about space or anything. So when I asked something about where they'd been, Grampa Pete and Mom jumped all over me."

That sounded crazy to me. "How on Harmony could anyone tell what you were talking about in your own home?"

"You know how we use our Talent to tune in to other people?" I nodded. "The government people could do that with tiny mechanical bugs that would send what they heard to a big machine where people could hear it."

"But why would they want to do that?" I stared at him.

"Because the people in charge of the country wanted to control what the rest of us thought and did, because, as Grampa Pete said, they were afraid of us."

"That is totally preposterous," I pounded the sand beside me. "Why couldn't you just talk in your minds?"

"First of all, Grandma and Grampa Pete never had any Talent, it was just from Grampa Allen. Second, we were trying to keep our Talent a secret because nobody else had any."

"Oh." I nodded my head. That made sense. I picked up a tiny pink shell.

Uncle Allen poked the fire. After sun down, it was getting cool.

"They all came to Pauli's birthday party the next day," he continued. "Mom had a hissy fit because Dad didn't like Aunt Lyn and Uncle Larry, so they pretended to be long lost cousins." He grinned.

"Aunt Lyn got all cozy with Pauli. The cake was good, though. You don't know what you've missed, never having had chocolate cake." He smacked his lips.

"I'm not even going to ask what that is." I sifted sand through my fingers.

"Anyway, a week later, we all went down to San Diego and met a bunch of cousins, who had Talent and somehow connected with Aunt Lyn. I thought it was neat, because we didn't get to go anywhere very much. The only thing I didn't like was that there was no boys my age to play with, so I tagged along with Bill."

"I'm sure he liked that," I said, thinking of Laurie and Ricky.

"No," Uncle Allen grinned again. "He found a room with a huge model train layout and told me to stay there. That was pretty cool."

"Is that when Grampa Bay and the others made plans to leave Home Earth?"

"Yeah. I didn't really know what was going on until I heard Pauli was going with them. She was all up in the air about Cousin Bay. I wanted to go, too, but she wouldn't talk about it."

Uncle Allen yawned. "Two weeks later, we went back down for Art and Betty's wedding. They made me carry the rings on this fancy pillow. I tried to get out of it but they wouldn't let me. The twins were flower girls."

He pushed himself to his feet. "I'm going to turn in." He rolled out his blankets.

"But I want to hear more." I yawned, disappointed.

"We have plenty of time. Good night."

"Goodnight." I curled up in my blankets. This was fascinating, new family history. We were all taught that the oldest generation had come from Home Earth, that they came to Harmony to escape people who wanted to use our Talents for their own purposes, that Aunt Lyn had met Judee, the Wati, on the city-world of Centralia, and that they had lived with the Bramites for a couple years in a big cavern before finding a way out, and eventually back to Earth.

We had even been taught some of the history of Home Earth, to remember our roots, Mama said. It was so totally different, it was hard to believe it was real. All those machines…

**

In the morning, we were up before the sun. We ate a hasty breakfast, packed up, and took off.

We didn't talk much, it was hard to carry on a conversation with the quines splashing and making noises.

After we reached the glade and passed through the Gates, I *called* Mama and let her know I was back. As it was almost dark, we camped there.

At supper, Uncle Allen continued his story. "After we got home, Bill and Pauli were having a lot of private conversations and watching me. I knew something was up, but they wouldn't tell me anything.

"In the middle of the week, there was an earthquake, and they shut down the roads. Dad locked Pauli in her room and gave me the key. He wouldn't tell me why. Then Grandma and Grampa Pete came over, and she took the key and let Pauli out. Grandma and Mom got on me for saying something I shouldn't have, and then they went home.

"Later, I heard Mom and Dad talking about locking me in my room with a pot to pee in until after Aunt Lyn and the uncles had left. That scared me at first, but then I thought maybe Aunt Lyn wanted to take me, too. It was really hard to hide my excitement."

He rose and walked around.

As I watched him, I thought, when I was twelve, I was trying to get away from duties and pesty little brothers.

Uncle Allen continued. "On Saturday, Bill took me to my little league ballgame as usual, and gave his car keys to a friend. I wondered why, but then got into the game. At an innings break, Bill called me over and we went out and there was Bay in his Jeep.

"'We're going for a ride,' Bill said, as we took off. We went back to the house and there was a cop out front talking to Dad so we parked around the corner. Pauli came around from the back and got in and we took off. Dad saw us, and he and the cop chased us up the mountain to Grampa Pete's cabin, which meant we had to go through the woods a lot. I *felt* anxiety from the others, but I was just excited. Bill brought my things, but forgot my little stuffed zebra because it had fallen under the bed."

"That must have been exciting," I said, packing up leftovers.

"Oh, it was. The uncles were at the cabin, and we all ran up the trail. Except Pauli. Bay had to half carry her. We met up with Aunt Lyn and the others, and went on up to where the shuttle was supposed to pick us up. It came, just as Dad got there. They shot at us as we flew away."

"Did you like being on the spaceship?"

"Oh, yeah." Uncle Allen grinned. "They had this neat game room with pinball and vid games. Bill and I spent a lot of time playing them. And a place where we could look out and see billions of stars."

He fingered a seashell. "We went back and picked up the Bramites, only a lot of them had been sick. Then Quinbar, the Centar, came and tried to get Aunt Lyn, but she outfoxed him somehow.

"Then we were put into deepsleep, and when I woke up, we were in orbit around Harmony."

"What was waking up from that like?" I couldn't imagine such a long sleep.

"Later." He yawned.

***

In the morning, up before dawn, I couldn't wait to start the trip back to Freedom One. I put my cloak on, it was cool up in the mountains. We made good time; the quines knew they were on the way home. A few of the trees were touched with yellow.

That evening, Uncle Allen said, "I'll never forget what it was like when I woke up out of deepsleep. My first thought was, 'this isn't my bed', followed by 'where am I?'. Then I became aware of all these tubes and wires all over my body. It scared me so badly I peed all over myself. Then I realized I didn't have any clothes on.

"I tried to yell and move my arms, but they wouldn't move. Then the cover above me swung open and one of the Bramite women looked at me. 'The kid's awake,' she said to someone else. 'We'll need a clean up here. How do you feel?' she asked me as she began pulling out the tubes and wires.

"'Ublub,' I mumbled.

"'It'll come back in a moment.' She pulled off the last one and helped me sit up. 'How does your head feel?'

"'Okay,' I said. She and another woman got me cleaned up and my clothes on. I was totally embarrassed and wouldn't look at her as she took me out to a bigger room where Bill and Pauli and Bay were waiting.

"'Oh, wow,'" I said. This room had lots of padded chairs and picture screens on the walls.

"We went to the dining room and ate, where I met Judee, the Wati. She looked like a grownup teddy bear. I couldn't keep from staring at her, a real live alien. Then Bay took me to the observation bay. 'Watch', he said. It was all stars, more than I'd ever seen before, except for a blue crescent at the edge. The blue part got bigger and bigger until I saw a whole world, blue and green and brown.

"' Is that the Earth?' I asked.

"'No, that's Harmony, our new home.' It took me awhile to get my mind around that." Uncle Allen sighed.

"I asked when we were going home, and Bay explained that we weren't, this was our new home for the rest of our lives."

"Didn't they tell you before?" I asked, moving a dish.

"Probably, but I guess it went in one ear and out the other. A lot of things did at that age."

"So what was it like when you went down to the planet?"

"Well, Judee, Aunt Lyn and Uncle Larry went down first. After all, it was Judee's ship. Then Uncle Adam and Bay had been down there several days when they woke me up.

"When I first got there, I ran around like crazy, trying to see everything. The next day, Bill put me to work, mainly as a go-fer. 'Allen, go get this, Allen go bring me that.' It wasn't until we'd been there several tendays that it sunk in I would never see my folks or younger sisters or brother, or my buddies again. It took me a while to get through that."

"I guess. It must had been hard for all of you from Home Earth."

Uncle Allen sighed. "It was. But we're all part of this world now." He sat back and stared at the fire.

I was moving to another world, too, but we could go back to the old one fairly easily. For now.

CHAPTER 33

The rest of the trip went smoothly. Uncle Allen told me some more about his family and the world he had begun his life on. He made it sound real.

Mama and Papa met us on our way in. No other major problems had occurred, and the boys were behaving. Granlyn and Grampa Larry were doing fine. As we approached Freedom One, I began to feel as if I were returning to a place I visited once a long time ago.

At the community, several people were harvesting early crops, and a group of kids were playing with a ball, batting it back and forth. I'd had a ball once, when I was little.

Roroy wasn't home when I dumped my pack in my house, so I visited Granlyn and Grampa.

"Glad you're back," Grampa said, sitting at the table. "I think we should go this time."

"Twins grow fast," Granlyn said, hugging me, "and I don't want to wait any longer. Also, Ruthie's expecting again, and I think she should go."

"That's what Uncle Allen said. I'm planning to take you two and Ruthie and Will. She won't go anywhere without him. Also, I promised Aunt Maria I would bring Dicky and Mindy this time, so it's going to be a crowd." I smiled at Granlyn. "How is everything here?" I dropped onto the couch.

"Nothing exciting," Grampa said. "The men are digging up some of the loovah plants and the women preparing them for storage and transport. The older kids are all excited about a new place, but at least, they're staying right here. Haven't heard anything from the Bramites for a while. Gabe says Amy tells him it's quiet there. He's thinking about going back and seeing his mother one last time."

"Do you think they'll let him?"

Grampa shook his head. "I think they'll have to meet this side of River Point. But we'll see."

We chatted a bit longer, then I excused myself. "I want to find Roroy," I said as I rose and headed for the door.

"Do. I know he misses you." Granlyn smiled at me. "See you at supper."

I found Roroy in the craft hall, carving a version of Beast. His back was to me, so I crept up and put my arms around his shoulders. "Boo," I said in his ear as he picked up his carver.

He jerked around, dropping his tool. "Goddess, you're back. I thought they said you wouldn't be here 'til tomorrow." He pushed his chair back and scooped me into his arms.

I hadn't realized how much I'd missed him. Maybe I would let him make me a baby, after we were all moved over to Peace.

Roroy put me down. "I'll work on this later." He tucked the little figure into a pocket and led me back to our house.

***

At communal supper, I told Dicky and Mindy they were going next. "So you need to start thinking of what you want to take. A backpack each, and another couple bags on the quines."

As I sat at the end of a table and looked around, I caught Uncle Art's glare before he wiped it off his face. It was common knowledge that he thought I was too young, and a girl besides, to have the responsibility of leading the move. He thought his Art Junior should be the one handling the move, but Junior said he had to stay to look after his papa. Uncle Art was becoming a crotchety old man, even though he had little gray in his hair yet. He'd never really gotten over the loss of his wife, Betty.

Art Junior asked me about the new world.

I told them what had been done so far, and added, "I'm going back in five days."

"I wish we could all go at once," Will said. "We'd like to go soon." He looked at Ruthie, beside him.

"You are." I looked at Will. "I told Ruthie to start packing."

Will looked at her, then at me with a thoughtful expression.

I winced. He couldn't be changing his mind after all this time, could he? I stared at my plate. The buried pain still burned inside me, but now there was a tendril of hope.

"Good. We'll be ready." Will picked up his mug and drank.

"We can't all go now," Grampa Larry said. "We need people here at least until all the crops are harvested and prepared to go. We can't afford to leave anything useful here."

After dinner, Mama told me, "Don't worry about cleanup. Go spend time with Roroy."

"Yes, Mama." Finally, she told me to do something I wanted to do. I found him and we trotted to our house.

***

I spent the next afternoon talking to people and answering more questions. This time we'd be taking a cart. Qione picked a pair of young males to pull the cart, and Papa, Mike, and Dick practiced hitching them up.

When I told Qione that Granlyn was going, she selected her sister, Qiola, and we had Granlyn ride her a few times. "I think I'll be able to manage this," Granlyn said, as we helped her off the quine. "I like this one." She patted Qiola.

At night, I had time with Roroy. "Why you have to go so soon, Marisa?" he asked. "Can't others go? Is much longer for me here than you there."

"I know you miss me, but I'm the one who knows the way the best. I miss you, too, Roroy."

He held me tightly. "I did not know I could care for a person like I do for you, Marisa. You are my life, now."

His words made me uncomfortable, but I didn't know why. I let him carry me to the bed.

***

By the next day, even though I would miss Roroy, I was itching to go back to my world. I worked as hard as I could, to keep my mind off the upcoming trip, helping out wherever I was needed. I looked through the carts and picked one to take this time.

Uncle Art and his son fixed the cart handles so that they could be pulled up to a vertical position. On the morning we were to leave, Qione picked out a placid youngster for Ruthie. Will took Quest because Kiong wanted to stay 'til the others were through.

I think he wants to go back to our world and find some more recruits, Qione told me.

Ruthie made her usual fuss about riding a quine, and Will had to put his foot down.

Qione hovered over her sons as Mike and Dick hitched them to the cart.

Mindy carried her baby in a snuggie on her chest, and the three-year-old rode with Dick. I rode Qione, as usual, and led the way.

The cart came behind, then Granlyn and Grampa Larry, followed by Will and Ruthie, and Dick and his family, all mounted, with Uncle Allen at the end.

This was the longest procession I'd ever led. As usual, the kids wanted to go faster, but Qione wouldn't allow it.

Actually, I wanted to go faster, too, but didn't dare say anything. Although sunny, it wasn't very warm, but luckily there was no wind.

When there was room, Grampa rode beside Granlyn and held her hand. He appeared right at home on his quine. Uncle Art had made a set of stirrups for Grampa, to hold his bad leg. The rest of us rode bareback, feet dangling.

At camp at the staging area the first night, Granlyn dismounted, bent over and rubbed her knees. "It's been a long time since I sat on a horse. How many days did you say this trip would take?"

"Probably four days to the Gate with the cart, and two days from the other end to Freedom Two. If we need to take longer so you can rest, we will." I patted her shoulder.

Uncle Art, who'd come up the day before, greeted us, and we set up camp. We women, except Granlyn, set out to prepare a meal. Ruthie excused herself to feed her baby.

As soon as we finished cleaning up after supper, Granlyn and Grampa settled down for the night. The rest of us stayed up a little longer, talking and singing.

***

The next day it was almost midmorning before we got underway. First, some of us slept later than planned. Then Uncle Art wanted to check out our cart and how it was packed. Ruthie refused to get back on her quine and said she'd walk back to Freedom One.

"You can't do that," I said. "We all have to go to the new place."

"No, Ruthie. You can't do that walk by yourself in your condition," Will added. "Come on, I'll help you up."

"You can't make me get on that beast," she cried. With baby Willie in a snuggie in front and pack on her back, she trotted back the way we'd come.

Will chased and caught her, carried her back, and put her on the quine. "Uncle Art, get me something for a harness, will you?"

The two of them managed to strap Ruthie on so she wouldn't be afraid of falling off.

Granlyn, already mounted, rode over to the crying girl and said, "Ruthie, calm down. She's an intelligent creature. She won't let you fall off. Getting all upset like this could harm your babies." She reached out and patted her. "If I can do this trip, so can you. The quines understand our situation, they're mothers, too."

"Can I ride with Will?" Ruthie asked.

"No," I said. "He's a big man and that's all they can carry."

Will mounted and rode up next to Ruthie. Taking her hand, he said, "I'll be right here, promise."

I felt his displeasure with her actions, and thought, I wouldn't have done that. I saw his back stiffen as the others gathered up the kids and settled them on their quines. Finally we were off.

It took us two more days than usual to reach the Mountain Gate. On the second day, Ruthie willingly mounted her quine, and Will stayed close to her.

My emotions twisted within me. I tried to ignore them, and him.

***

Everyone was eager to get going in the mornings. The trail had become well marked by now. We found a few places on hillsides where we had to move rocks or bushes to get the cart through, and we had to do more switchbacks than usual. Qione supervised the two young cart quines.

Every night, when Granlyn and Grampa turned in right after we ate, I prayed for the Oneness to be with them.

Finally, we made it to the Gate glade, and camped there. The glade barely had room for all of us and the cart. I looked around at everyone, my grandparents and friends, and thought, what the hell am I doing messing around with their lives? But I knew I could get them through the Gate and to my new place.

People were tired, heck, I was tired, so I chose to wait for morning to start going through.

CHAPTER 34

Next morning, when Qione opened the doorway in the hillside, we found the opening a little too narrow for the cart.

That's as far as I can get it.

I looked at her. I don't take 'no' for an answer, so I eased into the opening and pushed against the edge with my back. It widened a little more, and the quines pulled the cart in. Qione had to keep reassuring her sons that it was all right, constantly talking to them.

I lined everyone up according to the order in which they would go through the Gate. The cart first, with Will and Uncle Allen. Then Granlyn, Grampa, Ruthie, Quest and one of the cart quines. The next batch was Mindy and the girls with the other cart quine. Lastly, Dick and the boys, and me with Uncle Allen's mount.

Finally we started in.

"Oh my," Granlyn said, as we paraded down the long room. "Is this all part of the Gate?"

"I think so." It was always the same to me.

When we reached the screen room and opened our door, I discovered that the quines had no idea how to back the cart in. Finally, with Uncle Allen on one side and Will on the other, they somehow managed to get the cart into the room. After unhitching the quines and leading them out, the door closed.

The cart was still there when the door opened.

"I guess we need someone to go through on the cart to pull it out on the other side," Uncle Allen said. "Come on, Will." He and Will climbed up on top. I pressed the button again, and this time the room came back empty.

"Okay, Granlyn, Grampa, and Ruthie, you go on in, with the men's quines. The rest of us will come through with the kids next time." They rode in, and the door closed.

"Okay, people, we'll be going through in a few minutes." I prayed to the Oneness for their safety, and counted to a hundred twice. Taking a deep breath, I pushed the button.

The room was empty, and the next group entered. Finally, it was my turn.

The first sound I heard when I came to was groaning. Granlyn--I scrambled over to her. Grampa Larry was holding her tightly.

"What is it?" I put my hand on her belly. "The babies are fine."

"I know," she gasped. "I didn't know it was going to be like this."

"She'll be all right, Grampa," I said. "How are you doing?'

He shook his head.

"I think it's harder on older people. It doesn't seem to bother the kids at all." I looked at them running around and moved over to Ruthie, crying in Will's arms. Baby Willie bawled too. I touched her side. Will's face was close to mine. Something in his eyes made me wonder if he were having second thoughts.

"You and the babies are fine," I told the girl.

Dick and Uncle Allen were up harnessing the quines, who didn't seem to be as bothered with the trip through the Gate as we humans. I never seemed to get used to it, all the times I'd been through.

I *contacted* Aunt Maria and *told* her I was back, with Granlyn and Grampa, Ruthie and Will, Dick's family and a cart.

After we ate, we mounted our quines. On Qione, I led the way. The trail to the beach was a little tricky in a few places, with immovable boulders and large bushes with tiny pink flowers. In one area we had to dig out a bush, roots and all, to get the cart past a huge rock.

Qione and I were almost to the beach when I heard a crunch and a crack like a tree falling, men yelling, and a quine screaming. I jumped off as Qione jerked around. The cart lay canted on its side, several bags on the ground beside it. Grunting, Uncle Allen and Will picked themselves up off the ground. The screaming quine lay underneath the other one. I ran to the quine, put my hands on his shoulder and shut down his pain as Qione nuzzled him.

Uncle Allen pulled the other quine off, and I saw that this one, Qobbo, had a broken front leg. He was trying to push himself up with the bad leg and moaning. My gut knotted. This was a major disaster.

The other quine seemed to be okay. The men undid the harnesses, the unhurt quine scrambled to his feet and moved around behind Qione. Will went back to tell the others what happened. Dick, his oldest son, Greg, and Grampa came back on foot with him.

"Looks like this front wheel went up over this rock and tilted the cart over," Uncle Allen said.

Can we get the others by?

I looked at Qione. "Let me see." I peered up where the men went through. It didn't look wide enough for a quine.

"Hey, fellows." The men looked at me. "Can we move this enough to let the others get by?"

"Good idea. Come on. That back corner, I think." Uncle Allen led the way, and the men lined up along the back end of the side of the cart to push, and I tried to *lift* it. We managed to move it just enough. Granlyn followed by Grampa eased through.

"Oh, the poor thing," Granlyn said. "Down." Qiola knelt and let Granlyn off. She crouched beside me as I tried to get his leg aligned. "Do you think we can save him?"

"Of course. Who's got the healers' kit?" I asked her.

"Mindy, I think."

Ruthie, on her quine, and Quest came past. "Will, where are you?" she cried.

Qione said something to the other quines, and they trotted down to the beach. I could always tell when she was talking to one of her kind, in their minds, but not what they were saying.

The kids came through, with the other men's quines, and continued on down to the beach. Finally Mindy arrived.

"I need the healers' kit," I told her.

She jumped down and began pawing through her paniers. "Here it is. What do you need?"

"Are there any splints?"

She dug out a pair of narrow flat boards and a long bandage.

Granlyn and I put the splints under and over the break, and I wrapped the bandage cloth tightly around his leg, while she held the splints in place. Qobbo only whimpered a little bit. Qione talked to him nonstop, rubbing her nose on his neck and shoulder.

"Well, he certainly won't be pulling any carts for a while." I sat back and watched as Qione nudged him up into a sitting position. Qiola also nuzzled him. "Or even carry a rider."

"We can worry about that later." Granlyn patted her patient. "What are we going to do about the cart?"

Uncle Allen and the others were already unloading it. He caught my eye. "Get Ruthie and those kids back here. They can help."

I called them, and the kids came running, followed by Will and Ruthie on foot. Will had run down after her. Granlyn and I left Qobbo to his mama and auntie Qiola and went to help. Mindy brought an armful of clothes around past the quines and dumped it.

Finally Uncle Allen called a halt. "I think this'll do. Let's see if we can get the cart off the rock."

With everyone except Granlyn helping, some of us with our Talent also, we managed to get the cart off the rock and upright. Uncle Allen, Will, and Dick played around with it, looked it over and moved it back and forth.

"I think it's okay," Uncle Allen said. "How's the little fellow doing?"

"He'll live." I saw that Qione had rounded up Greg's quine to replace Qobbo to pull the cart. We still had to reload it. It could have been worse, I suppose.

"Now it's too high," Ruthie grumbled, bouncing Willie on her hip.

Uncle Allen grinned and stepped up on the rock. "Not any more. Just hand things up to me and I'll put them back in." Will, as tall as Uncle Allen, stood by the rock to hand items up to him. The rest of us started giving things to Will. It didn't take long to get everything collected.

Qione and Qiola had Qobbo up on his three good feet. He wanted to walk, but kept trying to put the bad foot down.

"Do we have a piece of cloth long enough to make a sling?" I asked Mindy.

She fished in her kit again. "This is the last one. Hope no one else gets hurt." We devised a sling over his back that held his broken foreleg parallel to the ground. Qione and Qiola led him down to the beach in a three-legged hop-walk.

The men hitched up the quines and accompanied the cart down to the beach. The cart creaked a lot more than it had before.

We all had to push to get the cart across the soft sand down to the hard area.

"Perhaps we can make a path down with rocks or something," Grampa suggested.

"I don't see any around here, but I think there's some up by the river." The sun hung overhead and I was hungry. "I suggest we rest and have some food here, before we continue on."

"Good idea," Grampa said. "I could eat a…" He stopped and ducked his head.

"Larry," Granlyn said. I hid a smile.

The quines were already in the water, and so were the kids.

We women set out the food, and everyone came up, sat down, and ate.

"We won't get to the halfway camp tonight, but I know there's a stream before that." I brushed crumbs off my chin. "I'm going to *call* Aunt Maria and tell her what happened."

Granlyn nodded. "Maybe they can send someone."

Aunt Maria *sent* that she would send the Chads, Mike and Susan, and extra quines.

"Okay. They'll be coming to meet us somewhere along the way. Now let's get moving." I jumped up.

Lyn may ride Qiola, but I cannot have a rider. I must tend to Qobbo.

I relayed Qione's message to the others. "I'll walk," I added. We packed up and the others mounted. Greg took his little sister's quine, and she rode with her mother. Between the creaking cart and Qobbo, I had no trouble keeping up with the riders.

The young quine developed a three-legged pace, and every so often I walked beside him and soothed his pain. When we came across a stream, Qione stopped. *Rest here.*

Although the sun was only halfway down the sky, I agreed. I couldn't stand any more of that creaking. I didn't want to think of what would happen if an axle broke.

Qione found a place for Qobbo to lie down in the grass at the top of the beach. Qiola and Granlyn stayed with him as Qione followed the rest of the quines into the sea. The kids were already in, and we adults followed. Will carried little Willie, and even Ruthie splashed with the rest of us.

"This is great. Can we come here often?" she asked.

"Not here, but further along below our new home," I replied. I was glad to see her smile.

After a bit, I splashed out and sat by Granlyn.

"This is wonderful, Marisa. Thank you. How far is our new place from the sea?"

"About a quarter day ride. We plan to have regular beach days."

"That will be nice for the kids." Granlyn drew in a great breath. "It even smells like the Home Earth ocean."

"How are you doing?" I asked her.

"Hanging in there. How many more days?"

"We'll get there tomorrow evening. When we do, you can just sit and watch. Maybe childcare, if you feel up to it."

"Good." She trickled sand through her fingers.

When everyone tired of the sea, we had supper. Qione told me she wanted to stay there 'til morning, her young one needed the rest. I checked his leg and *sent in* healing vibes.

***

The next morning, we all rushed through breakfast and left just after sunrise. Qobbo appeared to be feeling better, even sticking a foot in the water. The cart creaked even more ominously.

"I've checked everything and can't figure out why," Uncle Allen told me.

"Maybe it's because it wasn't packed as well as before."

"Possible. I couldn't reach the corners."

At noon, we found another stream, and stopped to rest and eat. I *called* Aunt Maria again and *told* her how we were doing.

'Our group plans to be at the halfway camp by tonight. Wait for them there,' she *sent*.

I told the others, and we continued on. This time, Qione let me ride her.

As we approached the halfway camp in mid afternoon, I heard a shout, and turned to see the left front wheel roll away and the front left corner of the cart sink into the sand.

Chapter 35

"Oh crap," I muttered. We all stopped and gathered around. I checked on the cart quines, who seemed to be all right, as the men unharnessed them. "We're close to the camp. If anyone wants to go on, I'll show you." Everyone except Uncle Allen, Dick, Will and Ruthie chose to go.

"Come with us, Ruthie," Granlyn said. "Will will be along in a little while."

"Yes, go with them. You and the baby need to rest," Will added. "I'll be along later."

Little Willie was fussing, so she gave in and came with us.

I led them to the camp in the semicircle of trees, with a stream near the firepit in the sand, and we all dismounted. Qione found a place for Qobbo, in the grass under the trees at the back of the beach, as the rest of the quines rushed for the water, followed by the kids. I helped Granlyn get settled near Qobbo.

I sat between them and rubbed the quine's upper leg. "The others probably won't be here until about sundown or so, so you'll have a chance to rest." I patted Granlyn's shoulder with my other hand.

"Good. I'll sit here and watch that nice blue sea and the beautiful blue-green sky." She smiled. "I think the youngsters are enjoying all this."

"I hope so."

Grampa came up, sand covering his damp feet, dropped his boots, and sat on Granlyn's other side. "This is wonderful, Marisa. I hope we can get to this beach often. With the big breakers way out, must be a reef, the waves are nice and easy close in."

"Is this like Hawaii?" Granlyn asked.

"Sort of. They have big breakers there most places." He looked at me. "The family was planning to go to Hawaii in the fall of the year we were abducted from Earth."

I nodded. "I want to go see what's going on with the cart."

I rose and dusted off my behind. Hawaii meant nothing to me.

Dick and Mindy, back at the cart, had started unloading it again.

"The axle's broken. I don't know whether we can fix it," Uncle Allen said.

"What'll we do?" I remembered the sled Uncle Peter had made for Roroy. "Maybe make a sled out of it?"

"That's a possibility. Let's start taking the small stuff over to the camp." He picked up a large box and started off. I grabbed a smaller one and followed him. We called the kids out of the water and soon formed a line carrying various items from the cart to the camp, like a line of ants. Furniture and such stayed in the cart.

Afterward, I collapsed on the grass beside Granlyn. At least I'd got her this far. Thank Oneness for that. I was so tired I could hardly think. On all the previous trips, I'd taken for granted everything would go well. And now this. The young quine was doing all right so far, but it would take a long time for his leg to heal enough so he could go running or have a rider. And the cart. I didn't even want to think about that. I wished I could turn this whole mess over to somebody else.

I awoke to yelling. Scrambling to my feet, I saw riders coming down the beach from Freedom Two.

"Mike," someone shouted.

I tried to run toward them, stumbled and fell. Someone pulled me to my feet and said, "Wait," into my ear.

"Uncle Allen, they're coming."

As they neared, two rode out in front. Susan and Mike. I almost cried for joy.

Susan pulled up, jumped off her quine, and hugged me. "Mari, are you all right?"

"Mostly." I gently disentangled her. "I'm not hurt, but as the leader, I'm pretty upset. We've got a quine with a broken leg and a cart with a broken axle."

"Oh, no." She pulled back.

"What happened?" Mike asked, coming up beside her.

I told them briefly. All I wanted to do was lie back down and go to sleep.

"You go get some rest. We'll take care of things." Susan could read me so well.

It was full dark when I awoke again.

I heard singing and the swish of the waves. Granlyn, next to me, was sound asleep. Good, she needed it.

Qobbo appeared to be asleep also, and Qione sat next to him.

Go to your people, Qione told me.

I rose and joined the others around the campfire. Stars twinkled in the sky, and the snap of the flames complimented the slap of the sea.

"There's food if you want," Susan said, patting a place next to her.

"So what have you been up to?" I took the piece of bread she handed me.

"We've got everything sorted out as to who will carry what. I *called* Aunt Maria, and she's going to send some more people down to the beach at the river. Will found a long log in the bottom of the cart, and he, Uncle Allen, and Dick are going to try to use it as a replacement. They want the rest of us to go on in the morning. Either they'll come with the repaired cart, or by themselves, riding the quines."

I nodded. "Sounds good. Now, what's been going on at Two?"

We talked for a while and finally crawled into our blankets.

***

In the morning, we packed up and took off. We had to pry Ruthie away from Will, he said he didn't want her hanging around while he was working.

"You'll probably see him tomorrow," I told her. "I'm separated from my mate for almost fifteen days at a time."

We traveled a little faster without the cart. Qobbo walked at almost his normal pace. His leg seemed to be healing nicely.

Aunt Maria, Joan, and Cory met us at the place where we left the beach. Granlyn rode over to Aunt Maria and they clasped hands.

"So glad you made it," Aunt Maria said, smiling.

"Glad I'm here." Granlyn looked up the slope. "It's up there, right?"

"Right. Okay folks, let's go."

Barbi and her kids chattered with Joan, and a sense of relief swept through me.

When we started off, the quines took their sweet time, and I didn't blame them. We rode past several new cabins to the plaza, where we dismounted.

Thank you, Marisa, for your help with Qobbo. I'll bring him over tomorrow for you to examine. Qione and the others ambled over to the quine territory.

Granlyn patted her quine. "You were a good girl, Qiola." The quine nuzzled her hair.

"I see you've been busy," Grampa said, looking around. The clinic was up, and the meeting hall roofed and walled in. "Is that the big river over there?" He pointed to the line of trees to the west.

"Yes. We'll take you over in a day or two so you can see it."

"Good. Now where do we sleep?"

"In the clinic, until we get your house finished." Aunt Maria led us over to the clinic and showed us the little room she'd curtained off for them. Granlyn sank down on the bed.

"Rest," she said, and leaned back.

"We can bring you supper later." I pulled the moss-stuffed comforter up over her. "Don't worry about anything. Grampa, I think you should lie down, too." He looked pale, and I watched as he stumbled around to the other side of the bed. I kissed them both, and Aunt Maria and I left.

Outside, I heaved a big sigh. "They made it."

Aunt Maria smiled. "Yes, it's a relief to have them here. I'll get on Chad to get everybody working on their house. Now we have to figure out what to do with all the stuff from the cart. Probably in the meeting hall, for now."

"We need a warehouse and communal kitchen built next," I said, noting several new cabins west of the plaza.

"That's on the list."

I showed Ruthie her cabin.

"How are we supposed to live in this tiny place? There's not even a bed for Willie," Ruthie complained.

"I know it's not very big, but you'll get a real house soon. At least, it's shelter and a place to put your stuff."

I left to go help Aunt Maria and Joan get everything sorted out. On a break, I went to check on my house site. As I passed Granlyn's house I saw the walls were up, and the roof on. At my place, the 'm' I'd made out of a twig hung by one end from the stick I'd planted. My house wasn't going to get built unless I stayed here and did it myself. Or what I could.

I hunted up Grampa Bay. "I need to start on my house," I said. "Who can I get to help me?" As the oldest, he was in charge of deciding who would be working on what.

"I'll get that taken care of in the morning."

The next day, Dick and Cory helped me lay out the house, marking the corners and doorways, while the Chads worked on Granlyn's house.

She and Grampa settled in chairs outside the clinic, watching the activity in the place.

CHAPTER 36

A few days later, when I went to see Qione, she told me she wanted to go for a long ride north, up the big river, just us two. *Something's going on up there. I want to see what it is.*

"Okay," I said. "Tomorrow?"

She nodded her head.

***

We took off early, after I'd checked on Granlyn and gotten permission to go, and headed over to the big river. Where there was a break in the trees, Qione trotted to the edge of the bank and stopped. I watched the water churning its way down to the sea. Across the river, stood more trees. Something like a log floated by.

I hate this body, Qione told me.

"What?"

My ancestors were biped humanoids like you.

I didn't know what to say. This was the last thing I expected to hear from her.

Many millennia ago, she continued, *my ancestors were forced to leave their home world and come to the one we lived on before we met you. The body scientists had to make changes in them so they could live on the new world. In the following generations my ancestors grew bigger and bigger. Finally, their backs grew too long to stand on two legs, so they began walking on four legs. The ancestors' jaws were always large, because we were always vegetarians. The head and jaw grew larger, and the fingers grew together.*

She stopped and sighed.

"Oh my," I said, trying to absorb this. Grampa Larry had taught us about evolution and how, back on Home Earth, men were trying to find out how to speed it up. Suddenly a thought struck me. Mama could move people, I could bend time, what if my daughter-to-be could change her shape? "No," I cried out.

What? Qione turned her head to look at me.

I told her.

You need to fold back your talent, she told me.

"Do what? How?"

Qione shrugged and trotted north.

Could I control my daughter's Talent in the womb, I wondered. This I would have to think about. I would have to know what to do before I got pregnant.

Sometime later, we came to another break in the trees, where the river narrowed. A bridge, a flattish 'u' shape, arched across, in some grayish-brown woven material. Even though there was a breeze, the bridge did not sway.

"The screen said there were no other people here," I said.

It could be very old, Qione told me.

I sat and stared at the other side. A wide meadow stretched to forest beyond, enveloped in a bluish mist. I *reached.* There was no identifiable danger I could sense, nothing manmade, but the strange uneasiness I'd felt before was very strong here. Animals of all sizes up to that of quines roamed the forest, but I could not *sense* any intelligent beings.

"Do you want to go across?" I asked.

Qione shook her head and turned back for home.

As we left, I felt a pull from the forest across the bridge, which faded as we moved farther away. I would have to come back and go across. I had to know whether there was any threat to our new world. Inside me, anger stirred at whoever or whatever had put this threat here. This was my world and I wanted everyone else, except my clan, to keep their hands or tentacles off.

Back at the settlement, I did not tell anyone about the bridge. That was my secret, for now.

"Something bothering you?" Will asked later when I slammed a plate down on the table.

"No." I took a deep breath and controlled myself.

Will raised an eyebrow and walked off. I stared after him. Part of me still wanted him.

I have to stop worrying about the bridge and what's beyond it, until I can do something about it, I told myself. I managed to keep a smile on my face the rest of the day. My future daughter kept intruding into my thoughts, though.

When I saw Granlyn that night at the clinic, she looked at me and asked, "What happened?"

"Nothing." I twisted my hands.

"You went for that long ride. Where did you go? What did you see? Tell me, Miss Marisa."

I shrugged.

"Now, Miss Marisa, I may not have your Talent, but I have

enough to tell that something's worrying you. It's not Qione, is it?"

"No, she's fine." I hesitated. The woman wouldn't stop until she'd gotten the secret out of me. "Okay, we found a bridge way up across the river."

"A bridge? But I thought you said there were no other people here." She sat up.

"That's what the screen said. Qione said it could be very old, and whoever built it was long gone."

Granlyn nodded. "Keep an eye on it and keep me posted."

***

The work on the houses continued. I helped hang curtains in Granlyn's house while the men were putting up my walls. Mike had co-opted Chad III to help him with his house, next door to mine.

Granlyn settled in as childcare coordinator. I could tell she loved the little ones. A few days later, Aunt Maria and I took Granlyn to see her new house. Grampa had seen it, but refused to tell her about it, not wanting to spoil the surprise.

At the house, Granlyn oohed and aahed. "This is wonderful, Marisa. Did you design this?"

"Aunt Maria and I did. We want you to be comfortable. Do you want to rest for a while?"

"Yes, please. Would you mind bringing us a bit of supper later?"

"No, of course not. Here's your bedroom."

"This bed is so soft," Granlyn said, sitting down and patting it. "Larry, come see."

"We found some moss over in the trees by the big river," I said, as Grampa came into the room behind me.

"This is very nice, Marisa. I think we'll be quite at home here." He sat beside Granlyn.

I returned later, and Granlyn and I opened her box of books and pictures and began decorating her house.

***

I was crossing the plaza two days later when Uncle Allen, Will and Dick showed up without the cart.

"What happened?" I asked.

"We got the wheel back on, but just past the camp, it came off again." Will dismounted. "We decided to leave the cart and come here for more tools and things, then I'll get a couple other men and go back and fix it."

Ruthie came running and threw herself into Will's arms. "You can't leave again, you can't."

"Don't worry, I won't be long." He looked at me over her head as he disentangled her.

***

After supper, I asked Uncle Allen, "I need to oversee my house being built. Would you mind going back to One by yourself?"

He picked up a stack of plates. "Not at all. Just give me a couple of days for us to rest. Yes, I know how to get through the Gates."

"Good. You'll have to take different quines." I led the way to the communal kitchen. I felt him watching me. "I'll check with Qione to see who else of her group can open the gate from the other side," I added. "If it's someone here, I'll let you know and you can take her."

"Okay."

Qione told me that Qiorna, back at Freedom One, could do it, and I passed the information along to Uncle Allen. Qione also told the ones going back to tell Qiorna.

We continued to build houses, and plant seed and loovah seedlings. The latter grew in just about any conditions, and quite rapidly. Mike and Cory devised a trap system to catch fish. The women put the finishing touches on the communal kitchen and clinic, and began classes for the children who were here.

I worked on my house when I could, and did my tasks, but always in the back of my mind hung that uneasiness at the bridge, and an ominous sense of coming disaster crept over me.

***

One day, Uncle Allen arrived with Aunt Maria's second son, Fred, and his family, and Granli. Megan, Fred's mate, was Granli's daughter. With them came Megan's brother, Bobby, and Aunt Beth with her three youngest. And another cart, which made it through without any problems. After settling in the newcomers and unloading the cart, the place bustled. I didn't see much of Uncle Allen, he was set to work on the mill, and I was busy between the classes I taught and working on my house.

***

When it was time for one of us to go back, I volunteered. Susan would stay linked with me until I reached the Gate.

I took several extra quines along, and Qione and I made an uneventful trip, except for Qione having to drag the other quines out of the water at the end of the beach.

***

At Freedom One, Mama and Papa greeted me with big hugs.

"It's been too long," Mama said, kissing my cheek. "How's Granlyn and Papa?"

"They're fine. They have their own house now and she's planning for the babies."

"I'm glad to hear that."

The boys clattered into the house, followed by Uncle Peter and his crew. After greeting everyone, I went to find Roroy.

"My goddess, you're back." He hugged me. "But for how long?"

"A few days." I relaxed in his arms. I always missed this. "When do you want to go? Can you ride Beast yet?"

"Yes. I rode him yesterday. He unhappy with all this packing and leaving. Can we go this time?"

"Probably. Let me think about it." I didn't think about much of anything for a while.

***

That evening, after supper, Mama, Papa, Uncle Gabe, and I had a meeting at their house.

"First, is there any way we can move more people through at a time?" Uncle Gabe asked.

"We're making several trips through the Gate with the carts now," I said. "I suppose we could try two carts and more people." I didn't care for the idea.

"The reason I ask," he tugged his beard, "is that we're catching some of the young Bramites trying to sneak into our settlement. A couple took some food from the warehouse. Officer Charley here is watching at night, along with the quines, but that means he's not getting as much done in the daytime. Uncle Art has moved up to the staging area and is watching the stuff we've taken up there."

"We need to move out of here as soon as possible," Mama said. "Take as many as you can."

"So this time it'll be John and his family. Roroy wants to go. He says he can ride Beast. Who else?" I asked.

"I want to come and bring the boys," Mama said. "Charley has to stay here, but we'll manage."

"Okay, that's two and six and three, eleven plus me. And Roroy makes twelve. And two carts."

205

"Thirteen," Uncle Gabe said. "How many do you put on a cart?"

I scowled at him. "Two men, to pull it out. We could probably get the two smallest children on it, too."

"So two carts with two men each. But Roroy can't get up on a cart, so that leaves John as the only adult male. I wonder if Bill would be willing to go. Then Laurie and Ricky could be the second men." Uncle Gabe tugged at his beard. "Then twelve quines plus the four with the carts. Do we have enough?"

"Couldn't the two men on the first cart also pull out the second one?" Papa asked.

"I suppose so." I shook my head. "I don't know. We'll have to see." So many things I still didn't know.

I decided to stay two more nights. I went through all the carts, rearranged the contents, and ditched some old items we didn't need. Mama had already packed up much of her belongings and gathered more supplies for the trip. Mama and Aunt Anne prepared crops for the winter as others worked on the harvest.

CHAPTER 37

Finally, the day arrived. We lined up in the plaza for our goodbyes. After Roroy and me, John rode with his family, behind the first cart. Then came the second cart, followed by Mama and the boys, and Bill. I prayed that my brothers would behave themselves.

Laurie and Ricky wanted to go faster, but again, Qione kept to a slow but steady pace. Ricky and his young quine kept trying to go off trail to see things, and Mama and Laurie were having a hard time keeping them in line. When we stopped for a rest, I made him come up and ride between Roroy and me.

The days passed.

Once again, we filled the glade to the point we had to sleep underneath the surrounding trees. I looked around at my mother, brothers, and friends, and wondered how I dare direct their lives like this? But I knew I could get them through the Gate and to my new place.

People were tired, heck, I was tired, so I chose to wait for morning to start going through.

***

I lined everyone up according to the order in which they would go through the Gate. One cart first, with John and Bill on it. The cart went through with no trouble. The second batch was Mama, Ricky, and three quines. Next was Mary, her kids, and John's quine, followed by the second cart. Beth, her kids, and Bobby came next, with Roroy and me and the second cart's quines bringing up the rear. We had to wait for a long time for the Gate to recharge.

"Takes longer after so many," Roroy said.

"I hope it's just that." I was glad that I had told John and Bill how to get to the new colony from the glade.

At last, the button worked, and we passed through.

***

I awoke to children yelling, sat up woozily, and looked around. Roroy lay beside me, with Beast sitting at his side shaking his head.

John and Laurie had already got one set of quines hitched up and were working on the other cart.

Roroy sat up and clutched his head. "Does it not get better?"

"No." I took a deep breath. "But you won't have to go through again. Let's get going."

After we ate a quick breakfast, I led the way down the path to the beach. Qione took it slowly and very carefully. It had rained, and the trail was muddy. The second cart got stuck in the mud.

"Not again," I said as the others groaned. It took all of us pushing and *pushing* to get it out.

At the beach, the quines marched down to the sea. The kids jumped off and ran into the water after them. The cart quines stayed on the hard sand. Qione told them they would get to play when we got to camp.

Mama looked at the sky, then at me. "I've never seen a sky like that. Blue-green. And a moon." She pointed to a pale disc hanging over one of the islands.

"I know." I wasn't used to having a light in the sky watching me. It was creepy.

I pushed us a little to get to the camp before dark. All the adults were relieved to dismount and walk around, and the cart quines dashed into the sea. Around the semicircle of trees at the back of the camp, the quines found plenty of grass.

We women began to fix supper while the men gathered firewood.

"This is weird," Mama said. "Here we are on a strange but nice beach, on a strange world, wondering where we are going."

"I know where we're going." I sliced a loaf of bread. "And you've got me and the boys."

"Yes. And Mama and Papa will be there."

I smiled at her and continued to slice bread.

After supper, I announced, "Tomorrow, we will reach our new home at Freedom Two. I've called them, and several people will meet us at the river. They'll bring fresh quines for the carts, as it is uphill from there, and will unload some of the stuff from the carts to make it a little lighter.

"So let's get a good night's sleep and tomorrow we'll be home."

***

Everyone was eager to get going in the morning, and we started off at a fast clip. It was a bright, sunny day with a few puffs of clouds in the blue-green sky. The moon was gone.

At midday, the trees began to thin out above the beach. Small plants with pink flowers appeared here and there.

When we reached the river, we found Cory and Barbi, Dick and Mindy, and their children, splashing in the water along with the quines.

"How's everything?" I asked.

"Fine," Barbi said, splashing out of the water. "The loovah is growing nicely. Marisa, your house is ready for you."

"Really? Thanks." I smiled at her.

The guys unhitched the cart quines, who ran down to the sea. After the new cart quines had been secured, Qione called the others back. We all took what we could carry out of the carts.

Barb and Mindy dragged their kids out of the sea, and we began the trek up to the settlement.

The rest of the clan greeted us in various places on the way up and took more bags out of the carts. We stopped in the plaza, dismounted, and let the quines trot back to their territory. The cart quines, unhitched, followed them. The men collected the panniers.

I told Roroy, still on Beast, to come along while I walked with Granlyn back to her place.

"Here we are," she said. "I love this house. Thank you again. How long are you going to stay?"

"I'm not sure. Excuse me, I've got to show Roroy our house."

Bill came with us. I saw that someone had built a ramp up to the front door. We helped Roroy off Beast and into his wheeled chair.

"I'm going to take a look around," Bill said, and wandered off.

Roroy and I entered our new house. The living room looked huge, mainly because there was only a double stuffed seat in there. Our furniture hadn't got here yet. Behind the living room was the kitchen with plenty of storage. Two small bedrooms, one with a bed in it, and a little bathtub room completed the house.

"Nice," Roroy said, and wheeled himself to the seat.

"It'll be better when we get our furniture." I didn't know whether it had come in the carts we'd brought, or not.

***

After supper, Uncle Allen pulled me aside. "I did some exploring upriver while you were gone. I found a bridge across the Grande."

"A bridge?"

"A strange bridge that shouldn't be here. My quine wouldn't go across. I had to dismount and walk over. It's much the same on the other side, but I felt a sense of wrongness that I couldn't put my finger on. I want you to come with me to see what you think."

"Okay." I couldn't decide whether or not to tell him I'd already seen the bridge.

Later, I told Qione that Uncle Allen wanted to go with me up to the bridge. "Will you go with me?"

She agreed to, but told me, *there's something bad about that place.*

***

Two days later, Uncle Allen and I rode up to the bridge.

"Do you feel it?" he asked

"Definitely an otherness," I replied.

"Do you want to go across?"

"Sure."

We dismounted, because we knew Qione and her brother would refuse to go over, and walked toward the bridge. Uncle Allen stepped onto it and nothing happened, so I followed. The otherness became stronger.

At the halfway point, we stopped and looked back. The trees along the river blocked our view of the settlement, but the land and forest we could see appeared normal.

When I turned back to the far side, a faint mist had crept over the land there. "Look," I said, pointing to the haze. "What's that?"

CHAPTER 38

"That's strange." Uncle Allen glanced at me. "What do you *sense* about it?"

I *reached*. There was something there, but nothing I could pin down, and no obvious danger. "I don't know what it is. I've never felt anything like this."

"Do you want to go any farther?"

"Yes." I had to find out more about this unknown. We continued on, and stopped at the foot of the bridge.

Uncle Allen held me back and took a step onto the land. "I think it's okay."

I took a few steps, keeping my *senses* on high. This place was like a mirror image of our side. I shivered. After all this to get our people over here, and now another threat to our community.

We walked a little farther, then turned and trotted back over to the bridge.

What was it like? Qione asked me.

"Like our side, but there's something there I can't pinpoint. Let's go home."

I didn't like it at all, little bugs tickled up and down my spine, but I couldn't *sense* any danger. I wanted it gone. I gritted my teeth and clenched my fists. Just when I thought everything was going well, now I had this to worry about.

***

Back at the settlement, I helped with sorting out the stuff I'd brought and did some more planning. Although I continued to do my tasks, the mirror world gnawed at me. It wasn't right, it didn't belong in our world; it was wrong.

***

The day before my next trip, I talked Qione into going back up to the bridge. I dismounted, trotted across the bridge, and walked along the edge of the forest.

I found marks in the ground opposite where our houses were. I found a fire pit, long unused. I also found the remains of a latrine, also long unused. Someone had lived here long ago. Who were they and where did they go?

I *reached.* There was something in the air, something foreign and yet not. I started for the forest. As I walked between the first two trees, *sensing* no danger, I was grabbed from behind, a hand over my mouth. My first thought was, how could I have not seen this? Terror rippled through me until I put a stop to it.

The being turned me around, hands clamped to my upper arms. I could not *sense* its mind at all. It, he, looked at me. Manlike, he had a round head with the usual adornments and a fuzz of dark hair on top; two arms and legs; his barrel torso and long limbs wrapped in a brownish green material. His eyes were deep blue, round, with vertical pupils.

He made a noise. I did not respond, still in shock. I couldn't remember my Talent not working, ever.

He put a wide, four-fingered hand on my head, just above my eyes. I saw him, the trees, the field beyond, and superimposed on it, a strange purple world, with people like him walking on a path through a yellow field.

"Oh," I said. He removed his hand, briefly touched my curls, and made the same noise as before. I shook my head, trying to understand. What was he doing here, what did he want, why couldn't I *sense* him?

He pounded on a tree. I *felt* frustration from him. And I was frustrated, too. I couldn't communicate with him by voice or mind. Basically, I was deaf like Mama, but without a mindlink to connect with others.

As I turned to go back to the bridge, I *felt* something coming from him. Something that I *sensed* as 'don't go'. I looked at him.

He made a noise that sounded like 'Otor'. I repeated it. Apparently it was his name.

I said, "Marisa." Slowly, accenting each syllable, as I patted my chest.

He made a sound that sounded like 'Maareethee'.

"No, Ma ris a."

'Meeritha.'

After a few tries, I realized he could not make an 's' sound.

'Mareetha.' Otor pointed to the ground, turned and walked away, fading into the trees. Literally.

As I ran back to Qione, the only thing I could think of was why hadn't the screen mentioned these people?

On the way home, I told her about it.

Is overlap of worlds from different dimensions. Must stop it before it takes over our world.

"How do we do that?"

Happened to our home world. We could not stop it. That's why we left.

"No." I couldn't believe this. Why had I not felt any danger? "We can't move again. We're not even all here yet. Granlyn's babies…"

Process is slow. You have plenty of time. You can stop it if you use your Talents right.

I was stunned. I wanted to talk to someone about this, yet I wanted to keep it to myself. My thoughts ricocheted off the inside of my head. I could change time, yes, but there's no way I could handle a planet-wide mess like this. What else could I, we, do?

Qione talked to me about her brood and how they were making their home in the groves. She prattled on about this land and the beach. Her people wanted regular days to go down to the beach often. The water refreshed them in a way nothing else could.

We had mud holes on our world, but no rivers. Much rain always soaked into the ground.

I listened, but could not stop thinking about the other world. When we got back, I ran to my house, and hid in a corner of the back bedroom, thankful Roroy wasn't there.

"Oneness, what am I going to do?" I cried out. "Help me." My mind shut down.

Roroy found me later, and I woke as he pulled me into his arms as he sat in his wheeled chair.

"My goddess, what is wrong?" He kissed me. "This not you."

"Ro," I murmured. The other world came back to me, but I decided to worry about it later. "I had a bad experience up at the bridge. I'm okay, but I can't talk about it yet." Maybe Qione was mistaken.

When he wheeled us out to the couch, I saw that he'd found some of our furniture.

"What have you been doing?" I asked.

He told me about his work with the crops and supervising Bill and some of the younger fellows as they moved the couch and bed into our house.

That night, I dreamed about a purple world with a tooth-filled gash in its side, coming down on us from the west. When I woke up screaming, Roroy held me and did not ask any questions. He was so patient with me. The thought seeped into my mind that I should try to have a child with him. I wasn't ready to be a mother, to have a child to care for, but maybe the only way I'd be ready would be to get pregnant.

***

At breakfast, Roroy asked me, "Are you still planning to go back to One today?"

"Oh." I put my hand to my mouth. I'd totally forgotten about that, but I realized the trip had been planned and I had to go.

"Yes. I'll be okay. Laurie's going with me."

We went down to the plaza where Qione and several other quines waited. Allen, Papa and others were attaching panniers. Most of the clan was already there to see us off. We said our farewells and mounted our quines. We were taking extra quines because I couldn't remember how many there were left at Freedom One.

We rode as fast as the quines would let us and made camp early. Qione refused to talk about our trip up the river. I kept the other-world problem tucked away in the back of my mind. The next day, we reached the glade early, and went on through the Gate. I *called* and *reached* Papa.

'We're on our way back,' I *sent*.

'Okay. Take care.'

When we stopped at the staging area, Uncle Art greeted us with, "So you're back. About time." I saw a row of carts to one side. "They're ready to go. I'm staying until the last trip."

"Good," I said. "How's everything?"

"Status quo."

At the plaza at Freedom One, Uncle Peter and Aunt Anne greeted us with hugs and kisses. "How are things over there?" he asked.

"Fine," I said. "So what's been happening here? Any more problems with the Bramites?"

"No. Our children are kept close, and Charley keeps a watch for the others."

After I left them, I went around to check the buildings. They were mostly bare. Only the clinic had a bed and a chair and a few boxes of supplies. Sadness enveloped me. This was growing-up home, and I would miss it. I didn't remember too much of River Point, but I know Mama and Granlyn did.

At supper, I announced, "Since there's so few of you left, most can go this trip and the rest next time. Who wants to go this time?"

"Us, for sure," Art Junior said.

"And us," Uncle Peter added.

"Gabe and I will stay," Papa said.

"How many carts do we have left to go through?"

"Five," Uncle Peter said.

"Okay. We'll take three this time."

The next two days I helped the others finish packing. I wandered around my empty house, picking up a few odds and ends. I recalled lying in bed beside Roroy, sitting on the couch with him talking about our new world, and at the table eating. Our new house on Two was larger and had a real bath tub room, but this was our first home.

***

On the third day, we packed up and prepared to leave. Art Junior and his family followed me, then Uncle Peter and his. At the staging area, we collected three carts. We brought all the quines except the ones for the men and the remaining carts. Kiong had brought a lot more of his people back from his world.

"Only one more trip," I said, with a sense of relief.

Qione set the same slow pace as before, but we didn't have to stop so often to clear things out of the way. We had to make seven trips through the Gate; three carts, two families, four cart quines, and me with the other two quines. I sighed as the blackness took me.

When I awoke in the glade, I felt a little less woozy. About time, I thought.

Christi held her head. "Is it always like this?" she asked.

"Mostly," I said. The men were already working on getting the quines hitched up. We gathered our bags, mounted our quines, and moved off down the trail. Dry this time, it was easier going, and we had no problems with the carts.

At the beach, we all relaxed. The quines let us off and splashed into the sea. Everyone oohed and aahed about the blue-green sky. Camp that night was rowdy, with loud singing, hilarious tales and rambunctious children.

***

The next day, we were met at the river by several people, including Uncle Allen. "Welcome home," he said.

"Wow, three carts." Cory began to unhitch quines.

215

"Only two more left." I looked for Susan, but she wasn't there.

The procession ambled up the hill to the plaza.

Everyone dismounted, removed panniers, and the quines trotted over to their territory.

At my house, Roroy greeted me in the doorway. "My goddess, you're back."

"Only one more trip." I fell into his embrace.

After a while, I *called* Susan.

Before I could say anything, she *burbled*, 'Mari, I'm pregnant. You did it.'

'Great,' I *sent*, feeling both gratified and appalled that I could do what I did. 'I'll see you later.' I turned back to Roroy.

"This house very nice," he said, taking me into the front bedroom and showing me our new bed. That night we slept together in our own bed for the first time in our new home.

***

In the morning, I pushed Roroy over to the craft house and found Susan at child care.

"How are you doing?" I asked.

"Okay. I'm getting real tired of throwing up every morning."

"Isn't it a little early?" I picked up a towel someone had dropped and folded it. "It'll go away in time."

"I've been nauseous since day one. Wait 'til you get pregnant."

I laughed.

***

The newcomers settled in, and Roroy found a place nearby for Beast. It was nice to be back with Granlyn, who was huge and mostly sat and watched, and Mama. She and the boys were staying with Granlyn until their house was finished.

One evening, Susan and I worked together on the vegetables for the communal supper.

"I can't figure out my due date, and neither can Ruthie," Susan said. "All this going between worlds."

"You only went once." I dropped a scrubbed potato into a bowl. "No way I'm getting pregnant until we're settled here. I'd never figure it out. Hey, I thought of something. Can't you control your morning sickness with your Talent?"

"Once in a while, if I really concentrate, but it usually sneaks up on me before I can. Just you wait." She grinned and punched me on the shoulder.

The meal went well, even though we did miss the few who were still back at One. Especially Papa.

I had told Granlyn and Mama about the bridge but nothing about Otor or what Qione had said about the other world. Granlyn told me, "Go up there every once in a while to check on it, and keep us posted. Don't worry about it."

Easy for her to say, but I couldn't stop thinking about it.

CHAPTER 39

Two days later, Qione and I went back to collect the last three members of our clan. I didn't want to leave, but it was my job, and I did want to see the place one more time. Grampa Bay had Art Junior go with me.

As soon as we came through the Gate onto Harmony, I *felt* something wrong, and *reached*.

Gabe *responded*. 'Thank Oneness. We'll meet you on the way.' He faded out.

'What happened?' I *demanded*, but got no answer. "Something bad's happened," I told Art Junior. "Let's go fast."

A little later, I heard from Uncle Gabe and he told me the rest.

'Sorry. Uncle Art was starting to slip off the cart and we had to tend to him. We've been going through everything in the settlement, even taking some of the buildings down. We built and filled another cart with shelving and other items.

'Some of the young Bramites came in the night and torched the buildings. All three of us got burns, Uncle Art's the most serious. The seven quines had disappeared, but only six came back. Since they were all needed to pull the carts, Charley and I put Uncle Art on one of the carts and we walked.'

Qione told me later that the quine who didn't return had died trying to jump a chasm too wide for him. *Kiong had told him not to, but what can you do with male adolescents.*

'We've used up all our salve and need to get to Freedom Two as fast as possible,' Uncle Gabe *added*.

I prayed to Oneness that their injuries weren't too bad. 'Art Junior and I are on our way as fast as we can. See you soon.'

We met them the next day. Uncle Art was burned down his left side and left arm. The others had minor burns on arms and hands.

I hugged Papa carefully. "Good to see you, sugar," he said. "Go help Uncle Art first."

He and Uncle Gabe brought Uncle Art down from the cart and put him on Art Junior's quine.

"You," Uncle Art muttered as he saw me.

From Qione's back, I stifled my anger, went in, and controlled

Uncle Art's pain. Then I dug out the salve we had with us, and used it liberally on him. The rest I put on the others. Papa said his pain didn't bother him, but I *went in* and toned it down.

Then I took care of Uncle Gabe. "Thanks, kid," he said.

Uncle Art smiled weakly, as Junior rubbed his good arm.

We changed out the cart quines with ones we'd brought, and all of us were able to ride.

"If everyone's ready, let's go," I said. We took off at as fast a pace as the cart quines could manage.

Every time we stopped, I treated the injured. I tried to be as cheerful as possible, but still hurt inside. How could those peaceful people do that? They'd come at night, while our men were sleeping. Uncle Art's cabin was the closest, and he always took the longest to wake up. Fortunately, almost everything of value was already over at Freedom Two.

At the glade, after we came through the Gate, Uncle Art took a long time to come around. I *reached* to Mama and let her know what was happening. The usual lightness was missing in the glade, and it was cooler than normal. I shivered.

'Take your time' she *sent*. 'We've had a bad storm through here, and a lot of the buildings are damaged. It's heading your way. I'll send Peter and Anne to meet you.'

'Thanks. We could use some salve, some food, and dry anything, if you have it. See you in a few days.'

I hadn't paid much attention to the breeze, but it quickly picked up. By the time we'd eaten, it was raining hard.

"I don't think we should go down that slope in this rain," I said. "Let's wait a bit." Waiting was the last thing I wanted to do, but I didn't want to risk the carts, or Uncle Art falling off the quine. *Please, Oneness, make the rain go away.*

We all huddled under the big tree that held the Gate. Both the rain and the wind grew stronger and stronger. I'd never seen a storm like this. This was all we needed, when we were in such a hurry to get back home.

"This may go on for days," Uncle Art muttered, glaring at me as if I'd caused the storm. He refused to let me go in and check for infection.

I ignored him and collected rain water for the cloths for his face and chest. We ran out of salve by nightfall. On the second day, we ran out of dry bandages. By then, everything we had was wet.

The quines huddled and shivered, but there was nothing I could do for them. Qiong let out a bellow of frustration every once in a while and talked to her group whenever one of them started to whimper.

"I'm sorry, Qione." I rubbed her neck.

Not your fault. I've never seen a storm like this. She nosed my cheek.

"Neither have I."

I tried to keep calm on the outside, but a seething mass of worries churned inside. Junior paced constantly, in between checking on his father, and threw stones whenever he could find one.

Papa kept telling us we'll be all right, and Uncle Gabe added, "There's nothing we can do about it, relax."

Oh, sure. Wet and cold was not good for the injured men, and we were running out of food. Everything in the carts was soaked, even with the plastic covers, relics of the ship that had brought Granlyn and the others to Harmony. When the frustration got too bad, I screamed, "Where are you, Oneness," and pounded on the tree.

At night, as we tried to sleep sitting up, backs against the tree trunk, I prayed to the Oneness to stop the storm. Papa held me close with his good arm, and Uncle Gabe sat on my other side. Uncle Art, on his quine, buffered by other quines on each side, moaned every so often. I tried to quiet his pain as best I could, but as soon as he realized I was there, he pushed me away.

Papa asked Uncle Art to tell us stories about Home Earth, to keep his mind off his pain. We learned a lot those few days.

I *kept in touch* with Mama; the storm had pretty much calmed down there. 'Peter and Anne left this morning with a pair of extra quines. I do hope they'll be okay,' she *sent.*

***

Finally, on the third day, the rain let up, although the wind didn't drop much.

"Let's go," I said. "Just be careful going down the trail."

Papa and Uncle Gabe hitched the cart quines, and we mounted our steeds. Qione told me, *We never had storms like this on our world. I sure hope it doesn't happen very often.*

Uncle Art felt feverish, even though I had made him drink lots of water. He wouldn't let me *go in* to check for infection. We inched our way down the trail to the beach.

Muddy and overgrown in some places, it was full of downed branches and twigs we had to clear out of the way. Fortunately, none of the carts got stuck.

At the beach, we stopped to rest and eat a bit. The sand was littered with storm debris, and we had to pick our way through it. Qione had the cart quines pick up any large stuff and toss it out of the way of the cart wheels. Although still overcast and windy, it looked lighter to the west, in the direction we were headed.

I walked with Papa and talked about what was going on at Freedom Two. When I told him about the alien I'd met on the other side of the river, he said, "I thought that thing said there were no sentient beings on this planet."

"It did, but maybe they couldn't sense them. I couldn't, until he was right on top of me," I shrugged. "But I never felt any kind of danger, so maybe it will work out." I wasn't ready to tell him the rest of the story.

"It better. I don't want to have to go through this move again."

"Neither do I."

***

We met up with Uncle Peter and Aunt Anne at the halfway camp. She had brought more salve and bandages, and immediately went to Uncle Art. "Oh my Oneness," she said under her breath. "We definitely need to get him home as soon as possible. At least, the clinic is still in one piece."

"Is he going to be all right?" Junior asked. I *felt* his terror.

"Oh, he'll live, but I don't know how much use he'll have of his arm," Aunt Anne replied, gently rubbing on salve. She put fresh bandages on him, and checked the other men.

We collected branches for the fire. The wind was down to a strong breeze here, with the sun peeking under the clouds. It should be even nicer tomorrow. I hoped.

I told Junior, "Don't worry, your papa will be all right," and *sent* soothing vibes his way.

"Thanks," he said. We ate and rested for a while, but no one could sleep, so we continued on. Everyone but Uncle Art walked, to save the quines. The moon shone on the water, a wide stripe of light, so we could see. I *called* Mama and *told* her we were leaving the camp.

***

At dawn, several others met us at the river, bringing fresh quines.

221

Aunt Anne greeted Uncle Allen and rounded up Uncle Art, Papa and Uncle Gabe. "We're going straight to the clinic. You, too, Junior." The five of them took off.

Qione and I followed. The settlement was a mess. Buildings half destroyed, boards and clothing strewn all over, boxes here and there. Aunt Maria and her daughters were trying to clean up.

Qione bugled, and other quines answered. I dismounted. "You go to them," I said. She trotted off, and I headed for the clinic.

Aunt Maria had Uncle Art stripped to the waist and lying on his right side. She was putting some kind of poultice on his burns. "Oh, there you are," she said as we entered the building. "Marisa, do your magic on his pain, would you."

I touched his cheek. "Come in with me, I'll show you how to do it yourself."

"Don't touch me," he growled and jerked away. "Ow."

"Well." I snorted and stepped back. I knew he didn't like me, I was the daughter of the one who had cost him his wife, but I *sensed* that he was in severe pain. I decided to get Susan to help him.

Mama ran in and saw Papa. "Charley, you're hurt." She put her hands on his chest.

Aunt Anne had put a poultice on his arm and covered it lightly with a bandage. "Now, be careful with that arm and don't get it wet, or bump it. You'll probably have a lovely scar."

"Thanks, Anne," he said. "Not bad," he added to Mama.

Mama kissed him, took my arm and turned me around.

Only then did I realize Granlyn had had her babies. She smiled at me from a bed by the window, the little ones in her arms.

"How are you," I exclaimed, running to her. "How are they?"

"Glad to see you back. Meet your new aunt and uncle, Leona and Curtis," Granlyn said. "Those were my mama's parents' names."

My first thought was, they are so tiny. About half the size of a normal newborn. Then I realized that Granlyn had had them early.

"Are they all right?" I asked Aunt Anne.

"Oh yes. They will need extra care for a while, but they're quite healthy."

The little girl looked like us, with tiny wisps of black curls, but baby Curtis had lighter hair, what there was of it, and Grampa's dimple in his chin.

"Hello, little darlings," I said. "How'd it go, Granlyn?"

"A lot easier than with your mama and Peter." She smiled. "What's with Art?"

"The Bramites came one night and set fire to the buildings, Uncle Art got burned pretty badly."

Papa came over to greet Granlyn. "Boy, we've missed you," he said. "How's the little ones?"

"What happened? Did you get burned too?" Granlyn demanded as she saw the bandages on his hand and arm.

"Just a little, getting Uncle Art out."

"How bad is he?" Granlyn asked.

"His left arm and side got it pretty badly, but Anne says he'll heal okay," Papa said.

"I hope so," Granlyn said.

Grampa Larry came in, kissed Granlyn and sat nearby, a big grin plastered on his face. "I have a son," he said. "Thank you, Marisa."

"My pleasure. It looks like the storm was pretty bad here."

"I think it was a hurricane," he said. "I experienced the edge of one once, when I was visiting my folks in Florida. Did you see the line of debris on the way up?"

"I wondered what that was."

"That's where the storm surge of the sea came up to."

"The sea came up there?" I could not picture it.

"Yes," Grampa said, looking at his son. "This place is wide open, and the wind came howling through. I think we should plant a row of trees as a windbreak below the colony."

Now we had storms to worry about, I thought. What happened to our perfect new world?

"Hello, goddess," said a voice behind me.

"Roroy," I said, turning. He was on his feet, with crutches. I hugged him. "I'm back for good, now."

"I stay here until we get house fixed."

"Is it that bad?"

"Most of roof gone. All wet."

"Oh dear." Then I noticed the piles of blankets around on the floor, with paths through them.

"Yes, many sleep here," Roroy said, moving toward a long seat by the wall. We sat side by side, his arm around me. I leaned into him. I was home now.

***

The next night, we had a feast to celebrate the fact that all of us were together again, plus two new babies and three more on the way. Papa and other men carried Granlyn and Uncle Art out and set them in chairs so they wouldn't miss anything. I sat between Granlyn and Mama, who each held one of the babies. Grampa Larry was grinning, too. There was no doubt that the little boy was his son.

Will helped Ruthie find a seat. She was huge. She would have hers soon. Susan was beginning to show. I'd have to get pregnant soon if mine was to be first born. I figured I could manage that with my Talent.

Grampa Larry rose to lead the toasts. "First, to give thanks that we are all together again. Second, to welcome the two new members of our clan. And third, for this wonderful place to call our new home." He nodded at me.

"Hear, hear," came from the group.

CHAPTER 40

Everyone set to cleaning up and rebuilding. Grampa Larry and Uncle Art worked on ways to strengthen our new buildings and houses. Granlyn's house, in the trees, only had part of the roof torn off and one wall half down. Roroy's and mine had more damage, but the back bedroom was habitable. I cleaned it out, then stored our things in there as I cleaned them. We needed to get the houses fixed, it was getting too chilly to sleep out.

The little ones thrived, Uncle Art and the others began to heal, and two tendays later, Ruthie had her baby, a bouncing boy, bigger than the twins put together. Will went around with a huge grin.

I heaved a sigh of relief. She could have all the boys she wanted, but my daughter had to be the first girl of the new generation. Granlyn was the first female to show Talent in her generation, Mama was the first in hers, and I was first in mine. So my daughter had to be first in her generation.

***

The storm and the new babies drove the alien out of my mind until one morning, as I was awaking, I felt a force drawing me to the woods on the other side of the river. I shrugged it off and went about my day.

It was hard to keep to my tasks, as I kept running to see the babies. There was no way I was going to call these little ones aunt and uncle. They were bright and alert, and Granlyn kept comparing them to Mama and Uncle Peter.

***

Every morning I felt drawn to the woods, and every day I tried to shrug it off. Finally, I gave in and asked Qione if she and another quine would be willing to take Ricky and me up to the bridge.

You sure you want to go?

"Yes, I have to. I feel a pull and every day it gets stronger." I stroked her neck.

She nodded, and selected one of her sons.

I took Ricky with me to get him out from underfoot of the others.

His task was to sort cloths, which had got all mixed up after the storm, but he didn't want to do it and was dealing them out like a hand of cards.

When we neared the bridge, Qione stopped and refused to budge. We dismounted and left the quines there, nibbling on tree leaves.

As we crossed the bridge, I felt such a strong pull I don't think I could have gotten away by sheer force. "Ricky, do you feel anything?"

"No. Where are we going?"

As we approached the woods, I started running and couldn't stop. The alien appeared and I crashed into him. At least he was solid. Ricky told me later that he thought I ran into a tree. He couldn't see or otherwise *sense* the alien. I didn't understand that. He could *sense* the creatures in the forest. Could this alien, Otor, have a block on himself somehow?

A feeling of warmth, of otherness stole over me. My eyes closed, and when I opened them, I was in his world, standing in a doorway, clinging to long, silver handles at the edges. Or they were clinging to me. Behind me was my world, my family, my clan. In front of me was a place I could barely see through the mist. Dark blues at the top and bottom, large orange blobs with greens, reds and purples.

Slowly the mist thinned out. The orange blobs became structures, mostly spheres and obloids stuck together in some random order. One sphere at the top of the tallest blob hung over space, attached to the rest by the tiniest of arcs. The blue at the top was sky, with a few stars twinkling. The bottom was, I don't know, it looked like sky also, but how could that be?

The purple wound in ribbons all around and through the structures, like walkways. The greens and reds were various size blobs here and there.

Something came down over my head, fitted itself around my body, and closed at my feet. A suit of some sort. Before I could protest, Otor and I were on one of the purple ribbons. It felt solid under my feet. And there was dark blue sky all around. I fought off dizziness and terror. Otor had a firm grip on me.

The orange structures were as large as mountains. We walked along the purple ribbon into one. "Ricky," I said, shaking.

In my mind, I saw him standing motionless by the tree I had supposedly run into. I understood that he was outside of time, waiting for me to return.

As I stepped inside, a dark shield came down over my face.

An inner door opened, and the walkway moved, taking us inside as we were standing on it. Even with the shield, it was so bright I could hardly make out details. We passed tables with brown and white objects on them, but I couldn't figure out what they were.

The walkway curved and rose, bringing us past a row of what looked like plants in bright colored buckets. Otor never said anything, nor sent anything into my mind, unless this whole thing was an illusion. He just kept holding my arm tightly as if I might fly away if he let go.

After a while my mind quit trying to decipher what these thing were, and began to wonder why he was doing this.

He *sent* me something I couldn't understand. Presently we came out of a tall opening into the dark blue, and the purple walkway stopped at a doorway in space, open but black on the other side.

As Otor pulled me through, and I *felt* a sensation of change, my eyes closed. He let go of my arm, and I opened my eyes. I stood in a small room, still shaking. White walls and ceiling hovered over the black floor and built in bench, walls that seemed to curve at the corners of my eyes. There was no color at all. Even the tall, thin woman standing there had white hair, skin, and black eyes. She wore a long, black gown that covered all but her face and hands.

I blinked. "Hello." I grasped my hands together and held them at my chest.

'Greetings,' came into my mind. 'I am Arisam. Welcome to my world.'

The alienness within me reached out and joined with her.

"What?" I was totally confused. It was hard to breathe. I wanted out, but my curiosity was aroused.

A door opened behind her, revealing a larger black and white room. I'd seen a lot of strange things in my time, but this was the weirdest. As I followed her out, unsuccessfully looking for color, any tiny bit of color, I wondered why this place was this way, and then I wondered how I was going to get back to my own world.

'Come.'

No, I thought, and turned back to the little room. The door would not open.

'Come,' she repeated. I had no choice but to follow her. We passed through a room filled with tables and chairs and people, all black and white. The floor felt more or less level, but the walls wouldn't stay put, moving in and out as if blown by the wind.

The air seemed the same as in my world, faintly warm, but with no odors, no aromas. And no sounds, just a faint buzzing in my ears.

One of the tables slid into my path, then slipped back to its place as I tried to dodge it. My innards twisted into knots. This place felt all wrong, and out of joint.

Dizziness crept over me, and my stomach jumped around. My feet followed Arisam to the end of the big room and into a small, roundish room with a narrow table and two chairs.

I sank into one of the chairs, whose arms were different heights and the seat not quite level. When I shook my head quickly, I glimpsed bits of colors at the edges.

"What is all this?" I asked, clutching the arms of the chair to keep from being pulled away.

She sat across from me. Her hands stretched over the table, fingers just touching mine. Something beyond my comprehension searched my mind and body, something that left my mind in a muddled state.

'There are many realities,' Arisam *sent* into my mind. 'Occasionally they overlap. When they do, a rare person from one reality can cross into the other one. You are one of these rare people.'

"Why?" I stared into her black, fathomless eyes.

'The why is not known. For our worlds, we can help each other. You have a problem with your mental abilities, we have a problem with our structure. If you use your Talents properly, you will stabilize our world and cease growing your Talents.' She inhaled. 'You have an unusual assortment of Talents which, if used properly, can benefit both our worlds. Do all your people have these Talents?'

I tried to hide my thoughts, to not answer, to shut down my mind, to keep my people safe from whatever this was, but she saw my 'yes'.

'We will need all of your people. We need to prepare for you. You will return in three days.' Her face showed no expression.

A great numbness held me. There were questions in my mind, but there was no way for me to express them. She stood, and my legs raised me to a standing position. I followed her out another door, and found myself alone in the woods.

"What was that all about?" I demanded of the trees around me, reveling in their greenness. How could those people live without color? Slowly the dizziness and confusion drifted away.

I *reached.* There was one person, in the distance. Ricky. I saw a trail heading in that direction and took it.

After a long trek, I reached the first tree, and Ricky, in front of me, opened his eyes. I looked about, but no one else was around.

"Hey, sis, are you all right?" His eyes were wide.

"I'm fine. You wouldn't believe…" I began, and stopped. From his point of view, I'd hit the tree, bounced off and was standing in from of him. "Never mind, let's go home."

"I wouldn't believe what?"

"I said never mind." I strode off.

"Why won't you tell me? Would you tell Laurie?" He bounced along beside me.

"Forget it." I was beginning to wonder whether or not it had all been a dream induced by running into a tree. I felt my forehead. No lump. There was no pain anywhere else. But did Otor take me there? Did I really meet a person called Asiram? It was so strange nothing really made sense. I couldn't tell what was real and what wasn't.

Ricky kept pestering and I kept saying no. I needed to talk about this, but with whom? I needed someone who understood my Talent and who would understand this weird other world stuff. First generation wouldn't understand my Talent, but who later would understand the rest?

I pondered this as we rode back to the settlement.

As we dismounted, I told Ricky to leave me alone. In my house, I plopped on a chair and put my head down on my arms on the table. What had happened to me? It was so vivid, all those colors and then the black and white, so real, yet it was so far away from anything I knew, my logical mind couldn't accept it as real. I would have to think about it for a while before I said anything to anyone else.

When Roroy came home, I told him about it.

"It was dream, from hitting head," he said.

"No, it wasn't. It was real. They had a different kind of time, so I could get back to the tree and Ricky shortly after I'd left."

"People do not believe you change time," he said, taking me into his arms. "I know you save me at swamp, and from poison fruit, but change time? No, no one change time."

I did not argue with him, but I wondered. Did he really think that? Did everyone else, like he said? In his embrace, I shut my mind.

***

The next day, Susan and I were making softened fabric out of loovah leaves for baby clothes. The loovah plants grew wildly no matter what the weather.

"You've got something on your mind," Susan said. "Give."

I couldn't hide anything from her. Granlyn and her. "Roroy says no one believes I bent time. Do you?"

"If you say you did, I believe you, but I don't understand how it could be done." She looked at me out of the corner of her eye. "I mean, time is just one minute after another. How can you change that?"

"I don't know. I don't know how I did it, but I know I did."

"Well, that's in the past. We're all here and everything's fine, so just relax."

But I couldn't, and I couldn't tell her why.

***

The next day, Uncle Allen came to see how my house was coming. The roof and the damaged walls had been replaced. It just needed finishing touches, like latches on the front door. Somehow, I ended up telling him the whole story of the other world.

"I have to go back tomorrow," I said. "What am I going to do?"

He looked down at me. "Do you think what you saw was real?"

"It sure seemed real, but sometimes I'm not sure what's real and what's not. Do you believe I did what I said I did when I bent time?"

"If you believe you did, then I believe you."

I looked up at him. He had his father's long face, brown curly hair down to his shoulders, his beard a darker, curlier brown, and his mother's dark blue eyes. I wondered why he'd never chosen a mate.

"I was always the odd man out," he said, reading my mind. "All the traveling and deepsleep screwed things up inside, my libido is practically nonexistent." He smiled at me. "Maybe someday I'll find the right gal."

A premonition came over me, but I shrugged it off. He was way too old.

I found Granlyn and told her briefly what I'd seen and what Arisam told me. "I don't understand how one world could take over another, but I sensed she was telling me what she thought was true. The whole thing scares me, but especially since I couldn't sense anything about that world with my Talent."

"Apparently, your Talent only works in this universe." She smiled.

"I'd like to go with you and see this place, but I can't take the babies and I'm not gpong anywhere without them. You go, find out everything you can, and come home safely."

CHAPTER 41

After breakfast the next morning, Uncle Allen said he would ride up with me.

Again, Qione wouldn't go anywhere near the bridge. We dismounted, left the quines in a grove by the river, and walked up to the bridge. Although the sun was bright, it was not very warm, and I wrapped my cloak about me.

I felt the emanations from the other world not long after we started out. "Do you feel it, Uncle Allen?"

"I sense something, I'm not sure what. And please, just Allen. There's too many uncles around here." He smiled.

At the bridge, he took my hand as we stepped onto it. In the center, the pull of the other world felt much stronger.

When I started trotting, Allen said, "Hey, what's the hurry?"

"Don't you feel the pull?"

"Not really."

I pulled away from him and ran into the woods. I heard his shout, then nothing. In sudden darkness, my feet kept running, my hands out in front of me. No, I moaned. I blacked out.

***

The next thing I knew, I was in the first little room where I'd met Asiram, and the door to the black and white room was open. I didn't want to go out there, but something I couldn't resist drew me toward it. As I stepped out into the larger room, I began to feel the dizziness and a sense of annoyance about these people moving me around like a doll. Nothing had changed here.

Asiram waited for me in the little round room. 'Greetings. Come with me.' A door opened at the other side of the room, and we stepped out onto a little gray porch, with a pair of posts holding up some kind of awning.

The world beyond was chaos. My brain could not absorb it. There was no horizon, nothing solid in one place I could use for a reference.

I clung to the porch post. At least it stayed in one place.

Black, gray, and white objects of all sizes and shapes moved aimlessly, as far as I could see, up and down, around and around, this way and that, against a pale gray background. Some moved faster than others, even below the level of the porch. Some spun and twirled in place, others moved in curved lines.

Dizziness overwhelmed me as I hugged the post and closed my eyes. A faint, deep humming filled my being. Oneness, get me out of here, I prayed. Asiram had stepped off the porch and disappeared into the whirling mess.

Something like a great pair of hands gently grasped and detached me from the post. We moved in some unknown direction. When we stopped, I peeked and saw an oddly shaped, half squashed box with an end open. The hands dropped me into the opening, and I slid down, screaming.

I landed on something soft and opened my eyes. Asiram stood in front of me, in a room with somewhere between nine and eleven walls, with a dark gray chair in a corner. I could sense the walls pulsing, and my heart pounding.

She blindfolded me and led me through a place full of murmurs of machinery and movement. After she sat me in a large armchair all out of balance, she took the blindfold off. The seat dipped in the middle, the back rose higher than my head. Several shades of gray, the arms were different sizes and heights. The chair wrapped itself around me, and I fell asleep.

When I awoke, still in the chair, Asiram sat nearby, watching me.

'Your sense of equilibrium differs from ours,' she began. I could see objects moving about behind her, in a large ovoid space beyond this small room. 'Close your eyes, this will help.'

I did. My stomach settled down.

'Your universe is static. Everything moves in ordered orbits or stays in its place. Mine is mobile. It is becoming unstable. We need your world as an anchor.'

"No," I cried. "Not again. We've gone through two moves in my lifetime. We're not moving again. This is our world, we're keeping it."

'Once set up, you will not notice us, unless you choose to. In my universe, the Gatekeepers have rendered our world unstable. My people each have anchor points we can reach with a thought.'

"Gatekeepers? You have Gates?" I tried to understand.

'Yes. Our world is an alternate to your Peace. A ship brought us here. The Gatekeepers on our world are using some sort of propellant through the Gates to move our world. At first we thought it earthquakes, then realized it was more. Our Talents saved us. They are similar but different from yours.'

"Oh." I knew of alternate universes, and she was saying I was in one. My brain couldn't keep up. "So you didn't have to go through all this moving. How did you find us?"

'I have a way of locating others of myself in other universes, and you were the best option.'

"But what can I do?" One chair arm dropped out from under my arm. I gasped.

'Ignore it. It will do no harm. You are not ready yet. You have young, yes?'

"Not yet." Why did she want to know that?

'How long does it take to process one?'

"One what?" I was still lost.

'Offspring.'

"Oh. About two hundred and seventy days, I think."

She made a humming noise. 'Can you not proceed more quickly?'

"No. It's a natural process, and we have no way of speeding it up. We grow our young within our bodies, and they won't come out until they're ready." I opened my eyes to look at her, and quickly shut them again. "One of our young women has two babies, and another is expecting."

'What about you?'

"I need to have a daughter soon. It's complicated."

'Figure it out. We have time yet. You will be called when time is right.'

The last thing I remember was everything stopped. Even time.

***

I slid out of a chaotic dream afraid to open my eyes. The bed I lay on felt familiar. A murmur of voices tickled my ears. I smelled trees nearby. Nothing moved. Cracking one eye open, I saw color. Blue walls and blue-green curtains.

I opened both eyes. I was home, in my own bed, Roroy hovering over me.

"My goddess, you're back." He lifted me in a great hug.

When he let go, I saw Granlyn, Mama, and Aunt Maria watching.

"How do you feel?" Aunt Maria asked.

I stretched. "Okay." I sat up on the edge of the bed. "How did I get here?"

"Allen brought you back on Qione," Granlyn said, wiping away a tear. "She sticks her head in the window every once in a while."

"Qione." I turned to the wondow.

She looked in. *I'm here.* I moved over and stroked her neck. *You're well. We couldn't wake you. So scared.*

"Didn't mean to scare you. I don't know what happened, but I'm okay now."

Qione nodded. *I go eat now. You come later.* She trotted off.

Appalled, I sat back on the bed. She'd been out there all night, with nothing to eat or drink, just to stay with me. How long would she have waited for me to wake?

"Where were you?" Roroy demanded.

"I was in another world," I began, then stopped. I couldn't access the memory. "It was chaotic, everything constantly moving. No color, just black and white and gray. There was someone…" I shook my head. "Sorry, it's gone." I felt vaguely relieved that I could not remember. "How long was I out?"

"Allen brought you back last night." Aunt Maria checked my vitals. "You appear to be your normal, healthy self. Just keep an eye out for any changes."

"Okay."

Mama hugged me, and she and the other women left.

I shook my head, pottered around the house, and finally sat by Roroy on the couch.

"Do you still not remember where you were?" he asked, arm around me.

"No. It was so weird I don't think my brain can handle remembering it."

He kissed me.

***

After supper, which we all ate together on the plaza, we had a meeting. Allen told what had happened to me, and added, "That bridge is strictly off limits for now. The quines won't go near it. And neither should any of you."

"There's nothing there, anyway," Ricky piped up.

I glared at him. "What's going on here?" I asked, shivering. It was getting cold at night.

"Most of the crops, except the loovah, have stopped producing," Grampa Larry said. "We need more traps for longears, more fishermen. We may have to ration our food. Pregnant women and new mothers will get what they need. The rest of us eat what's left."

"Are there any shellfish at the beach?" Granlyn asked.

Grampa Larry grinned at her.

"Marisa, you've been there the most often, have you seen anything?"

"Not that I remember. Just tiny shells. Has anyone been along the stretch between our river and the big one?"

"Good question. Who wants to go down tomorrow to check?"

Laurie and Ricky volunteered. "I will," Will said.

"Okay, Will and Laurie. Look for any kind of edibles large enough to be worth bringing up." Grampa Larry rose.

***

That night I woke several times in the night from chaotic dreams, of which I could not remember any details.

***

In the morning, I talked to Susan and Mama to find out what tasks I needed to do. As I sorted tunics, I tried to keep my thoughts on the new twins, but Asiram's world kept haunting me.

That afternoon, Will and Laurie brought back a couple of bowl-sized clams. "There's lots of these," Laurie said.

I checked them out. Nothing poisonous, but not a whole lot of nutrition. I turned to Susan. "You were talking about changes in your body. Do you think we could change ours to get more nutrition from these things?"

"I don't know. Let me think about it."

We cooked the two clams, and all the adults had a taste. Granlyn and the others from Home Earth said it was very good, and at least it would help fill the stomach. The next day, we sent Allen and Laurie down with big bags to collect more.

We began to prepare for cold weather, having no idea how long it would last and how cold it would get.

***

A few days later, I woke to see Roroy putting extra tunics in a bag.

"What are you doing?" I asked, sitting up.

"I go explore this world."

"You can't leave." I rose and went to him.

"I must, my goddess. I do not belong here. I cannot give you a child." He held out his hands.

"Of course you do. You're an important part of this community." I put my arms around him.

"I am not like you. You people talk too much in your heads."

I looked at him. "We do?" I'd never realized it.

He took me in his arms. "Yes. And you need a daughter."

"Why?"

"To continue your people."

"We have plenty of children."

"Freedom Two needs your child."

I sighed and pushed away. He wouldn't give up. "So what do we do now?"

"When I am gone, you can choose other mate."

"No," I blurted out.

He pulled me back in. "You will find someone." After a kiss, "I go north. I will return someday."

He let me go, took his bags outside to where Beast was waiting.

"I'll miss you guys." I ruffled Beast's fur. He made a little purry sound. I watched them head up the river until they disappeared.

I understood why he left, to give me a chance to have a child, but it still hurt. A lot. I sat and wept for a bit, then I went to Granlyn and told her about Roroy leaving.

"You have been trying to conceive?" She sat beside me on the old green couch.

"Yes. We're just too different."

"You must have a daughter. Who do you want to father her?"

"Oh." Allen popped into my mind. I hadn't thought about that part of it.

"It should be Will, he was supposed to have chosen you." Granlyn looked out the window.

"What about Ruthie?"

"She doesn't need to know."

"Let me think about it." I kissed her and left.

She told the others that Roroy had decided to do some exploring.

***

A few days later, Will caught up with me at my house. "I hear Roroy has left. Is he coming back?"

I looked at him. "Why?" I still felt uncomfortable around him; the knot of pain throbbed.

"I was wondering," his eyes looked everywhere except at me,

"what you are going to do to get a daughter. We need her for the next generation."

"He didn't say." My heart sped up. Was he offering to do the job? "Come on in."

He followed me in and settled into a chair near the couch where I perched.

Finally, I broke the silence. "So why did you pick her instead of me?" I couldn't help asking. The question was never far from my thoughts.

After a pause, "Because I was young and stupid, and afraid I couldn't control you." He looked at his hands wrestling each other.

"Oh," I said.

Will looked up at me. "I felt your pain when you lashed out with your Talent. I wanted to take it back, but didn't know how."

My heart flipflopped. "You did?"

"Yeah." He crossed his legs, then uncrossed them. "You left things in a bit of mess, you know."

"I don't remember much of that. Just running forever, hurting my ankle, and Papa carrying me home." I didn't want to remember. The pain was bad enough.

"Uncle Allen was there, too. You sort of disappeared after that for a while."

"I guess I couldn't face anyone." The knot began to unwind.

"Since your mate is gone, I thought I'd offer you my services." He looked at the shelves in the corner.

A thought struck me. "Did Granlyn send you?" I demanded, sitting up straight.

"Oh. No. It was my idea. Really." He crossed his legs again.

I stared at him, into him. I had to know the truth. Was he serious, or just needy because Ruthie had just had a baby? I thought of all the times we'd bumped into each other, especially on their trip to our new place. I could find no reason to disbelieve him. My thoughts tumbled. I wanted him to give me a daughter, but I wasn't sure I was ready for that yet. Guilt by betraying Roroy, even though he wanted me to do it, mixed with a strong desire for Will.

"Okay," I said finally. "This one time."

"What if you don't..."

"I will," I cut in. "What are you doing in three days?"

"Three days?" He dropped his leg and sat up. "I thought we'd do it now."

"My eggs are not ready." I stood. All of a sudden, I had to get him out of my house.

Will rose, hesitated, then put his hands on my shoulders and kissed me. "See you in three days," he said, and left.

I sat down hard. Did that really happen? Of course it did, I told myself. Now I had to get ready for something new.

'Marisa,' Mama *called*. 'Get down to child care right now.'

I trotted down, putting Will in the back of my mind.

***

Three days later, we did the deed. I had told Granlyn, because I knew I couldn't keep it from her, but no one else.

CHAPTER 42

A few days later, when I felt the pull of the other world, I went to find Allen to see if he could go up to the bridge with me. He was working on a house below the plaza.

"Sorry, honey, I can't leave this job right now," he said. "Maybe tomorrow."

"Then Qione and I will go alone."

"Oh no you won't."

"How are you going to stop me?" I turned to go find Qione.

Allen grabbed me by the shoulder and pulled me around. "You are not going anywhere without me. You could lie there unconscious and who knows what could come around and hurt you. We will go tomorrow morning, and that's final."

"Since when do you own me?" I snapped, jerking away.

"I'm concerned for you," he muttered, looking at the house.

"I can take care of myself." I ran to Qione. When I told her what I wanted to do, she refused to go.

Too dangerous, she told me. *And I will not go on any long trips for a while. I am going to become a mother again.*

"Oh," I said, staring at her. She did look a little rounder than usual. "Is there anything we can do for you?"

She shook her head. *My sisters and aunts will be with me,* she told me. *I will let you know when the time comes.*

"Okay." I rubbed her neck and returned to the plaza.

Now I had her to worry about. Although I was sure she could handle it. As I returned to my tasks, I thought of the both of us becoming mothers at the same time. Our daughters would bond.

***

The next day, Granlyn *called* me to her house. As I passed Will on the way, we exchanged smiles.

"What's up?" I said as I entered.

"Sit down." She patted the old green couch beside her. "Allen came last night and asked if you could be his mate."

I sat up. "He did?" For some reason I wasn't surprised.

"Yes, he did," she said. "Do you have any idea how long Roroy will be gone?"

"No, but he told me he thought I should go ahead and have a daughter with someone else." I twisted a curl.

Granlyn sighed. "All right. Your child will be Allen's. Only you and I and Will will know the truth. We will have a mating ceremony in two days. If Roroy returns, you will have to deal with it." She *called* Allen to come to her.

As we waited, I told her about Qione.

Granlyn's face lit up. "How wonderful to have a young one," she said. We talked about the quines until Allen arrived.

When he saw me, his eyes widened.

"Yes, we've agreed. We'll have the mating ceremony in two days." Granlyn smiled at us.

He took my hands, pulled me to my feet, and crushed me in a bear hug. For the first time, I felt like I could be part of the clan.

Some people were surprised when we announced our mating, several wondering about the age difference. Uncle Art said we were a couple of idiots. I knew he disliked Mama because she'd been unable to save his Betty from the alien, but what did he have against me?

At the ceremony, I wore great-grampa's scarf and had the jitters.

Afterward, Allen moved from his little cabin into my house. That night, in bed, I realized that he too, had felt like an outsider at times. He had been the only child among grownups, out of phase with the other generations, having to distance himself because of his Talent.

It was wonderful with him. I wanted to be with him all the time, drawing on his experiences. I asked him once if the age difference bothered him.

"No." He smiled at me. "Your youth keeps me young."

I enjoyed working on the same projects with him. Our Talents meshed. I almost forgot who the real father of my child was.

I continued to dream of the other world, but could only remember bits and pieces.

***

Granlyn had Mama and me take an inventory of the foodstuffs we'd brought over, and determine what food we would have here.

We were to figure out how much we would be getting from the loovah plants and what the hunters and fishermen brought in. Pregnant and nursing women would get what they needed, but the rest of the clan would probably be on rations.

***

A few days later, I finally checked, and knew for sure I was pregnant. Now I would have to wait. I still wasn't ready to be a mother, but I hoped I would be by the time the child arrived. It would be a long winter.

That afternoon, at the craft hall, Susan said, "You're pregnant."

"Yes. How did you know?"

"That's one of my Talents," she smirked. "Welcome to the pregnant club."

As I went about my tasks, community and wifely, that other world lurked in the back of my mind. I knew I couldn't go up there until after Qione and I had our babies. It would take three days to walk it, and what if I passed out again?

***

I tried to *reach* Asiram, but only *sensed* the barrier between our worlds. She would have to reach to me if she wanted me.

***

At first, I wasn't sure I was ready to be a mother. I had long talks with Mama about it, which basically came down to you just have to live with it, and we'll be here to help. I managed to keep my nausea down to a bare minimum, and Susan and I talked about our babies constantly.

It wasn't until I heard in my mind a tiny 'm' that I knew came from baby Janny, that the fact I was going to become a mother felt real. I sat down on my bed hard and whispered, "I hear you, sweetie." From then on, every once in a while she'd make an 'm' at me. Every time I heard it, a frission of joy enveloped me.

CHAPTER 43

Fall deepened into winter. We had rain every now and then, but it didn't get any colder than it had on Harmony. Most of the men spent their time hunting, fishing, or repairing their gear. We made covers for our little fruit trees, almost hip high. They wouldn't give us fruit for another couple years or so, though.

At the midwinter feast, Uncle Art announced, "I've been watching the stars move, and I believe that the year here is about a quarter longer than at Harmony."

I groaned. Almost all of the food we'd brought was gone, and the hunters were having a hard time finding any longears. Fortunately, the fish and loovah were still plentiful. Mama said the fish here weren't as tasty as the ones on Harmony, but at least they had sufficient protein for us, after Susan and I had managed to change some of our protein converting cells to use it. We saved the chickens for special occasions.

***

The winter stretched on and on. It grew cold and rainy, and the sky remained overcast even when it didn't rain. We women were stuck inside most of the time, with the children, making clothes, mending and weaving baskets. The men alternated between making repairs on the buildings and going fishing. Laurie and other boys his age were sent down to the beach every tenday to collect what we called clams. We ate the last ones at the midwinter feast.

Mama had put away a goodly amount of dried vegetables, and every once in a while she invited Susan and me over for supper. Back on Harmony, I would have pushed the veggies aside as tasteless, but here, I gobbled them down.

The loovah continued to grow even in the cold, rainy winter weather. Susan and I felt guilty eating fish and chicken while most of the others survived on loovah mash. Granlyn said she wasn't going to feel bad about the others as long as there was enough to eat. I don't think Ruthie had a conscience. I sure didn't see any sign of one.

***

One morning, we had another problem. Baby Leona was under the weather. Aunt Anne *called* me to Granlyn's, where she was examining the babies.

"All her signs are normal, but she seems to be hungry."

"I'm not producing as much milk as I used to," Granlyn said, a worried look on her face. "Maybe we could get Ruthie or Dottie to help? At least until Susan has hers."

"Dottie's been having trouble making enough milk," Aunt Anne said. "But Ruthie has plenty, and she should start weaning Willie, anyway. Where is she?"

I took off to find Ruthie and bring her to Granlyn's. Aunt Anne explained the situation to her.

"What if I don't have enough for Brian?" Ruthie asked.

"You will," Aunt Anne said. "That's why women have two breasts. For two babies. I think Aunt Lyn can handle one. Willie's old enough to be weaned."

"Um," Ruthie mumbled, looking around.

"At least, let's try it once and see if it helps her."

"Okay." Brian hung in a carryall on her back and Granlyn had Willie sit beside her. Ruthie perched on a stool and took baby Leona. "She's so tiny." She opened the flap on her tunic and began nursing the baby.

Brian started to fuss, bombarding all of us with cries of 'No, no.'

'Hush, Brian,' I *sent*. 'There's plenty left for you.'

When he didn't quit, Granlyn and Aunt Anne joined me, and we managed to sooth him. Ruthie agreed to come twice a day to feed little Leona.

***

I began dreaming of the other world, dreams of which I could only recall bits and pieces. Gray and white movement, Asiram, and something threatening. As I became constantly aware of my child in the back of my mind, the awareness of the threat of the other world also grew.

My baby was growing fast, but not fast enough. Every few nights, I would speed up her time a little, so that she grew twenty-four hours' worth in eight hours. It cost me a lot of energy.

When Aunt Anne asked me if I was getting enough to eat, I told her, "Yes, I'm fine. It's just the pregnancy. She's growing so fast."

"I know, but from what I can tell, she's perfectly normal. Just eat as much as you can."

***

Some time later, at my house, Susan and I were making baby clothes. She had grown heavy, and I teased her. "Are you sure you're not having twins?"

"Just you wait," she retorted. "I can't believe you haven't had any morning sickness."

"I was surprised, myself." I hadn't thought it would work, keeping my stomach under control. Or maybe it was something they did on that other world. Susan was the only one I told about my trip, besides Granlyn and Allen. The threat was still there, and growing stronger. I still could not *reach* Asiram. When I focused on the other world, I could feel the pull, so I tried not to.

"Yeah, sure." She punched me lightly in the shoulder.

"Back to work," I said. We had already gotten Cory and Uncle Bay working on cradles for our babies.

A little later, Susan yelped, "Ow. I hear you, sweetie."

I looked at her.

"She kicked me." Susan's eyes widened. "Mari, she's in my mind." She grabbed at me. "I thought that didn't happen until after she was born."

"No. Mama said I told her my name before I was born. And I know my baby's name will be Janny."

Then I heard Susan's baby in my mind. 'me Glori want out.'

"Oh, my word," I said, staring.

"You heard it too?" Susan asked, hands on her belly.

"Yes. Just keep telling her no, it's not time yet."

"Mari, I'm scared. I can't handle this."

"Sure you can." I rose and rubbed her shoulders. "Mama and I will always be here for you. Why don't you talk to her? She can tell you all about what a problem I was."

"Okay. I'll finish up this shirt and go see Aunt Perri."

***

That night in bed, I thought about what had happened with Susan. I was continually aware of Janny and her little sounds, but she wasn't ready to connect fully with me yet. I'd found I could use my time Talent to push my baby to develop faster. Now people were asking me if I was going to have twins.

Susan's Glori sounded as pesty as I was, but I wondered what Talents she would have beyond mine. I shivered.

I'd always been able to control everyone else; could I control her, or Janny?

I sensed trouble ahead. Big trouble. As if the threat from the other world wasn't enough.

I also felt very alone. Everyone else was living their own life, but I had to live everybody's. I felt that I'd been put in charge for a reason, but no one else knew about it. Grampa Larry was our leader, with Granlyn advising him, and I let him lead, but I felt the responsibility of the whole clan on my shoulders. And it kept getting heavier.

To get my mind off this, I thought about Ruthie's babies. Willie and Brian, placid children, were both mindlinked to most of us. Mama had the most Talent of her generation, and Granlyn before her. So it was always the first born girl that had the most. But Will's Talent was stronger than Ruthie's. Did that mean Willie and Brian's Talent would be more like their papa's?

We had to stop this progression. I had to stop it. But how? Qione had said something about folding back our Talents, but I still had no idea how to do that, if it were even possible.

***

I visited Qione on days it didn't rain. Some of the other females were also carrying young.

I dislike this rain and having to stay under the trees, she told me one day.

"I know. We're all tired of the rain. Maybe we can get the men to rig up some kind of a shelter for you. I'll ask around."

Thank you. The trees let too much in.

There was still plenty of grass and other small plants for them to eat, but many of the trees were mostly bare. I took my leave and returned to the settlement.

A few days later, Laurie, on Quest, rode up to check on the bridge. "Don't go across it," I warned him.

"I won't."

When he returned the next day, he found me and pulled me aside. "Mari, something's going on up there. There was a blueish mist from across the river way over on our side. Quest wouldn't go anywhere near it. I got off and walked and was half way to it when I felt something pulling at me. I fought it for a bit, then turned and ran back to Quest." He rubbed at dark specks on his cheek.

"What's that on your face?"

"I don't know. I think it came from the mist. The wind was blowing my way." He rubbed the other cheek.

"Does it hurt?"

I dropped the cloth I was folding, took his arm and led him toward his house.

"What are you doing?" He tried to jerk his arm away.

"Taking you home. You need to wash yourself thoroughly, and bundle up what you're wearing and put it outside. If it did come from the mist, we have no idea what it is and what it can do to us."

"Oh. Okay."

I let his arm go. "Thanks, Laurie, you did good. We're definitely going to have to do something about it before it gets down here."

"Like what?"

"I have no idea. After you get clean, let me know if there's any black spots left."

"Okay." He ran off to his house.

Now I knew we were in trouble, and it scared me silly. When Allen came home, I told him about Laurie's trip.

"Oh, no. Did he get all the stuff off of him?"

"Yes. Papa said he checked Laurie thoroughly. He's going to keep a sharp eye on him the next few days in case there's any aftereffects." I prayed to the Oneness to keep my brother safe.

"Good. It looks like we'll have to do something soon." He pulled me into a hug.

"We can't until Susan and I have had our babies."

"And how long will that be?"

"A while yet."

"Can we wait that long?"

"We have to. We need the babies' Talents beside all of ours."

***

That night, in my dream, Asiram told me to prepare to bring my people up. I tried to explain about Susan and me, but she drifted off.

In the morning, I told Mama and Granlyn about Laurie's trip and my dream.

Granlyn wandered about her living room, twitching a curtain here, a tablecloth there. "Why does this alien want us? How do we know they are not trying to destroy us?"

"Yes," Mama added. "You can't trust those people."

"Asiram wants us to come up and separate our two worlds."

"Who wants what?" Grampa limped into the house and tossed his toolbag on a chair.

I explained.

"Asiram thinks that with our newest generation, we can do it with our Talents. I tried to tell her we couldn't do it now, not until Susan and I had our babies, but she was gone."

Grampa dropped into his big chair. "What exactly does this person want us to do?"

"I'm not sure, but it's about getting rid of that mist from her world." I told him about Laurie's trip.

"Oh, Christ." Grampa held his head in his hands.

"I know," I said, shivering. The terror was back.

He looked at me. "Obviously, we can't go any time soon, but I wonder, should we let the others know this is coming up?"

"Yes," I said. "They have to be prepared."

"Not yet." Mama fidgeted. "When the girls have their babies."

"I think sooner," Granlyn said. "Remember, only a few of us even know about the bridge, let alone this other world."

"I agree with you, babe."

We agreed to talk about it some more, with Allen, and plan how and what to tell people.

***

Now I had something else to worry about. Probably the younger people would accept it, but Aunt Maria, Uncle Chad and Uncle Art? Especially him. They wouldn't. How could I convince them?

That night, in my dream of the other world, I had a feeling Asiram was in the dream, telling me to hurry up. Although I was pushing my pregnancy as fast I as dared, I didn't know what else I could do. The more the baby crept into my mind, the stronger the pull of the other world. I tried to keep focused on whatever I was doing.

The dreams continued. I tried to ignore them.

CHAPTER 44

Finally, the days grew noticeably longer, warmer, and the rains stopped. The men began preparing the crop fields and the grampas dug out seeds from storage. I hoped they would grow fast; I was really tired of loovah mash. We'd eaten all of the older chickens, and the boys hadn't caught any fish for days. The pull from the other world was always in the back of my mind.

I stayed home a lot. It was hard to carry my weight down to the plaza. I knew Susan felt the same way. It was a good thing she lived right next door so we could visit. And Granlyn on the other side. The twins were crawling everywhere, and we had to keep a close eye on them. Curtis put everything he came across into his mouth, and Leona constantly picked objects up and put them down.

***

One day I asked Mama if she would go with me to see Qione. I knew she was doing well, but I wanted to see her.

"Sure," Mama said, grabbing a wrap. "I'd like to see her too."

We walked slowly. Qione whickered when she saw us. She was huge around the middle, too.

You are well? she asked me.

"I'm fine. It's just hard to walk. I brought Mama in case I fell or something."

Good. I feel the other world sometimes, she told me.

"You do? So do I."

We can't do anything until we've had our young.

"I know." I stroked her neck.

You raised a fine daughter, Qione told both of us, in our minds.

"Thank you," Mama said. We chatted for a few minutes, then Mama and I headed for home.

***

A few days later, Mama and I told Uncle Peter and Aunt Anne about the bridge and the other world.

"Oh wow," Uncle Peter said. "How on Peace do they expect us to stop it?"

"She must have seen something in Marisa," Aunt Anne replied.

"She thinks we can with the new generation of babies." I patted

249

my stomach. "But I don't know if we can wait that long. Laurie says the mist has moved down here a lot more since I was up there."

"What does Uncle Larry say," Aunt Anne asked.

"He thinks we should plan on doing it, but first we have to tell everyone." Mama looked at me. "We can talk to people our age, and Marisa to her friends."

"Okay, but I think we should have a general meeting to plan for it." Uncle Peter rose.

***

Several days later, Grampa Larry called a meeting, insisting that everyone attend. Will had to drag Ruthie out of the house with the babies, and Papa had to round up a couple of the boys, but finally everyone showed up at the meeting hall.

As Grampa settled himself in his chair at the front, Uncle Art stood up. "What's this nonsense about another world?" he demanded.

"That's what this meeting is about. Please sit down."

Grumbling, Uncle Art sat.

Grampa held his hands up for silence. "As most of you probably already know, Marisa and Qione found a bridge way up the Grande. Marisa crossed it on foot, the quines won't go near it, and met an alien being."

Voices erupted. "She's dreaming," I heard Uncle Art say loudly.

Grampa put his hands up again. "Please let me continue. The alien took Marisa to a place she believes is another world. There, an alien appearing to be a woman told her that their world is somehow intertwined with ours, and that they need our Talents to unravel this mess. Laurie went upriver a few days ago and found a strange, bluish mist creeping down the land along the river. Allen went up yesterday and confirmed it."

"Nonsense," Uncle Art bellowed.

I saw Aunt Maria shake her head.

Allen stood up and looked at Uncle Art. "Are you calling Laurie and me liars?"

"Probably just a land mist."

"No." Allen shook his head. "Laurie's quine, Quest, told us that there were particles in that mist that should not be in the air on any world. We have to get rid of it before it gets here."

"What does a dumb quine know." Uncle Art glared.

I jumped up. "Quines are not dumb. Most of them are smarter than you."

"Marisa," Mama cried.

"Well, it's true. Qione knows all sorts of things. Just because she doesn't have hands to work with doesn't mean she's dumb."

"Okay, calm down." Grampa stood and raised his voice. "Marisa is right about how smart the quines are. If Quest said that, then I believe it's true." He paused. "Marisa, what can you tell us about this other world and the situation there?"

"Um, I don't remember all of it, but the main thing is the person I met and what she said. Her world is all black and gray and white, no colors, and things don't stay put like on our world, but keep moving around. She said her world is in another reality, another universe. My Talent doesn't work over there."

I looked around and saw several sceptical faces. "Anyway, she says our worlds have got hooked together somehow, and we need to separate them. That's what that blue mist is, her world creeping into ours. If it comes too far, it'll take over our world, and us."

"And you believe that?" Aunt Maria asked skeptically.

"Yes, I do. I feel the pull of the other world even now."

"How do you know it's not something you dreamed when you were knocked out?" Uncle Art demanded.

"It's real. Ask Allen and Laurie. If you don't believe me, go see for yourself."

"I think we can safely say that we have a big problem on our hands." Grampa Larry stood and motioned for me to sit. "Now we can either sit here and wait for it to swallow us up, or go deal with it. I understand this person wants all of us to go, even the babies."

"Especially the babies," I said. "But we can't go until after Susan and I have had ours."

"Okay, that gives us a little time." Grampa fingered the dimple in his chin, hidden in his beard. "It takes two days to get up there, right?" I nodded. "So we will need to take provisions for several days. Are there enough quines for everyone to ride?"

"I think so. The little kids can ride with older kids if necessary."

A thought hit me. "I need to talk to Qione about this. Several of the quines are pregnant, so we'd have to wait until they've had their babies, too. I think it'll be about the same time as us."

"Okay. So we need to plan food and supplies, and fashion carriers or harnesses for the babies and little kids. And plan our schedules to allow for several days without tasks."

"What exactly are we going to do?" Will asked.

"I don't know yet. I'm trying to reach her to find out. I'll let you know when I do."

"Okay, Marisa. Anyone who wants to see for themselves is free to go up and look. Now let's get back to work." Grampa Larry sat down and rubbed his eyes.

Susan and I waddled back to my house. Our times were getting close. We had our supplies of baby wrappers and necessities, and the beautifully carved cradles sat in our nurseries.

"I can't wait for her to come," Susan said, rubbing her stomach as we settled on the couch.

"Me too." The babies echoed us.

"We'll have to wait a tenday or so after we have them before we can ride that long distance."

"I know. Especially since they're our first." I patted my belly.

We chatted a little bit longer, then Susan heaved herself to her feet and waddled home.

That night, my dreams of the other world were much stronger, and I remembered more of them. The background a grayish blur; the only thing clear was the round room and Asiram. She asked me how soon and I told her about Susan and me, and the quines.

'Too long.'

'We can't do it any faster.'

'You have Talent to move time.'

'For me, a little. No way I could do everyone.'

She sighed, and the dream faded out as I woke.

CHAPTER 45

A few days later, I woke up with cramps and called Aunt Anne.

"They're contractions. Come to the clinic when they get close together. It won't be long." She paused. "I'll get things ready. Walk around if you feel like it, but don't go too far. I'll tell Bay you'll be off duty for a while."

I wanted to talk to Allen, but he was down at the beach. I toddled out to the porch and sat in the swing. We had a supply of baby clothes and things, and I had a couple of nursing tunics.

"Now I'm just waiting for you, Janny," I said. Her head pushed, and I felt another, stronger contraction. "Please don't take too long." I couldn't sit still. 'Susan, I'm in labor,' I *sent* to her.

'I know,' she *returned*. 'So am I. You're not having false labor, are you? Isn't it a little early?'

'No, she's ready. Oooh. Keep in touch.'

I waddled off to find Mama. She was at her house, taking a break.

"So, it's time," she said as I clumped in. "Come here." I let her wrap her arms about me. She *sent* me a picture of my birth, and the joy we had both felt at the time.

"There will be pain and discomfort," Mama said, as she led me to the couch. "But it will be worth it."

I believed her. I spent the afternoon with Mama and occasional contractions, while she told me stories of my childhood. Later, I went by Susan's, and we commiserated together.

"I wish we had more than one birthing chair," she said.

"Yeah. I wouldn't want to have mine on the bed." I looked at the sky through the window. "I'd better go, Allen will be home soon."

"Okay. Take care."

I'd just got supper laid out when Allen walked in and hugged me from the rear.

"Oof," I said, turning. "Our daughter will be here tomorrow."

"Oh," he said, shrinking back and staring at my bulging abdomen. "Here?"

"Of course not. I'll go to the clinic when it's time." I moved to give him a hug. "Anne said I could probably sleep here tonight, and go down there tomorrow."

After I woke him a couple of times with contraction moans, he kissed me and moved out to the couch. I drifted in and out of sleep, uncomfortable in any position. Finally, as the sky was beginning to lighten beyond the forest, I rose, donned a nursing tunic, and waddled out the front door.

'Me come out now,' Janny *sent*. I clutched myself as a contraction hit and my water broke.

"Anne," I gasped, and staggered toward the clinic. When I barged in, Susan was just settling into the birthing chair.

Aunt Anne looked at me and then at Susan. "You too?"

"Yes," I gasped. "My water broke."

"Let me take a quick look at Susan."

Susan and I had contractions at the same time. I *sensed* Aunt Anne *calling* Aunt Maria as I held onto the back of the chair.

"Okay, Susan, you've got a little while yet. Let me look at Marisa."

Aunt Anne helped me into the birthing chair and settled in front. "Oh my, I feel her head," she said.

I screamed and Janny popped out. As I panted, trying to catch my breath, I heard Janny yelling.

"Is she all right?" I gasped.

"Fine, dear. She's just exercising her lungs."

"Hurry," Susan moaned.

Mama and Aunt Maria ran in, followed by others. "They're both fine," Aunt Anne said, standing and stretching. Aunt Maria took over from her, to deal with the afterbirth and move me to a bed. Aunt Anne got Susan in the chair, after a hasty wipe, and Glori arrived.

After Glori finished yelling, Janny made an 'oo' sound, and the two connected, linking in a way not even I could access.

Granlyn and Grampa Larry, with the twins, came in.

I *sensed* only curiosity from the two little ones, but Janny and Glori ignored them. Oh boy, I thought. These two are going to be a handful and then some. Finally the aunts shooed the others out so Susan and I could rest.

Later, Allen and Mike tiptoed in to see their new daughters. "They're so little," Mike said. Allen just stared at Janny.

"Okay, you two," Aunt Maria said a little later. "Marisa and Susan need their rest. You can come back tomorrow."

After they left, we slept a lot, in between feedings, and adjusted to our new motherhood the next few days.

***

After Janny and I had settled in back at our house, and I was up and about, I heard from Qione. *'Come see.'*

Mama and I trudged over to the quines' compound, with Janny in her snuggie on my chest, and found Qione in the center of a mass of quines, a lot more than before.

In between Qione's legs stood a tiny, blond, wobbly-legged version of her. I *felt* Qione's pride in her new daughter.

"She's beautiful," I said. Janny made a welcoming sound as I showed her to Qione.

Can she stand? Qione asked me.

"No, not for many tendays."

"Oh, how precious," Mama crooned, watching the little one.

Two other females stood nearby with new foals. One youngster was a female, the other, a male. Janny *sent* something to him and he snorted.

"Where did all these other quines come from?"

Kiong went back to our other world and brought all who would come. This is our world now. Qione nodded her head.

"May others come and see the young ones?" I asked her.

Mothers may. No males yet.

"Okay, I'll tell them, and we'll be back tomorrow."

***

That evening, the sunset was more vivid than ever. Several people remarked on it. Glaring yellows and oranges, deep reds, violent pinks and purples were a background for slashes of deep greens and blues. It hurt my eyes to look at it. I shivered; I knew it meant the other world was close.

***

Meanwhile, Janny, short for Janice, chattered at me almost constantly while she was awake, which drove me nuts. Fortunately, she slept most of the time. When she and Glori were close together, their bond kicked in, and she went silent as far as I was concerned. I often wondered what was going on in those little heads. I didn't like being shut out by a couple of babies.

The dreams continued. 'You have your offspring, come now,' Asiram sent that night.

'Not yet. Too soon.'

'When?'

'Five days.'

'Too long. Three.'

'If I can.'

***

I asked Aunt Anne what she thought. "If there is no bleeding or discharge, I would say you'd be okay. Just watch bouncing around."

At home that night, I *went in* to my body and made sure all was healed. My body was ready for the ride, but was my mind? I still didn't quite understand exactly what we had to do or how we were to do it. I knew this was the most important task of my life, to lead my people in saving our world, but I felt totally inadequate for the job. Someone like Papa, Allen or Uncle Gabe should be leading this expedition. Thoughts roiled in my head until I forcefully shut them down so I could sleep.

***

The next day, I talked to Grampa Larry.

"We need to go tomorrow. Is that enough time?"

"Make it one more day. It'll take time to get everyone ready." He looked down. "I'm concerned about Lyn riding for that long. I know I'm not particularly looking forward to it."

"I'm sure Qione will take it easy, she's got her little one, too."

"Okay, I'll make an announcement." Grampa smiled at me.

After supper at the plaza, Grampa Larry called for everyone's attention.

"The time has come." He gulped a deep breath. "The day after tomorrow we must all follow Marisa up to the bridge to save our world."

People groaned and refused to go.

Allen stood. "I went up yesterday. The blue mist is a lot closer. We have to do this, or it's the end of our colony and everyone in it. Let's give the kids and babies a chance at life."

Most everyone agreed, and the next day was spent in tying up loose ends and putting together backpacks. Uncle Art hid in his workshop and didn't even come out to eat. I knew Ruthie would be a problem, but I'd let Will handle her.

That evening, the sunset was even more garish than before. Again, I shivered.

256

CHAPTER 46

In the morning, a sense of purpose filled me, almost hiding the fear. This was the day I would save my people. I hoped.

"What's up?" Allen asked, rubbing his eyes.

"Today we will all go up to the bridge and move the other universe away." Even as I said it, I realized how ridiculous it sounded. Me, move a whole universe? Come on. But I had to, to save our world.

"Oh, right." Allen reached for me. I lay back in his arms for a moment. It would be much easier to stay here with him, where it was safe. Except there was no safe place on our world any more.

"Not now," I said, wriggled away from him, and rose. "First, I need to feed Janny." I picked her up out of her cradle and sat in the nursing chair with the padded arms. "You go tell the others we'll all meet in the plaza in an hour."

"Okay." He got up, dressed, and left.

As I held my baby, the jitters attacked me. How on Peace was I going to do this? I could see us riding up there, but after that was a blank. I prayed that I could *reach* Asiram and find out what to do when we got there. But my baby was here and now. After Janny finished, I took her to the potty pot, then laid her back in her cradle. I dressed and ate some bread and loovah mash.

'Wanna go,' Janny *sent*. She liked to be out and about with other people. I dressed her, put on her snuggie bag, so it hung down my front, and her into it. I carried her over to Granlyn's, where she and Mama were dealing with the twins.

"So this is the day we all go," Granlyn said, trying to hold Leona's leg so Mama could get her snuggie tied. Mama was already 'wearing' Curtis in his snuggie.

"Yes. I hope you're ready."

"As long as I get to ride Qiola, I'll be fine." Granlyn patted the baby. "You're getting too big for this. Next time, you'll have to ride on my back."

We trooped down to the plaza. Half the people had already gathered there, and more were coming every minute. Qione arrived with her people, including her little one. She, Qiola, Kiong and Quest directed the other quines to each rider. As people mounted with their packs, Qione moved them out to the north. Ruthie, of course, refused to mount, and Will and another fellow wrestled her up on top of her quine.

As people mounted and moved way, I checked them off the list in my head. One rider quine was left. "Where's Uncle Art?" I asked.

"We'll get him," Allen said, as he, Papa, and Uncle Bay took off for the workshop.

"Leave me alone," Uncle Art yelled as the three men dragged him to the plaza. "I've got work to do."

"Everyone has to come," I said. "Including you."

"Brat," he muttered.

The men wrestled Uncle Art up on the quine, who made a variety of moves, twitching and wriggling, that calmed him down.

It's a talent we have, Qione remarked. *We can send calming vibes into anyone who is touching us.*

Finally everyone was mounted, and those who needed it were harnessed. Qione and I rode through the pack to the front, the north side, followed by Allen on Quest. The two quines bellowed, and Allen and I raised our hands. The rest of the group stood still.

"Okay, folks." I projected my voice. "Time to go. Let's go save our world." I trembled with anxiety and the need to get this done.

Qione turned and started off at a slow walk. Allen rode at my right, and Will, on Kiong at my left. I felt both high and scared. In the clouds because I, Marisa, was leading my people to save our world, and scared witless because I still didn't know how we were going to do it.

I tried to *reach* Asiram to let her know we were coming, but could make no contact.

The quines, led by Qione, walked at a steady, even pace. Granlyn, Grampa Larry, and Mama rode behind us, Ruthie behind Will. Her mother, Aunt Beth, had Willie. Susan, with Glori and Mike rode on the other side of Allen, and Dottie, with her baby, Harry, and Freddie behind them. The babies, soothed by the rhythm of the steeds, mostly slept. I, too, dozed. Unable to tell what was going on up ahead, I decided I would enjoy my first ride with my baby.

It was still cool, and I had my cloak wrapped around us. The sun shone on us and the blue-green sky was clear.

Still, something didn't feel right.

258

'Are you sure you know what you're doing?' Susan *sent* privately.

'All I know is that unless we do something soon, her world is going to take over ours, and because their Talent is stronger than ours, even at this young age, we need the babies.'

'The twins aren't, because their father has no Talent, and I don't see much in Willie, Brian, or Harry.'

'Yes, but look at our two,' I replied. I tried not to show my terror and uneasiness.

Qione's little Qilla wound in and out of her mother's legs as we moved along. I wondered whether she would be able to keep up. One of the men could probably carry her if necessary.

We moved over toward the Grande and headed north, stopping every now and then for a rest break. It was too difficult to feed the babies while riding. At occasional streams, Qione halted so the quines could drink.

At the second stop, where we had our midday meal, Qione asked me if I saw anything ahead.

"No, do you? I do feel the pull."

Yes. The blue mist. Most of day's ride up. I do not like it at all.

"None of us do." I bit my lip.

We will camp well below tonight.

"Okay."

***

That night, the children went to sleep easily enough. For them, this trip was just an adventure. However, for the rest of us, it was an uneasy camp. We lay restless and fearful. I dreamed of Asiram and told her we were on our way.

'What do we do when we get there?' I asked.

'You will push the mist.'

'What? How?' I thought I heard a sigh.

'Meld your people's Talents and you will find a way.'

'Okay.' I'd figured that we'd have to merge all our Talent, but the other... 'Asiram?'

She was gone as I awoke. Oh my Oneness, I thought. Now what am I going to do? How does one push mist? I tried to think of something as I did my morning business, but nothing came to mind. I wandered aimlessly, trying to figure it out.

Allen tapped my shoulder and handed me a piece of bread.

"Come on, Marisa, we need to get going."

As we started out, a knot developed in my stomach, along with the pull of the alien thing within me. I sensed the growing unease in the others. Even the children were quieter than usual. Qione's disquiet and that of her people also strengthened. Qilla whimpered.

'Hush,' I *soothed*, as Qione nosed her.

Janny hid her mind within mine, and the other babies did the same with their mothers.

We kept going, but the rest stops were closer together and longer. The knot in my belly kept growing. At noon, only the younger children were hungry.

I found Art Junior. I knew his father would not talk to me. "How does one push mist?" I asked.

"Push mist?"

"That's what Asiram said we have to do."

"I don't know offhand. Papa might, but you know how he is."

"I know." I *heard* in Junior's mind that Uncle Art had said he'd rather die than let that brat of Perri's save his world.

"But he's a scientist," I said aloud.

"Yeah, but he's never been the same since he lost Mama."

"Come on, let's go," Allen yelled at us.

We packed up, mounted, and moved off.

***

The sun was still high when Qione stopped.

Not a rest stop, she told me. *Look.*

A line of dark blue-gray mist with flashes of color covered the land ahead, although the blue-green sky remained clear, even though we weren't anywhere near the bridge. As Qione halted, so did everyone else.

We drew close to each other. Allen reached over and took my hand. I contacted everyone with my mind. Even little Janny and the other babies joined in.

An arm of the mist reached out and grabbed all of us in a giant fist. I screamed, "Fours." Allan's hand squeezed mine as I flipped the flap down over Janny's face, squeezing my own eyes and mouth shut. The knot within threatened to choke me.

The Fours weren't working. As soon as I connected with one person, another would disappear.

And then there was nothing. No Talent at all. Anywhere.

As I clutched Allen's hand and my baby with the other arm, I heard scattered bits of cries and wails, the scuffling of the quines' feet, and Allen telling me that he was there. Qione moved uneasily beneath me, and I heard quines whimpering. The smell of fear swirled strong.

I tried to breathe. Something in my throat cut off my air. I puffed as hard as I could, and gasped in a little air. By the third and fourth puffs, I was only panting. I cracked an eye open. The air right in front of me was a little clearer.

"Puff," I yelled. "Blow out as hard as you can." I heard those near me pass the message back.

Qione bellowed something and I heard her blow out big breaths. It worked for a while, but when we had to stop and rest, the mist began creeping back. If only we had our Talents....

"Back," I called. "Keep the babies covered." I continued to puff until I could breathe normally. I knew the people near me were sending the message to the others.

Qione told her people, and slowly the quines stepped backward. *I will not turn my back on that thing,* she told me.

Before I could fully comprehend that she and I could still communicate, I heard a tiny voice in my mind.

'Mama?'

"Janny?" I whispered, turning her so I could see her little face. She reached out and patted my cheek. "Oh, my little sweetie," I cried, holding her face to mine. A place in my mind began to unfold. I linked with Janny, and then with Susan and Glori.

'Susan.'

'Mari, our babies did it.' Joy swept through us.

I linked to Mama and Granlyn, then to Allen and my brothers. The links spread like wildfire as everyone's mindlink Talent returned. I was aware through Qione that her people's links had also returned.

'That's one for us,' Uncle Chad *sent* to everyone.

Only Grampa Larry was silent. He'd never had any Talent.

"Grampa, you have your own kind of talent," I told him as I turned in my seat.

"Thanks, Marisa," he muttered.

We continued backing and blowing, but that was only slowing the mist. The terror in my spine and the knot in my stomach wrestled with each other. I *felt* Will bring me into our Four as the other Fours united.

That helped me relax a little, but didn't solve the problem.

Then Uncle Art reported, via Allen, that according to his pocket analysis kit, the mist consisted of something of which we had no record.

"But then, how can it exist?" Allen asked.

"It can't."

I felt a jolt of excitement. "Are you saying that something is making us think we're seeing it?" I demanded. I realized that I had only sensed the mist with my eyes. I had not felt it as it surrounded us, I had heard nothing but our own movements, smelled nothing but ourselves.

"Could be." Allen squeezed my hand.

Qione stopped moving backward.

"There is no mist," I said. The blue continued to advance.

Just then, Asiram *sent*, 'We are here.' I felt a mass of people with her. 'We are ready. Turn to face the sun. You push forward, we will pull. We have a mechanism, but we need help from your side. As soon as you are in position, begin.'

I *sent* her message to everyone, and Qione turned to her left. The other quines followed. Our Fours converged into Twelve plus two. As the power began to build, we pulled in all the rest of the people, including the other babies.

I felt the quines joining with us, all of them, even little Qilla. I laid my hands on Qione's shoulders. As the sense of us becoming one grew, I thought, I am the leader of all these people. A sense of the exhilaration of the situation drew over me, with an underlying element of terror. I'd never done anything like this before.

What am I doing, I thought.

I took a deep breath, raised my right hand, then brought it down as I shouted, "The mist does not exist." Others repeated it until everyone was shouting and *sending* with their Talents.

Qione took a step forward, the others following, as we 'pushed' against the mist.

The front bit faded, but more filled the space from behind.

"No," I whimpered. The word 'time' came into my mind. Of course, I thought. 'I'm going to stop time out there ahead of us,' I *sent* to all. 'Fours, with me.' I focused on an area in front of us as wide as our entity and as far forward as I could reach. The world flickered and the mist stopped moving. In the area of no-time, the mist disappeared.

'It has to keep moving to keep appearing to us,' someone *sent.*

'Go,' I *sent.*

Qione took a step and the no-time zone moved ahead of us. The feeling of all of us pushing at once and those of my generation holding time was extraordinary. It was much deeper than just the Four. Surrounded by power, I felt split in two. The leader of the entity, the hundreds of people with me; and myself, Marisa, underneath, who could still think my own thoughts.

The mass of us shouted and pushed as one, as we took each step. I *sensed* Asiram and her people moving back, pulling.

We continued on, stopping every few steps to catch our breath and relax a little.

Slowly, the mist retreated. Time became immaterial. This being I was a part of became all encompassing. I could sense the others like berries in a pudding, but I also felt as if this whole being was me.

I noticed the trees thinning along the river and realized we were getting close to the still obscured bridge. Suddenly a section of mist drifted across the river, approached our side. No, I thought, in panic. We could not expand our no-time zone, we were beginning to lose energy as it was.

Qione turned slightly to her left, so that only a tiny sliver of mist was outside the zone on our right. The no-time zone covered almost all of the new mist.

A few steps later, two barely overlapping gray circles popped into my vision. As we proceeded, the overlapping grew less, the circles darkened and became filled with sparkles. I understood that they were representatives of our universes.

Suddenly, there was a pop, the circles split from each other, and darkness enveloped my group.

***

When I came to, I heard small movements of people stirring, and quine mutterings. I opened my eyes and sat up. Beside me, Qione moaned. Little Qilla lay motionless as her mother nosed her. Before I could say anything, Janny woke up and began making 'ooo' sounds. I *felt* her *touching* the little quine. Soon Qilla opened her eyes, lifted her head.

'*Ah,*' Qione murmured, and moved so the little one could nurse.

"Look." I pointed to Qilla's front foot. Where the front of

Qione's foot was round and smooth, Qilla's was scalloped.

Qione peered at the foot, looked at me, and put her front foot and leg around her baby. I knelt and rubbed her shoulder as euphoria wrapped itself around us. Qione made a low murmuring sound.

A moment later, Allen pushed a pouch of water into my hand. After I drank, I held it out. Qione opened her mouth so I could dribble the rest of the water between her lips. As I brought Janny to my breast, I sensed a new link between Qione and me that only mothers could understand.

The mist was gone. So was the bridge. With a fleeting thanks from Asiram, I knew her world was back where it belonged.

As the others awoke, people fumbled for water pouches, and the quines staggered to their feet and headed for the river.

Will yelled, "Everyone, drink water and eat. Parents, feed your little ones."

Janny looked up at me and said, "Mama." I *looked into* her and saw that her children would have no more Talent than she did.

Then I *looked into* myself. The alien thing was gone. Thank Oneness we can be a complete clan again. Thank Oneness I finally belong.

I sat up and looked toward the forest on the other side of the river. It was gone. Farther away were ripples of low hills in front of higher hills. Beyond them towered purple mountains.

On top of a hill straight across from me, I saw a tall rider on a large, black beast with a round head and ears.

"Welcome back," I whispered.

ABOUT THE AUTHOR

Lorna Hopkins Keith was born in Hollywood, California and now lives on a lake in Florida with her husband and calico cat. Besides writing two practice novels and many stories, she has published this trilogy.

With a BA in math, she also loves to play with numbers and puzzles. Her occupation is as a bookkeeper.

Contact me at lornavkeith.com or lornavhkeith.com

www.ingramcontent.com/pod-product-compliance
Lightning Source LLC
Chambersburg PA
CBHW070801200626
46811CB00023B/315